MY PIGEON FAMILIAR

BRIDGET E. BAKER

Copyright © 2022 by Bridget E. Baker

All rights reserved.

No part of this book may be reproduced in any form or by any electronic or mechanical means, including information storage and retrieval systems, without written permission from the author, except for the use of brief quotations in a book review.

❦ Created with Vellum

For Whitney

*my best friend and my lifelong mate
you bring magic and laughter in my life
just as I hope this book brings those into the world*

PROLOGUE: MINERVA

It feels really, really good to have my wand in my hands again, and I can't help stroking it just a little bit.

Witches shouldn't be parted from their wands. We don't *need* them, strictly speaking, but after using them to help us focus our magic for so many years, they begin to feel like an extension of our body.

"You're so pretty," I whisper.

"I hate to interrupt the two of you." Xander's eyes are wide and his mouth twitches with suppressed mirth. "It looks like things are getting interesting, but I had to shift into a wolf three times today, and I really want to sit down."

"Sure, take a load off your paws." I tuck my wand into my shoulder bag and scooch toward the armrest of the enormous, oversized corduroy sofa we always hog at Grand Central Gloffee.

"Anything you want to share?" Xander plops down in the center of the sofa and leans back. All joking aside, he has no paws. He's just your average werewolf—shaggy hair that never stays neatly combed, golden eyes, and a rangy build that's deceptively strong. "I could use some good news."

Bevin tucks one of her blonde dreadlocks behind her ear, setting her peace charm spinning. "Minerva just finished her Institute of Magical Justice classes and they gave her wand back."

"Whoa." Xander straightens, his bright gold eyes flashing. "So you've been reinstated?"

I shrug. "It takes some time for the paperwork to get processed, but next week, probably."

Clark pushes through the front door and drags himself over to us, stopping next to the sofa. He sighs dramatically, his shoulders slumped, and his face drooped like a basset hound. It's been like that way too often lately. "Hey."

Xander coughs. "Looks like someone needs a joy spell cast on their glatté again."

"No, I'm fine," Clark says. "Really."

"You just don't want your sister to do it," Xander says. "Who knows what might happen? It could singe your nose hairs."

Clark unhooks his shoulder bag and drops it next to the sofa. "I could cast my own joy spell, but that's not going to work. Not today. Work finally processed the court order and gave half my savings to Carly, which means I'm both broke and officially single."

"That doesn't sound so bad," Izaak says. "I mean, half of a savings account's still better than no savings at all." He's sprawled out in the big orange lounger near the counter. Even when he's not using his vampiric charm, there's still just something about Izaak that draws magical people to him. I can't tell if it's his impressive build, killer smile, or his gorgeous dark brown skin. Of course, something also repels the humans—maybe the same thing. That's why he can't seem to get the jobs he wants no matter how hard he tries.

Xander stands up and nudges Clark into his spot on the

couch. "But hey, buddy, at least that's over, right? The misery has finally ended."

Clark's shoulders slump even more, which I hadn't thought was possible, and he sighs. "But I didn't want to get divorced at all."

When Xander circles around me and perches on the arm of the sofa, he meets my eyes and rolls his. I can't blame Xander, even if Clark is my brother. His celebrity lookalike was always Eeyore from *Winnie-the-Pooh*, but Clark has come to resemble him a bit too much in the past few months.

Maybe Xander's right. Even if I wind up roasting Clark's nose hairs in the attempt, I may need to cast a joy spell.

"I even offered to quit my job in spell research and follow her anywhere she wanted to go," Clark says for the nine millionth time. "I offered to live as a human entirely. Why wasn't that enough for Carly?"

"Because humans don't like our world, not deep down," Xander says. "They know they'll never belong here, whereas you live and breathe magic."

"Actually, I kind of get why he's all 'woe is me.'" Bevin smiles.

"Thank you," Clark says. "At least someone's trying to see it from my point of view."

"I mean, being married would be nice," Bevin says. "Then I wouldn't have to clip my toenails anymore."

"Huh?" I turn to stare at her blankly.

So does everyone else.

I even glance down at her toenails, to see whether they're like super long or crusty or something. I'd have thought in the time we were roommates I'd have noticed if that was the case, but who knows? Maybe demon-spawn have particularly gnarly toenails.

But no, they look perfectly normal. They're even polished a very non-threatening shade of baby blue.

"My future wife will definitely do that for me," Bevin says, as if we should understand what she's talking about. "It's my least favorite thing in the world to do, and isn't that what marriage is all about? Having someone to do all the things you hate doing yourself?"

"Like, eating your broccoli?" Izaak asks.

"You're an adult, Izaak," Clark says. "You can choose not to eat any broccoli at all."

"Tell that to my mom," Izaak says.

"No, you're all wrong," Xander says. "Being rich is about telling other people to do stuff you don't want to do. Being *married* is about having the same person to complain to all the time. But then you're stuck pretending that you're not annoyed about all the things they do that drive you crazy."

"Gee, your future wife is in for a real treat," I say.

"No, Bevin's right," Clark says. "I mean, I hate having to call in take-out orders, and Carly always did that for me."

Izaak groans. "You've got to stop the crying, fam. You're better off without her."

"He's right," I say. "I can call in to-go orders for you, and I promise not to take half your retirement account in exchange."

"But you work nights." Clark somehow looks even more depressed. "You're usually busy when I want something to eat."

Everyone looks anywhere but at Clark. I can't totally blame them. He's been a bit of a black hole of whiney need lately, but after a few minutes it gets awkward, so I take action.

I kick Xander.

"Oh, fine," he says, "when Minerva's busy, I'll do it."

"No," Clark says. "You know what? Don't bother. Clearly none of you want to be there for me."

"Fine." Bevin groans. "Out of all of us, your toenails are probably the grossest, but I'll clip them, okay?" She starts rummaging around inside her purse.

"Yeah, thanks," Clark says, "but that's okay. I'll just keep clipping my own."

"Let me get you something to drink." I wave at Gavin, and he sets his empty tray down and trots over.

"What can I get you?" Gavin grins at Izaak. He always looks annoyed... unless Izaak's around. He's had a crush on Izaak for so long that it doesn't even irritate me anymore. I just take advantage of the superior service and premium seats.

"One glafficino," I say, "extra foam, and put a flower on top."

Clark perks up a little. "And maybe a dash of cinnamon?"

"And a muffin," Izaak says. "One of those blueberry ones."

"Actually, I don't really like blueberries," Clark says.

"I know." Izaak bites his lip. "The muffin's for me."

I roll my eyes.

"And one blueberry muffin," Gavin says with a smile, "for the best-looking actor in New York."

Izaak really should stop flirting. He couldn't be less gay if he tried, but since he keeps turning down every part he gets that's a villain—which is all of them—he's so broke that he'd do most anything to keep the free muffins coming.

Someone in the back corner turns on the television. I barely register what they're saying, because the Supernatural News Network, or SNN, is usually such shoddy news that I'm accustomed to ignoring it.

Until Bevin squeals. "Oh my holy Gabriel, it's about the royal wedding."

"For the last time, it's not a royal wedding," Xander says.

"Roxana Goldenscales *is* a princess—her mother Althea was the last princess of Maynila, daughter of Rajah Sulayman." Like demon-spawn who live a very long life, dragona can live upwards of a thousand years.

"Wait, where's Maynila?" Izaak asks. "Have I never heard of it because I didn't pay attention at school, or because it's like super old?"

"Super old." Bevin sighs. "I can't believe she's marrying that gorgeous Russian Prince. It's like a fairy tale."

"He's not a Russian prince," I say. "Russia isn't ruled by princes anymore. He's just a dragona prince, which is more like a mob boss than actual royalty." I've kept up with the whole thing a little, since I know Roxana. Or maybe it's more accurate to say that I *knew* her.

"His mob runs Russia," Bevin says, "which is basically the same thing as being a prince. And he's so hot, he could almost turn me straight."

"Hey," Izaak says. "You said I was the only one hot enough to turn you straight."

Bevin blows Izaak a kiss. "You know I love you the most."

Izaak leans back in his chair with a confident grin. "Yeah, you do."

"But if that man walked through those doors?" Bevin points. "Have you *seen* his wingspan? You do know what they say about a dragon's wingspan, don't you?"

"Eww. Impressive wingspan or not, Roxana doesn't look very happy in any of the interviews about the wedding," Clark says. "And I read that they still haven't even met face-to-face."

"They meet in a few days." Bevin claps her hands. "I can't wait to see how it goes."

Xander bats his eyes. "Oh yes, I won't be able to sleep a

wink until I see whether that dragon shifter and his lovely bride are really the match made in heaven they appear to be."

"Hey, did you ever get an invite to the wedding?" Clark asks. "I could be your plus one."

"No matter how handsome you look, she's not going to call off her wedding for you," I say. "Not even if you blew all your savings on that countenance upgrade spell."

Clark rolls his eyes. "Please. Not everything is about looks. When you're as beautiful as her, you transcend stuff like that."

"You're saying that you'd like her if she looked like Janet Reno?" I ask.

Clark frowns. "Janet Reno? Really?" He sighs. "She and I had a moment a few years ago, you know, and she might remember it. That's my point."

"Oh, please. You had an eyelash on your cheek and she brushed it off," I say.

"Before you barged in, her fingers were *lingering*."

"You're delusional," I say.

"I wouldn't mind clipping her toenails for the next forty years," Clark says. "That's all I'm saying."

"Me either," Bevin says.

"Actually, count me in, too," Izaak says.

"You're all crazy," I say. "In less than a week, she'll be married, and she'll fly away to Russia, and none of us will ever see her again."

1

MINERVA

Most mistakes in life are no big deal, even the big ones. After an apology, restitution, and a little time or training, eventually everything is fine.

But occasionally, a tiny error can land you in hot water.

Or boiling water, in my case.

Three months ago, while trying to apprehend a vampire who was feeding on blitzed people in a hot tub on the rooftop of a residential building, one of my spells misfired. Instead of a freeze spell, I let off a heat flash. . .and everyone in the hot tub boiled like lobsters. Thanks to a few strong potions, everyone survived, and were mostly fine within 48 hours, but the vampire I was trying to arrest, well. He was the son of their Sublime Chancellor.

Yeah, it's a really stupid name. Magical organizations are kind of famous for those.

But vampires vote as a bloc, and the New York Paranormal Affairs Chief is an elected position. So when his daddy called my boss, Chief Lumos had to do something.

I've been on probation ever since, and let me tell you, having to take remedial magic courses really sucks. Usually magic is fun—spell casting, potions, circles, wards, I like most all of it. But getting sent to remedial magic class is like a plumber being sentenced to spend three months unclogging toilets. Boring, embarrassing, and it stinks.

If I'm being honest, the class hasn't even really fixed my problem. My magic has been erratic and unreliable since I was a baby. These classes may have helped me learn how to mask my failures more effectively, but I'm pretty sure the real reason I was finally cleared is that my instructors got sick of me.

Until my recertification paperwork comes through, I have to earn my paycheck somehow.

Which is how I got stuck as the NYPAD liaison to initiates from the human world. In general, the sharpest crayons are not assigned to coordinate departments.

"You're saying that there are cops out there running around who are actual *vampires?*" The chunky man with ruddy cheeks leans back in his chair, his disbelief palpable.

There's an art to explaining the supernatural world to people who only know about parodies, like *Twilight* or *Interview with a Vampire*. I usually start with vampires, because most humans want to believe they exist. It makes for an easier transition.

But sometimes, like with this guy, it's better to just rip the Band-Aid off.

"I think I got ahead of myself." I sigh. "A war has been waged for more than a thousand years."

"A war has been waged? Isn't that a little melodramatic?" He looks around the room. "Are you recording the introduction to *Star Wars* here?"

Do not smack the fat, rude human, Minerva, not when you're already in trouble. "This is real." I cross my arms, expecting another interruption.

He, miraculously, stays quiet.

"The akero, embodiment of all that is light and good,

and the daimoni, the epitome of all that is dark and evil, have clashed over and over and over. You'd think they'd have realized the futility of it, but they never did. It's like an epically bad marriage, where the husband and wife are both taking out life insurance policies and making plans."

Officer Stevens drops the front feet of his chair back to the ground. "Wait, are you actually serious about this?"

I pull out the laminated photos of the akero, who look like the most gorgeous angels you could imagine, and drop them on the plastic card table in front of him. "I'm not a stand-up comedian."

He splays the cards out and hunches over them, finally stopping to stare at the most predictable card, the image of Raguel, the akero who embodies joy. The priestess who snapped the photo managed to catch a shot where she has her arms raised, her face upturned toward the Northern Lights, her expression rapturous. It's a moving photo. I've seen grown men cry while looking at it.

Not Officer Derpey here, but you know, emotionally intelligent ones.

"You're saying the angels and demons are here? On Earth?"

"I haven't explained that part yet." He's wrecking the rhythm of this, and that kind of thing matters with stories. "Their most epic battles happened in many different places. They're so evenly matched that neither side could gain any advantage. It was sort of like two kids leveling each others' sand castles, over and over and over."

"Sand castles?"

Mental note: analogies are wasted on Officer Derpey. "Something shattered the delicate balance between light and dark, and neither of them will fess up to what that was."

"Something?"

"That's when the angel Gabriel, their leader, directed

the akero to flee for the first time. And of course, the daimoni have doggedly pursued them ever since."

Officer Stevens blinks.

"First, the daimoni caught up to them on the dragon shifters' planet, and they fought again, until they destroyed that whole world."

"Like another sand castle?" He smirks.

Maybe there is hope for him. "Exactly," I say. "The akero saved what dragona were still alive and took them along when they fled."

"Okay, and the dragona?"

"They look like you or I." Although they have significantly less flop sweat than he has right now, but I don't feel like I need to make that distinction. "The male dragona can shift into the form of a dragon—enormous, magical beasts who can fly and breathe fire."

"Like Smaug?" He raises his eyebrows. "Seriously?"

"They don't stay that way, and they don't ravage towns anymore, but yes. Kind of like that, actually."

"Did you say only the males?"

"Dragona are born more than twenty to one, male to female, hatched from eggs only a female dragona can lay. The women, in a fit of universal injustice, can't shift into dragon form. The dragona claim it's only been that way since they came to Earth. It's one of the many things I'd like to bug the akero about if they ever deigned to talk to a lowly NYPAD officer like me."

He's spluttering, but I decide to move along anyway.

"Anyhow, the akero reached the werewolves' home next, and the story played out in exactly the same way. And then verse three with the vampires, too. Each time the akero fled, they dragged the weary and broken survivors from the last place they destroyed along with them, earnestly seeking a new, sustainable home in a place where the daimoni couldn't reach."

"And now they're here?"

"Ding ding," I say. "They've been here for over a thousand years now, actually. They finally found what they were looking for on Earth."

"The daimoni can't come on Earth?" He's clutching his badge like it's a strand of rosary beads or something, his eyes hopeful. At least he's not scoffing anymore.

"Ironically, it wasn't the akero themselves who found the solution. Apparently one of the akero, the stories disagree upon which, did something they'd never done, something the angel Gabriel had forbidden."

He leans forward, and I realize I've got him. In human movies and television, the most unrealistic part is how much characters struggle with accepting the paranormal world. Most humans at their most basic *want* to believe in fairies and werewolves and magic. The second they catch a whiff, they're like a kid with an empty Pez dispenser, begging for more.

"One of them banged a human and made a baby."

His jaw drops.

"Angel-spawn, they called them."

I can see it, like I always can, the second it occurs to Officer Derpey that he might one day hook up with an akero.

"Don't hold your breath, dude. It hasn't happened since the first decade they were on our planet."

His disappointment's palpable. I almost feel sorry for him. It's like I offered him the best of all hope and then snatched it away. I probably shouldn't show them photos, but they usually don't listen until I do.

"The good news for us is that creating a little horde of angel-spawn worked. They were able to cast the daimoni out and set up wards to keep them out permanently."

"So the demons can't come to Earth. . .because of the

angel babies? Are you sure they don't need any more, because I'd be more than willing to—"

"You know what? I think they're good." I'm about to use my cold shower spell on this guy if he doesn't stop.

"How do we know someone's angel-spawn? Do they have wings like the akero do?"

"They looked like normal humans, as I understand it, no wings. The bigger problem was that the angel-spawn couldn't find mates among humans—they were too different—and they obviously didn't belong with the angels. So they married one another, and that created the race of humans known as mages. Witches and wizards, who can cast spells with power that's linked to but different from the akero's magic."

"That's what you are, right?"

I cringe a bit. "Yes, I'm a witch."

"So, it's not like *all* the angel-spawn are super hot."

I am going to punch this guy. Two chops right to the throat. "I'm not angel-spawn. I'm a mage, but good call insulting someone who can turn you into a toad." It's not strictly true, but he's getting on my nerves.

"But the paperwork I got said there's demon-spawn, too."

Right to the dark side. Guys like this are the reason the New York subways smell like a sewer. "Yes, and that's where things turn south. The wards created by the angel-spawn, and maintained by the akero ever since, can be broken."

"Like Smaug's missing scale." He grips the table with both hands.

It's like he thinks we're part of a movie. "This is my life, dude, and it's about to be yours. Stop comparing it to *The Hobbit*."

He nods his head, almost chagrined.

"The daimoni can be summoned here temporarily,

although being inside the warding spells causes terrible pain, like, worse than stepping on a Lego, I hear."

He frowns.

No sense of humor, this guy.

"But they come anyway because they want to create demon-spawn. That's their only chance of breaking the wards. Once born, demon-spawn long to descend, which they do by committing sins that will help their nature shift toward that of their fathers."

"Are you saying all demons are male?"

Maybe he's not a complete lump after all. "Good question. No, they're not all male. Half of them are, but obviously a female demon can't stay here long enough to become pregnant and have a child, so all demon-spawn are children of the male demons."

"Huh. That's wild."

"These children, the demon-spawn, literally become more and more like demons themselves as they do bad things. It hasn't happened yet, but their ultimate goal is for one of them to Descend, with a capital D. That's when a demon-spawn literally becomes a daimon, but because it started as a human with a right to be on Earth, its existence would shatter the wards."

"And then those things could all come in and that same battle would level Earth?"

I nod. "Exactly."

Officer Derpey's command of swear words is fairly impressive, really. His parents must've been from Jersey.

I wait for him to calm down enough that I can continue. "There are eight deadly sins, and a demon-spawn would have to commit each one in order to Descend. Each time they accomplish one, they gain a new power, and a burst of magic is released. At the NYPAD, we track those, and we ensure that no demon-spawn are allowed to descend past level six."

"How? How do you do that?"

"There's an elite group within our organization, the guardians, and they eliminate demon-spawn when they descend a sixth time."

"Why not just kill them all immediately?" He's got crazy eyes. Slap some camouflage rubber boots on him and give him a shotgun, and he could play the part of a paranoid prepper in any movie Hollywood has made.

"There are thousands of demon-spawn living constructive lives and not-so-constructive lives, all over the world. We can't kill them for how they were born. You should know that already. That's what makes us the good guys."

He mutters, "Sounds like that's what makes us the stupid guys."

"Believe me when I say, we all agree that no demon-spawn can be allowed to Descend. If the daimoni had access to Earth, it would mark the end of *everything*."

That's why I've always wanted to be a guardian myself; it's why I've been desperate for it.

But there's no way they'll ever select a magical flunkie like me. My own personal Everest? Figure out how to stop flubbing all these spells so I can fill my real purpose: protecting the world from the daimoni threat just like my dad did.

"If all these creatures are out there, how will I know—they could have been walking all around me before now?"

"They *have* been walking around you before now."

"But how can I know which ones they are?" He's showing the whites of his eyes, like a panicked horse.

"We all drink gloffee daily—it's like your coffee, but it tastes way better, and it works to disguise us from the humans. It's a glamour spell, basically."

"So I won't ever be able to—"

I point at his badge. "That's charmed. When you're wearing that, the glaffour berries won't work their magic."

He swallows. "So I'll be able to tell—"

"Vampires move a little too fast. They almost look blurry around the edges when they're in a hurry. Werewolves usually look a little hairy and sound a little gruff. And witches and wizards usually carry a wand."

"That's the only way I'll know?"

I shrug. "I can sense them—it's a magical thing. Werewolves, dragona, and vampires can smell each other. Humans—you just need to keep your eyes open and watch for the cues. Eventually you'll start to pick up on it, too."

When the door bangs open, I start.

"Officer Lucent?"

My partner Amber never calls me that, but with a human around, she's acting all formal. It's kind of cute.

"Yes, Officer Crimson, what can I do for you?"

"We just caught a case," she says. "An urgent one."

I blink. "But I won't be cleared until next week."

She thrusts a paper at me. "Looks like your paperwork got expedited. You're back on duty."

Oh, thank Gabe. I stand up. "Alright, Officer Struppins—"

"It's Stevens," he says.

"Whatever. I'm out of here. If you have questions. . . don't ask me."

2

MINERVA

It's not like zombies are universally adored. Most people dislike them, and for good reason. They're gross, they smell, and they usually have weeping sores that don't heal until the tainted blood has left their system and their bodies can heal. Oh, and they mumble even worse than George W. Bush at a press conference.

But me?

I really *despise* them. It's probably because as an NYPAD officer, we're always the ones getting called to deal with them so that humans don't get bothered.

And they're so shuffly, and slobbery, and just. . .ugh. They smell *so* bad.

You'd think that with a vampire partner, I'd be a little more tolerant, but Amber's actually way jerkier to them than I am.

"Just give up already, you lousy leech." Amber body checks the shuffling zombie, and he slams into the brick wall in the alley and slumps to the ground.

I crouch behind him, an extra strong zip tie in my hand.

"Really? You're still using zip ties?" Amber groans. "But you were cleared to cast spells again."

I was hoping she wouldn't notice. "It's been a while, and I'm rusty." I slide the zip tie around the zombie's wrists and cinch it tight.

"I thought you cast the same six spells over and over in there. Didn't you?" Amber lifts his arms a little too much and he moans. She bites off the extra plastic sticking off the end of his zip ties and spits it on the ground.

Sometimes I envy the vampires and their superhuman strength—and razor sharp teeth. I'm stuck using a pocketknife or scissors for things like that. Let me tell you, carrying around a pair of scissors is *not* a way to look cooler at the department.

"Let's go, slug." Amber wrenches the poor guy's arms backward and uses the pressure to lever him to his feet.

"At least our squad car's parked just down the alley," I say. "I don't think I could stand to watch him lurch and fumble very far."

"Mraaow." The zombie sounds almost like Charlie Brown's mom. He keeps turning toward Amber when he tries to talk, like she'll be more lenient. That's his biggest mistake.

"Don't look at me with those glossy eyes," she practically spits. "You were taught in kindergarten what would happen if you drank the blood of someone who's impaired, so this is on you. I'm sick of cleaning up after you, and taxpayers shouldn't have to pay for you to sit in the zombie tank until all that blood has left your system."

We finally reach the squad car and Amber shoves him into the back seat and slams the door with a sigh. "Why do we always get zombie duty? I swear, if one more of those gluttonous slobs pukes boozy O positive in the back of our car—"

"We can't leave them on the streets. They're too baked to drink gloffee and then the humans can see everything."

"We get great TV shows and movies from it, though," she says.

"Great? That word might be a little strong."

"Hey, *The Walking Dead*—"

The magical blast hits us both at the same time, and I rock back on my heels. Amber lunges for the driver's side door, blocking me from taking the wheel like a vampire meat-shield. "No. Not this time."

I don't bother trying to kick her out of my seat. The last time I tried that, it was like wrestling with an octopus. Instead, I climb into the passenger side like the polite partner that I am. "Can we go? It's so close. Please? If the guardians are already there, no big deal, we can just leave. But if we don't go and the guardians are too far away, the demon-spawn could escape."

She folds her arms and shakes her head. "I promised the Chief."

"What?" I blink. "What does that mean?"

"It was the only way he'd clear you." She sighs. "Did you know that ninety-nine percent of your misfires come when we're onsite after a demon-spawn descends?"

Probably because that's when I'm in the biggest rush. "I misfire plenty, even when there aren't descending demon-spawn around." That doesn't seem like it strengthens my argument. "That came out wrong."

"We're going back to the department. Right now." She turns the car on.

With no time to waste, I yank out my trump card right away. "If you take me, I'll let you drink my blood."

Her eyes flash more golden than I've seen in weeks. Her manicured fingernails circle the steering wheel and dig into the palms of her hands. Mage blood is almost impossible for vampires to get, and they all love it.

"You can drink it right now, in advance. That way you'll be at your strongest when we reach the site." I slice my forearm and grab a Dixie cup from this morning's gloffee.

Her moan when the smell of my blood hits is not unlike the noise the zombie in the backseat was making a moment before, and I feel a little dirty offering it to her. But with my magical dysfunction, I need to catch a descending demon-spawn to be taken seriously as a guardian prospect.

"Do we have a deal?"

She practically rips my arm off, she grabs the wilted paper cup so fast, but then she takes forever sipping on the little bit of blood.

"Come on, let's go!" I don't want my hustle to be a complete waste.

Which, as usual, it totally is. By the time we reach the scene, only a few blocks away, it's already crawling with Land Rover Defenders—the official guardian car. "Mother Feather."

"Hey, don't be mad. It's good they're here," Amber says. "We all want to make sure we catch and register the demon-spawn. As long as that happens, we all win."

"Oh, shut up," I say.

Amber pats my hand, like my granny used to when I struck out in t-ball. "There will always be more demon-spawn breaking the rules. It's a constant in life, like werewolves shedding on the sofa, men peeing on the toilet seat, and cockroaches hiding under the fridge. Demon-spawn descend. It's what they do."

It always irritates me when she makes those kinds of generalizations. "Some demon-spawn are trying to be good, and one day I *will* meet a man who lifts the toilet seat."

"That kind of naiveté is the real reason you'll never be a guardian." She puts the car back into gear and heads back toward the precinct.

"Whoa, we're going back?"

"In case you forgot." She jams her thumb over her

shoulder at Mr. Shuffles. "I'll run him downstairs, and you can dive into all the files."

I've been so busy with liaison work and remedial spell training that I haven't touched the files in weeks. Amber knows it's been taunting me. "Stop using that as a lure," I complain. "I'm good at other stuff, too. For instance, I'm great at fieldwork."

"Sure you are," she says. "Of course."

And it's like t-ball all over again.

She's not really being that mean. Amber knows that I *love* organizing the files. Paranormal Affairs Officers are disgusting slobs who can barely fill out a form, much less give it the care it requires to be easy to access later. After two years of being the only officer with organized and efficient records, the Chief finally begged me to take over the whole system.

Not that anyone thanks me for it.

"I did get approved for casting again."

"I'm the one who found out you were cleared, but you used a zip tie just now. Remember?" Amber sighs. "Maybe next time, you leave them in the car and take your wand."

I don't bother making excuses. With someone else, maybe, but Amber has been there for every misfired spell, every overcast one, and all the underpowered ones, too.

"You're so smart. I don't get why—"

"The class the Chief put me in worked," I say with a confidence I don't entirely feel.

"Did it really?" Amber looks pretty unsure.

I don't completely blame her. The last freeze spell that misfired left her standing stock still with her hand out in an alley for three hours. By the time she regained use of her own limbs, the other PA officers had magicked a mustache on her. It didn't disappear for two days.

"Repetition is the key," I say. "I cast the spells so many times that I can't overthink them."

"That's what they think the problem is?" She frowns. "You're overthinking them?"

No one really knows what the problem is. I'm smart enough. My aptitude and magic levels are plenty high. But just like in school, I'm erratic at casting. "It'll be fine. I certified in the main six spells, and they signed off for me to come back." Or, like SpongeBob's driving teacher, mine passed me because my instructor never wanted to see me again.

"Well, I'm really glad you're back." Amber smiles.

I should be counting my blessings—not many partners would be so willing to take me back after obligatory magical rehab, or so supportive after my frequent failings. It's not even like the last incident was an anomaly. Poor Amber has been zapped, frozen, put to sleep, forced to spill secrets, and stunned more times than I can count. "Thanks for always having my back."

Amber shrugs. "You're the smartest officer we've got. If you were great at casting, you'd have been made guardian years ago. You'd probably be gunning for the Chief's job."

I hate that she's right. If only.

The mood's unexpectedly somber back at the precinct. No one's laughing, no one's even speaking loudly. It makes our zombie friend especially irritating as he fumbles and groans and moans his way through the front entry. I glance at Amber to see if she has any idea what's going on. A quick, small shake of her head tells me she's as lost as me.

"I'll take him." She eyes the three-foot tall stack of files on the edge of our shared desk apprehensively. "You better get started or we might die under an avalanche of paper."

Outwardly I groan, but the little organizer inside of me squeals with glee. Sometimes I put off organizing the files just so I have more to do all at once. After I start, I stop paying attention to much else. But the four hours it takes me are glorious! When I come up for air, Amber's still playing on her phone.

"Plants versus zombies again?" I roll my eyes. "That app is so old."

"They added new levels," she says. "And look?" She spins her phone around. "The new zombies have fangs! They finally got it right."

"We have, what? An hour left on our shift?" I yawn—sometimes night shifts suck, but if I switched to days, I'd get assigned a new partner. Vampires are too sleepy to work day shifts, and in spite of her flaws, I do love Amber.

The front door of the precinct opens, and a burst of air puffs through the department. "They really should've added double doors," Amber says. "It's annoying how every single time someone comes in, the entire room gets windy." She shivers.

But we all look at the door to see who's entering out of habit, and maybe that's why they never bothered with the double doors.

I'm rewarded with the face I like most in this world. He's wearing his usual black shirt, dark jeans, and a black leather jacket. His hair's clean cut and combed, as always. He looks like every male detective in America *wishes* they looked. Muscles, clean jawline, deep chocolate eyes. "Ricky," I whisper.

"Ooh," Amber says. "Look who's here. Guardian Eye Candy."

I shove her.

"Wonder what he's here for." She wiggles her eyebrows.

As if. He barely even knows I exist.

"Hey Minerva." Ricky waves, but he doesn't walk toward our desk. He heads straight for the Chief's office.

I hate that I'm disappointed.

He pauses outside the door and pulls something out of

a slim briefcase. I wouldn't have thought he'd even own a briefcase, but he manages to pull it off. He presses a paper against the Chief's window, whispering a silent sticking spell, and then pushes through into his office.

"What'dya think that is?" Amber points at the sign.

I squint, but I can't quite make out the words.

When I finally edge close enough to read it, a pulse of excitement runs through me. GUARDIAN POSITION OPEN. INTERNAL APPLICATIONS WELCOMED.

My timing couldn't be better—cleared for duty just as they open a new spot? "It's fate," I say. "It must be."

"Fate?" Amber rolls her eyes. "That demon-spawn today killed a guardian—didn't you hear? Or were you too enraptured with the files?" She shakes her head. "That's not fate. It's shizzy luck, which by the way, is kind of standard for guardians."

"But they caught him," I say. "Or her."

"Yeah, and they registered another demon mark and *let them go*." She scowls. "They should just kill them after a single mark like they used to. All this PC crap is obnoxious."

For as different as they are, she sounds a lot like the human I was educating at the beginning of my shift. I didn't bother with him, but I never let it slide with Amber. "They don't really get dangerous until they've got three or four marks," I say. "A few might be accidental."

"Demons descend when they sin," Amber says. "One mark is one sin—I still think allowing them to register each new one and then not eliminating them until they have six is a huge mistake."

"We didn't make that call," I say. "The akero did—"

"But we're the ones out here carrying out the mighty akero's dictates, and it's our butts on the line," Amber says.

She's always been a little sacrilegious, but this feels

worse. I drop my voice to a whisper. "Please tell me you haven't been going to any more of those meetings."

Amber shakes her head. "I promised you, didn't I?"

If I didn't love Amber so much, I'd already have turned her in. Radical anti-angel secret societies and PA officers shouldn't mix. "Good. Don't."

"Not going doesn't change my irritation. Why don't *they* keep the world safe from the threat they brought here? Why do we have to do all their work for them?"

"They created the wards," I say. "It's our job to keep them intact by preventing any demons from Descending on Earth." Arguing with her is a waste of time, but sometimes I forget.

I redirect to what matters. Ogling Ricky with sideways glances while preparing my guardian application. Since I've saved most of the component parts of the application over the years, it goes together quickly, which is good. It's almost shift change. I'm just waiting for Ricky to stand up and leave, and then I can hand him my application directly. "I've about got this finished."

"You know I think it's dumb, but I really do wish you good luck," Amber says.

"It can't hurt to be the first one who applies, right?"

Her snort tells me that she feels the same way about my application as I do about her unpopular opinion on our angel overlords, as she calls them.

"What's that I hear?" Peter Chester sneers. "Officer Floppy Wand's applying to be a guardian again?"

"Why do you care?" I ignore his crass jabs. "You're still too afraid to apply yourself."

"Not being insane isn't the same thing as being afraid." He folds his arms. "But you just keep right on banging your head against that wall, expecting a different result."

"I just completed—"

"Remedial magic." He laughs. "That's like Hogwarts Pre-K. Bravo, you can cast level one spells with reasonable competency. I mean, joining the guardians makes sense to me. You're exactly the kind of officer who should become cannon fodder for some filthy demon-spawn."

"Look—"

Amber bares her teeth at Peter and snaps.

"Keep your bloodsucker on a leash," Peter says. "Or when Rufus gets here—"

"I don't need to use a leash. You're the one with a dog."

"Very original," Peter says.

"I still can't believe your new werewolf partner's named Rufus," I say.

"Oh?" Peter asks. "In addition to misfiring spells, you're struggling to remember names now?"

"Actually, I think the name's perfect for him. I had a dog named Rufus," I say, "and he drooled on everything and took dumps while squatting, just like your partner."

I know I got to him, because the dumb falcon that always sits on his shoulder fluffs up and squawks. "You have a better chance of being crowned Miss America than you do of making guardian."

The door cracks open and Ricky walks out, closing it behind him.

"I guess we'll see," I say. "Because I'm applying right now." I walk toward the guardian and hold out my application. "Here."

"Thanks, Minerva." If Ricky's voice was candy, it would be dark chocolate syrup. Rich, thick, and deep.

"You can just toss that in the trash on your way out and save everyone some time," Peter says.

Ricky eyes Peter up and down slowly. With the two of them standing side by side, the difference is incomparable. If they were in a Hollywood movie, Peter would be played by Chris Evans before the Captain America serum, and Ricky's definitely the after.

Peter's mouth, previously quirked up in disdain, flattens under the inspection.

Ricky slides my application into his briefcase. "Only one new recruit has applied every single time we've opened a position." He tosses his head at me. "Every single guardian in New York knows the name Minerva Lucent. She's brave, she's energetic, and I think that one day, she'll serve the akero as a guardian." He snorts. "You, on the other hand? I have no idea who you are, and I bet I never do."

I wait until Ricky's gone before I start to fan myself.

"He's just being nice, you know." Peter shrugs. "I couldn't care less whether they know who I am. Guardians' average life expectancy is thirty-five. Did you know that?"

I did, actually. "But what they do for the world can't be measured."

"Okay, Sparky," Amber says. "Let's go check on Mr. Shuffles."

I know what she's doing—trying to defuse this situation before I wind up on probation again. But guys like Peter have mocked me my entire life, and I always have to be the one to stand down. I'm sick of it.

"You're an interesting guy," I say. "When you were in school, did you learn what a Venn diagram is?"

Peter frowns.

"If I were to make one with a circle for stupid, and a circle for bully, and a circle for unattractive, you'd probably be the only officer here who managed to be in all three."

Peter frowns, but he doesn't look as apoplectic as he usually would. I'm guessing he doesn't know what a Venn diagram is and didn't really get my insult. Even so, he fires back. "You better rush off to check on that filthy vampire you put in lockdown before you really make me mad."

"Uh-oh, Peter Chester, really mad. What must that look like? More spluttering? An even redder face?"

"Keep making jokes," he says. "In the meantime, I'll tell the Chief that he'll have yet another chance to write a recommendation for the only mage on the force who can't even bond a familiar. I bet he only recommends you in the hopes he might finally get rid of you."

That one stings. I've tried more than six times to bond a familiar, but that particular spell never takes right for me, even when I tried it with a dog, and they're so eager to bond that humans can practically do it. "I just haven't found the right animal yet."

"Thanks to a hunting accident, my uncle's a little slow," Peter says, "and even he has a rat."

"It doesn't surprise me that your relative bonded a rat," Amber says. "Like calls to like, after all."

Peter's lip curls, and his partner, a brand new recruit, one of the burliest werewolves I've ever seen, is striding across the room toward us.

The Chief's door opens abruptly. "Shift change." He tilts his head at me. "First night back went alright?"

I nod.

"Great. Now go get some sleep so you'll be fresh tonight." I often wonder whether the Chief has auditory spells cast around the precinct. He casually opens his door in the middle of escalating fights a little too often.

Or maybe it's just part of being a good Chief.

"Yes, sir."

Amber walks out with me. "Don't let them get to you. That guy just has an inferiority complex—"

"He's not wrong, though." What committee in their right mind would select a mage who can't even bond a familiar to be a guardian?

Amber knows me well enough not to argue any further. Sometimes I just need to wallow. "See you tonight."

Most people think the eight p.m. to eight a.m. shift is brutal, but I don't mind working four twelves a week. I get eight hours of overtime, and I still have a three-day run of days off every week. Not too bad.

Usually I spend the drive home listening to classical music so that I can wind down and go to sleep. But this morning, even that doesn't help. I'm just as keyed up when I exit the subway near my place. Peter's a jerk, but he's right about one thing. I can't keep applying to be a guardian and being shocked when I don't get it. The definition of insanity really is doing the same thing over and over and expecting something to inexplicably change. I may not be the most talented or consistent mage, but I'm bright.

Unfortunately, that's not enough.

Smart people can't catch demon-spawn and neutralize them—if that's all it took, normie accountants and lawyers could be doing it. No, I need something else. I need to show the Chief and the committee that chooses the new guardian that I've changed.

But how?

It's not like a cuff spell or a brilliant freeze spell's enough. Those are baseline requirements.

The flashiest way would be to bond a really amazing familiar. It needs to be a brilliant one. A hawk, maybe, or a bobcat? No, bobcats are hard to tote around the city— maybe if I lived in the mountains.

When I notice the light's on at Bevin's Boutique, my best friend's secondhand magic shop, I decide to stop in. Most shops have a bell that jingles when customers come inside. My crazy friend Bevin has a charmed chicken that sings an egg song.

It starts cackling like a lunatic the second I walk through the door. Even so, there's no Bevin in sight. I wouldn't be shocked if she just forgot to lock up the night before. It's happened—and she lost a bundle of stock, too.

Since it's a secondhand shop, it's not like she can just order more inventory, either. She has to acquire it slowly, through her magical contacts and brokers. "Bevin!"

Two seconds later, her head pops through the back door. "Sorry! Just finishing up a seance. Be right there."

No wonder she's here early. Some of her clients hate the nighttime, but spirits are reticent to come out during broad daylight, so that leaves early morning. I hope it went well. She gets the bulk of her revenue from seances. She's quite good at them.

The hunched old woman who finally toddles out in front of her looks pleased, at least. "Next time, you can't pay me in dried glaffour berries," Bevin says. "I said that last time too, but I really mean it."

Her magical hen doesn't differentiate between going and coming, so the second the woman walks out the door, it starts flapping and singing again. "You need a new doorbell. I'll buy you some chimes."

"Chimes are boring." Bevin tosses a chunk of some kind of food to her front door chicken and it stops singing. "You're here early."

"I thought you swore off the early morning seances." I shake my head. "And that lady paid you in glaffour berries? Really?"

"She's so old, her teeth have fallen out," Bevin says. "And that's not a great place for a vampire to be, but she misses her husband, and I can't seem to tell her no."

"You're the worst demon-spawn I've ever met," I say.

Bevin beams at that, of course. She's made it her primary directive to utterly fail at ever descending. Even if it means she has virtually no power, she won't give in to her demonic side, except as a conduit to reach out to departed spirits, that is. "I'm actually here as a client today," I say.

"Oh?" Bevin leans on her counter. "What can I do for

you? Finally ready to splurge on that magical love potion for Ricky?" She wiggles her eyebrows.

"For the love of Gabriel, stop."

"The new one works really well, I hear."

"No, look. There's a guardian position open—"

She can't contain her groan. "Minerva—not again. Really? I know you want to be a guardian like your dad, but—"

"No buts. I realized that to catch the Chief's eye, to show him I'm ready, I need to do something big. Something splashy." I pause for dramatic effect.

Bevin grabs a nail file and starts buffing her nails.

"Mother feather, look, I really need to bond a familiar."

Bevin actually bangs her head on the top of her counter. "Not this again."

"What?" I can hardly believe what she's saying. "My best friend doesn't even have faith in me?"

She straightens. "Minerva Lucent, we've been friends for more than six years now. You know I love you. I'm grateful to you for your guidance, for your nonjudgmental attitude—for a mage—and for your unfailing support. But you will never be a guardian, and you need to be okay with that."

If even Bevin doesn't believe in me, maybe Peter's right. "I can't just bond any familiar," I say. "I need to bond a flame lizard."

Bevin freezes.

"Come on. If anyone can find me one, it's you."

"Do you have any idea what those cost?" She laughs. "Even if I could find one, you could never afford—"

"I'll sell my akero feather."

This time, her jaw drops.

"I mean it," I say. "You've been begging me to sell that for years, and I'll finally do it."

"You can't get it back if you change your mind," Bevin says.

She's actually trying to talk me out of it?

"And do you know how rare it is to bond a flame lizard? They're unpredictable, they're capricious, and they're foul-tempered."

But if I walked into the precinct with one of them on my shoulder? I'd make guardian by the end of the week. "I'll risk it."

"It's not like I even know where to look for a flame lizard egg. They say from the time you get one, you have less than 24 hours to do the ceremony. They're notoriously fickle and—" Bevin's eyes widen. "Wait. Don't you have an old friend who's dragona? I'm sure—"

"I can't call Roxana. We haven't even spoken in. . ." I do the math in my head. "At least two years, and that call was just because I sent her a holiday card and mentioned a guy she used to go out with. She wanted to see how he was doing."

"She's still your best bet. You might even get a good deal if she helps. You could buy it for a hundred thousand or so instead of giving up your feather."

"I don't have a hundred thousand dollars!"

"Between your life savings and your wedding fund? Really?" Bevin shakes her head. "It would be better than selling your akero feather."

She's probably right. I hate asking for favors, but if she happens to have any connections. . .I scroll through my phone until I find her number and hit talk. Of course, it doesn't work. "The cell reception in here is awful."

"Clark owed me for digging the imps out of—you know what? Doesn't matter. Having amazing wards has downsides, but I sleep way better at night this way."

I hold out my hand for her landline. I probably can't

mock her for having one anymore, not after this. "It's not likely she'll even answer this early in the morning," I say.

But she does. On the very first ring. "Hello?"

"Roxana?"

"Yes, who's this?" She humphs. "If you're calling about the charmed bags, they already sold."

"What?"

"The caller ID says it's a secondhand magic shop?" Her bored socialite voice sounds exactly like I recall. "If that's all you needed, I'll hang up."

"No, wait, Roxana, it's me, Minerva."

"Minerva?"

"Right, Minerva. Your old friend, Minerva Lucent, from Perfectly Poised, the magical finishing school."

"I know who you are." She sighs. "Look, I'm so sorry I didn't send you an invite, but the thing is, Mom's been a real drag about the guest list and security and—"

"An invite?"

"To my wedding. Isn't that why you're calling?"

She's clearly still assuming she knows everything. "No, I mean, congratulations on marrying a prince and all that." I didn't expect an invite, but it's been in every single supernatural paper and news report for months. "Actually I was calling to ask a completely-unrelated-to-the-wedding favor." Although. Maybe I can use her guilt to my advantage. "I was really bummed I didn't make the cut, though. I guess we're not as close as I thought we were."

"Oh, no, Minerva, we were."

"We *were*?" I sigh, heavy and long. "I guess it's true what they say—nothing really lasts."

"I'm so sorry. I didn't mean to say *were*. But, wait. Did you say you need a favor?"

"You were the first person I thought of, since we *were* so close."

This time, my dramatic pause helps. I can tell.

"It's a flame lizard egg," I say. "I figured even if you couldn't get me an invite to the wedding, the least you could do for an old friend was try to help me locate one."

"*Grabe*! Why on earth would you want one of those? They're horrible creatures, always setting things on fire and shrieking." I can practically hear her shudder through the phone. I forgot how crisp-sounding a landline can be. "Trust me, I'm doing you a bigger favor by telling you not to get one."

"But the thing is, I really need it. Any chance you can help?"

"There's only one person I know who sells those, and he's...unsavory."

"I don't mind," I say. "I'd love his contact information."

She gives it to me. "If that's all you needed?"

"It is," I say. "But I really do wish you the best with the wedding. I'm sure, knowing you, it'll be fabulous."

"That's true," she says. "It will."

I'm almost a little bit sad when I hang up. It's not like she and I are close now, but we were, once. She was my life raft in the middle of a stormy, miserable ocean for a while. It's sad when people drift apart.

"Wow, you're really going to do this?" Bevin picks up the paper on which I scrawled the name and number of Roxana's broker.

"You're going to do it for me, right?" I make prayer hands.

"As if I'd send you to negotiate this alone." She rolls her eyes. "You'd come back an indentured servant to a genie."

"Wait, are there really genies?"

Bevin laughs. "See?"

"I'm not that bad," I say. "I'm a cop."

Bevin pats my head and smiles condescendingly at me. "Yes, you are. And don't you forget it."

"I'm not a dog," I say. It's like t-ball all over again.

"A dog!" She claps her hands. "Let's try one of those again."

"Bevin." I plead with my eyes.

"Fine, but your princess friend Roxana was right—flame lizards are awful. And if it doesn't work, you'll be out either a lot of money or your akero feather, and either way. . . It's just a bad idea, that's all."

It will work.

It has to.

3

ROXANA

My mother Althea, at six hundred and nineteen years of age, is the most beautiful woman I know. Her gorgeous ebony hair shines. Her golden eyes sparkle. Her skin's luminescent. Her limbs are long and elegant, and her smile practically knocks men over like bowling balls smashing dead center into a stack of pins.

She was born just before the Spanish invaded our islands and named it the Philippines. At first she hated my father for what he did to her people, but eventually he won her over. As the president of the United States dragona, the CEO of the Dagobar Group, and the reigning champion of the local sparring ring, he's about as savagely successful as they come.

He's not someone you'd pin as a lovesick romantic, but that's the kind of relationship they have. It's probably entirely my mother's doing. She's effortlessly charming and gracefully elegant, all the time.

But their love for each other isn't the reason they could arrange a marriage for me with Ragar the Ruthless, the oldest and most terrifying son of the leader of Russia's dragona king, Mikhail the Marauder. They did that entirely thanks to my dad's similarly savage reputation, and the successful empire he's built.

Of course, seeing as he runs a horrifying mob of dragona in a savage part of the world, he's kept fairly busy. That's why today's our first time meeting in person.

I had such high hopes. It's really too bad that I absolutely detest him.

"I learned English for you," he says. "So that your delicate brain isn't required to strain itself."

"Strain itself?" My delicate hand's currently itching to slap him, but I've been trained my entire life for this moment. I don't know much about literature or science, but I know exactly how to be the perfect dragon-shifter bride.

It doesn't involve slapping my groom across his handsome face.

"The most beautiful female dragona are always the most delicate." When he grins at me, his teeth practically gleam. His cheekbones are just as high and sharp and his eyes just as bright as they looked in his photos. His is a bright and deadly beauty, perhaps more so in real life. He's even less warm than my own father, which I hadn't thought possible.

But Dad warms up around Mom. I need to remember that.

"I think you'll find that we Goldenscales dragona aren't nearly as fragile as you've been led to believe."

He wraps an arm around my shoulders, dragging me up against his muscle-rippling side. "That's cute, but I had killed a dozen other dragons by the time I finished with what you call high school. You can feel safe, knowing that I will never fail to protect you, no matter who must be slain."

Slain? Who taught him English? Did they use the Bible as the work text? It's an effort not to roll my eyes. "Oh, that's so good to hear—a dozen dragons, dead, by the time you turned eighteen." Maybe he'll take my shudder as a sign of how impressive I think he is.

"Does that not please you?"

Or maybe not. It's too bad he's not a little dumber. "Uh, no, I mean, yes. It does make me happy. How could it not?" I clear my throat. "Just think about all those bloody corpses." My lips twist. "I mean, that's hot."

This is not going well.

"It may take me some time before we can eliminate these communication errors." He beams down at me, like he's extremely generous. "I should have known you'd be impressed. What dragona would not be pleased to learn her future husband is the strongest, scariest, most powerful man in the world?"

"Right." I force a laugh. "Who wouldn't?"

Me. That's who.

Maybe it's because I've been surrounded by testosterone-dripping dragona my entire life. Maybe it's because no one even bothered to ask me if I wanted to get married. But in this moment, the meeting I've been groomed for my entire life, I've never wanted to disappear from my own life more.

"I trust you'll be pleased with the spectacle that we have arranged for our wedding. There will be hundreds of fire-eating dancers, dozens of the very best singers, and thousands of dragona from your father's realm and mine, all coming to pay tribute. The pile of treasure downstairs is already quite large."

Tribute.

When Mom first told me we'd be getting heaps of jewels and other fancy gifts, I could hardly contain my excitement. Now, the thought of smiling as thousands of people swear fealty to us and bind their oaths with gold and gems makes me a little ill. "Do we really need all of that?"

Ragar's face blanks, as if he can't understand the words

I'm speaking. Perhaps I should repeat my question in Russian for *his* delicate brain.

"Ya ne khochu etogo," I say.

"You learned Russian?" He looks even more surprised by that than he does by my declaration that I don't want any of their pledges and treasure.

"Do you really want all those people to swear to serve us? Is it really necessary, in this day and age?"

"You've been kept sheltered and safe." Ragar nods. "That's as it should be." He strides around me in protective circles, as if an attack could come from any direction at any time. "But it means you don't understand the true nature of our people. Your instincts are to nurture and to make beautiful. Leave the rest to me."

Right now my instincts are to gouge and to scream, but I manage to keep from saying that out loud.

"It's the oaths they offer that will keep our people together. With more than twenty men for every single female, they all crave the chance to protect you, and that's why they will serve me."

Not us.

Him.

His smile is downright wicked. "Because I'm marrying the finest among all our females, I will usher in a new generation of strength and vibrancy."

Again, with the 'I.' Is he planning to lay dragon eggs himself? This guy's the worst.

He steps closer to me and puts a hand on my belly. "I can't wait to start. I'll have more children than any other ruler before me."

Oh, goodie. I'm about to be a dragon egg E-Z Bake Oven.

Usually I like dark and handsome things, but instead of sending a thrill through me, his touch fills me with increasing dread. I should tell him that I can't marry him. I should tell him that, although I greatly regret it, I need to call off our wedding. But he's right about one thing. I was raised with great care and sheltered from everything. Mom and Dad never taught me to do hard things, so I can't quite force the words out.

After he finally leaves and Mom comes in, I can't keep a tear from sliding down my cheek.

"Anak ko, what's wrong?" Mom wipes the tear carefully from my face. "Crying will make your face puffy and red. We can't have that when you're getting married tomorrow. Do you know how many reporters will be there? The entire world will be watching."

No, we can't have anything mar the perfection of my appearance. That just won't do. Rage floods my entire body. Why is the only thing that matters my looks? Why didn't anyone ever ask me if I wanted to marry Ragar? Without that uncharacteristic anger, I'm not sure I would have been able to force the words out, even with only Mom in the room.

But I do say them. "I don't want to get married tomorrow."

Mom frowns. "It will be difficult to postpone the wedding, but—"

"I don't want to get married to Ragar *ever*." The words are barely a whisper, but I said them.

Mom heard it, too. I can tell. Her entire face is frozen.

"I know you went to a lot of effort to set the wedding up."

"Not just effort. Great expense," she says.

"I am sorry about that, and I know a lot of dragona have travelled from Russia—"

"From all over the world," she corrects.

"Right."

Mom takes my hand gently and drags me over to the plush chairs in the corner of my room. "It's normal to be nervous about starting a new life, but it's important to remember that this is about more than you."

"My wedding is about *more than me?*"

"You know I didn't choose to marry your father, and my mother told me the same thing I'm telling you now. Sometimes it falls on you to fix things when they go wrong. It's part of being a princess, a dragona, and a Goldenscales."

"What could I possibly fix by marrying a blockhead?" I shake my head. "He literally spent five minutes bragging about how many people he'd *slain.*"

"Your father wasn't always the gem he is now, either."

"Oh, please. Dad was never as bad as Ragar."

Mom rolls her eyes. "Dad came to conquer, and he saw our country as spoils of war. But how about now?"

"It's not where we'd like it to be, but Dad has helped the Philippines a lot."

"Every balikbayan should thank your dad for their job overseas. Why do you think he helped create jobs for Filipinos all over the world?"

I shrug.

"They're integral to the cruise industry, the healthcare industry, and many, many more. I convinced your father that in addition to Tagalog, my citizens needed to learn English, preparing them for the chances we created. I've improved the standard of living for all of my people by advocating for them."

Mom's saying now that those changes helped, but in the past she's complained that sending Filipinos around the world was only a superficial solution. Dad wouldn't do the work necessary to create more jobs in the Philippines, and that's the problem. He didn't *really* listen to her—not to what her people actually needed. He did what she wanted on *his* terms.

She stares at me pointedly. "You have the chance to do the same thing."

Which is exactly my problem—I don't want a marriage like hers. I want *more*. "So you know Ragar's terrible, but I have an obligation to marry him and keep him satisfied. . .so that I might one day convince him to help people? Is that really what you're saying?"

"He's not that bad. He's fairly handsome, for one, and his dragon form is—let's just say that it's much better than your father's." She shivers.

"Gross."

She tilts her head. "Perhaps you have questions about tomorrow night."

Tomorrow *night*? Ew, no. "Mom, look." I scooch toward the inside of my chair, moving a little closer to her. "Dad's pretty tough, and he yells, and he demands everyone listen to him, and they do. But you love him."

Her smile's half-hearted. "What are you saying?"

"I don't love Ragar. I don't even like him. I hate Ragar," I say. "He's arrogant, and he's rude, and he doesn't care about me at all. He doesn't know anything about me, and he doesn't seem to care to learn. He doesn't even listen when I speak."

"You'll figure that part out. The important thing is that no dragona alive can better protect you than he can."

"Not you, too." I stand up and start pacing, my footfalls making no noise at all on the plush carpet. It's very unsatisfying. Why couldn't I have tile or at least wood? "Mom, I can't possibly marry him."

"He's the fiercest, most battle-proven dragona in the world," Mom says.

"Oh, I heard," I wail. "He'd killed a dozen dragons by the time he graduated from high school."

She doesn't know what to say about that.

"I don't want a butcher for a husband."

"You're a female dragona. You may not like it, but that's what you need." She purses her lips and folds her hands in her lap. "You have no idea how many dragona will pursue you—would have already, if you weren't engaged to him five years back." She sighs. "He may be a little rough, but he's barely a hundred years old."

"By Gabriel, Mom. I'm twenty-four and I have better manners."

"Anak, dragona don't care about manners." Her nostrils flare. "He's strong enough to defeat his own father and take control of the dragona for the entire Asian continent, but he's loyal enough that he hasn't done it. That's a rare combination."

"Oh good. Savage, but loyal. That would be exactly what I was looking for—in a guard dog."

She stands and tilts her head. "You'll be even more pampered than you have been here, and you won't ever be in danger."

I stomp my foot, but again, thanks to the stupid carpet, it's like my foot is muzzled. Every part of me feels wrapped up, tamped down, and muted. "I don't want that," I say. "I want an equal partnership."

Mom laughs, the same trilling laugh she's always laughed. "You think I have a partnership?"

"Don't you?"

She sits again, and pulls the chair I was in closer to her. She pats the seat cushion. "Sit and listen."

I do as she asks, but my fingers dig into the armrests. "Fine."

"You know that male dragona have the power among our people."

Sadly, that's true.

"They can transform into great beasts. They can fly. They can breathe fire that will melt a building or forge metal into weapons. They can decimate towns, the larger and more powerful of them. Ragar's one of those. With that power comes a terrible ferocity and usually a very bad temper."

"If you're trying to change my mind, you're doing a terrible job."

"But you haven't paid enough attention to your power. Rivers aren't flashy. They aren't terrifying. Most people ignore them, but that's stupid. The river carves the land, changing its shape, providing life to its occupants. Wars are fought over rivers, and they should be. It's the river that has the power of life and change. Rivers endure."

"Mom, get to the point."

"You're a river," she says. "All the children of our people come from you and will be raised by you. You have the power to call your husband to you unequivocally. Don't underestimate the importance of your *charm*. With time, you will shape and mold him, and he'll do as you ask, always. He'll cherish you as your father cherishes me. It wasn't your dad who pulled for this match. It wasn't your dad who chose Ragar for you."

"Huh?"

"It was me." Mom drops her hand over mine and squeezes. "I gave you a tremendous gift, and once you tame him, once you use your charm to bring him to heel, he'll do anything you ask." She stands up and smooths her skirt. "Don't ask to stop this wedding again. Think on what I've said, and instead of wasting your time fighting it, come up with a plan to tame that raging inferno who will soon be your husband." She drops her voice to a whisper. "Make your mother and your grandmothers proud. You don't have to wield an axe to rule the world. You just have to direct the one who holds it."

I think about what she said for the next twenty-four hours, but it doesn't help. I don't want to *charm* my new husband. I don't want him as a husband at all. I want to wield the axe myself or not at all.

As if she can sense my ongoing misgivings, my mom never leaves me alone. She's always close, or my insipid bridesmaids are, or one of my many brothers, or worst of all, my future spouse. Someone's always around, always there, always forcing me to do the things that need to be done before the wedding ceremony.

Until, for the first time in more than a week, I'm finally alone—standing in my handcrafted Versace wedding gown, my hair twisted into complicated coils that represent the sleek twists and turns of the dragon body I'll never actually be able to shift into myself. My wrists, my ears, my fingers, they all bear the symbols of that same dragon body that I can never take. It's the reason we dragona women are kept in towers, hidden away in rooms, and generally sheltered from everything that life has to offer.

The males pick fights with everyone, and we're too weak to fight off the enemies they make. So we're stuck hiding all the time. Yes, they protect us, but it's their fault we need them to.

I hate that females can't shift.

I hate that the men are powerful while we are so very weak.

I hate that my dad makes all my decisions for me, and that starting tomorrow, Ragar will take over.

I hate that my only value in my family, in my marriage, and in this world comes from my ability to produce dragon eggs.

And so in this moment, my first moment alone for days and days, my final moment before becoming the oath-sworn property of a marauding, patronizing, controlling dragon shifter, I decide to do the only thing I can.

I decide to escape.

Even if I can't possibly break free for very long. Even if they'll catch me before the ceremony was due to start. Even if it's the feeblest attempt ever made at taking my own life into my hands, for the first time in my life, I have to do something.

I look around the room, at the window of the stupid high rise tower I'm stuck inside, and I evaluate my options.

Dragona love tall buildings.

They love being up in the sky, in a place that's close to the clouds and the stars. A place attackers can't easily reach. I suppose I should clarify. Male dragona love it.

Males can shift into a powerful form, one with enormous, armored wings that will hold them aloft. But me? I'm unable to do anything. I'm only a little stronger than a normie. I'm a lot prettier, and I draw men of all kinds to me like a lodestone, but otherwise, I'm powerless.

I've never hated that fact more than I do right now.

But do I hate it enough?

Most normies don't have windows or doorways from the top of skyscrapers that swing open freely. It's considered a safety risk. But the dragona office buildings and condos all boast huge, open air patios on their lodgings and in all their conference rooms. How else would they spread their wings and launch if a negotiation goes sideways? How else would they show off, by arriving late, landing shuddering on the patio and storming into the meeting with fiery eyes and rippling muscles?

We dragona do love our dramatic moments.

I suppose my desire to run and hide instead of posturing and attacking is yet another thing that makes me a miserable failure among my kind. If I were a little more bold, a little more fierce, I might not be stuck here, but I am who I am, no matter how I may wish the opposite. I open the window and walk out onto the expansive patio, the cool New York autumn enveloping me on all sides.

Wedding guests jostle and chatter below me, shouts and squeaks and cheers rising upward and combining into white noise, like smoke wafting away from a bonfire. The feeling that I must escape only grows inside of me.

But how can I?

A knock at the door sends my heart hammering. This can't be it. This can't be my summons. Have I missed my chance?

"Yes?"

The door opens, a terrified head poking around the edge of it. "I'm supposed to check on you every ten minutes, per the orders from Ragar the Ruthless." He swallows, his Adam's apple bobbing. "Are you alright?" His eyes finally find me, and they widen. "Aren't you worried the wind might ruin your hair."

"Don't worry," I say. "If you were standing close enough, you'd see that even a hurricane couldn't dislodge my hairdo."

He laughs, and his whole face softens. He's not a bad looking guy, for a wolf. If we had more dragona that Ragar and my father trusted, I'm sure we'd never have hired wolves to act as security. But all the dragona see me as a prize, and until I'm mated, I'm a lure to any single dragona male. So, wolves it is. "Well, now that I know you're alright. . ." But his eyes struggle to break away.

It's been like this my entire life. I may be completely useless, but men will do nearly anything I ask.

Except dump me, that is.

"Can you help me with something?" I ask.

His face brightens, his wolfy-yellow eyes widening. "Of course. Your wish is my command." His lips twist a little, as if he hates himself for being so pathetic. Clearly he has a sense of humor when he's not caught in a web of dragona charm.

"What would a normie do right now if there was a fire?"

He glances side to side. "Did you set something on fire? I heard that the female dragona rarely—"

"Nothing's burning," I say. "But if something *did* light on fire, what would they do? Would they just die up here?"

He laughs. "Buildings like this have to have fire escapes." He glances at the patio and shudders. "Not that I'd be keen on using one from this height, especially on a windy night like this."

A fire escape. Brilliant. "So they'd just have to cling to a little ladder all the way down to the street?"

He shrugs. "I suppose so. Places like this don't typically have fires though, not anymore. And *you'd* never need to do something like that. I'm sure dozens of dragona would literally fight among themselves for the right to fly you down to safety."

"Thank Gabe," I say. "Because I am just *terrified* of heights."

He steps toward me then, his masculine desire to protect me at all costs kicking into high gear because of my mock terror. Sometimes I really hate being me. "Don't worry. You're safe."

Oh, good grief. "Yes, yes. Well, thanks for your help." I look pointedly at the door.

"Right. Good." He clears his throat, and looks at the door. "This is a strange question, but would you mind posing for a photo with me?"

I glance at the clock. Thirteen minutes until they're coming to get me for the ceremony. "Uh, sure." Whatever gets him out of here faster.

The poor werewolf's so nervous that he nearly drops his phone trying to snap a selfie of us.

"What's your name?" The more that men talk around me, the less awkward they become, usually, especially if they're talking about normal things.

"Xander," he says. "Xander Binnigas." He beams at me.

"Right. Look, I'm happy to take the photo, Xander. I'm not great at many things, but—"

"Oh, I'm sure that's not true." He's deep in it now, grinning like an idiot.

"Okay, well, here we go." I snatch his phone before he can stop me, snap a photo, and hand it back. "I'd better go to the bathroom, if you don't mind. Not much time left before I head down."

He's stammering and apologizing as he backs out of my room.

The second he's gone, I peel off my wedding dress off, wincing a bit as it tears. It was ludicrously expensive, but nothing could possibly make me stand out more than that thing. I breathe a sigh of relief as I slide into the designer sweatpants and t-shirt I wore last night as pajamas. My heart hammers in my chest as I race back to the balcony.

Xander's not wrong about the wind. It whips all around my head, practically tearing the veil away from my frightfully sprayed hair. Which reminds me—I need to get rid of the veil as well.

After chucking it into the shower and turning it on, I toss my cell phone into the toilet so they can't track me, and put on some sensible shoes. It's not like anyone in their right mind would run from their wedding in high heels. I throw a few critical things into a bag—maybe a few more things than I need, strictly speaking. But a girl never knows what kind of situation she might encounter, right? And having spent most of my life in what amounts to a very posh cage, *I especially* don't have a clue.

Once I finally make it to the edge of the balcony, I find the iron ladder just like Xander said I would. I can hardly believe it's true.

The adrenaline racing through my system starts to wear off about four floors down, and I panic. I'm not especially terrified of heights like I pretended to be, but I doubt any sane person would enjoy clinging to the side of a building a hundred floors above the ground.

The wind whips through my hair, as if it's trying to punish me for saying it couldn't ruin the hairdo. *Touché, wind. You win.* The ladder's slippery, and I'm grateful I'm not in heels. One of those would have slipped off and brained someone down below for sure. And losing it would also probably have killed me. When I freeze up, too nervous to move, I think about Ragar's patronizing face.

And how he wants me to bake him a dozen perfect little dragon eggs.

That keeps me moving.

When I panic about the fall that threatens to end me if my feet just slip a rung or two, I think about my dad ignoring my protests.

A bird flies by my head and I shriek, but I focus on the look on my mother's face when I told her I wanted to cancel the wedding. None of them cared about what I wanted, so why should I fear for my own life? I'm sick of being a human incubator. I want to become someone who can defend myself, who can advocate for myself. I want to matter for something other than my scaly, dragona lady parts. (I'm actually not sure whether they're scaly. But it sounds more dramatic, doesn't it?)

I worry about every thirty seconds that someone will notice a woman slowly making her way down the side of the building, but the wedding itself saves me. As it turns out, the flashing lights on the rooftop of the building, the bands and singers and fire-eaters outside the front of the building, and all the general hoopla my parents and my in-laws set up keep anyone from paying any attention to me. It's ironic that their own sense of importance is my saving grace.

I've rubbed a blister on the palm of my right hand, and my biceps are ridiculously sore, but the second my feet hit the pavement, I dart off. If I circle the building toward the front I'll be caught immediately, so I head for the back and follow the line of the alley.

The bags of trash smell terrible, but I don't care. A rat darts across my path, and I stifle a scream. It's a side of New York I've never seen and I'm not too keen on, but freedom is too exciting. I won't turn back over that kind of stuff.

When another rat shoots out of a trash can, running across the toe of my shoe, I change my mind. I mean, how bad could Ragar really be?

But I only backtrack a handful of steps before regaining my resolve and turning back around. About six blocks away from my wedding, I realize that I have no idea where I'm going.

I don't even have any ideas for where I *might* go.

It's fall in New York City, and all the clothing in my apartment was appropriate for my supposed honeymoon in Maui. I have no money, no wallet, and no phone. Even if I did have a phone, I have no friends I could possibly call. Any dragona I contacted would simply hand me back over to my parents.

Frankly, in my wildest dreams, I never thought I'd get this far. At any moment, I expect sweeping patrols to show up and take me back. Then an idea hits me.

Bevin's Boutique: Secondhand Magic.

That's the name of the business that Minerva called me from two days ago. I have no idea where it is, but if I can find it, maybe Minerva will help me. She may not agree to let me stay with her, but at least our friendship should be worth the cost of a train ticket out of town, right?

I wish I'd gotten her that flame lizard egg. I'd almost be willing to give her my first-hatched dragon egg to secure my future.

Why was I so stupidly selfish? I should've been nicer my entire life so that people would be willing to help me now.

At least, thanks to my idiotic charm, I find a dozen men willing to help me locate Bevin's Boutique. One of them even hands me a wad of cash. I shouldn't take it, but beggars can't exactly be choosy, and neither can runaways.

"Thank you." I stuff the cash in my pocket, wondering what things precisely cost money. Mom and Dad have always paid for everything, so I've never paid much attention.

But now that I know the address of the place I'm headed, that cash comes in handy, paying for my cab fare. And suddenly, I'm standing in front of a bright white and blue sign that says, "Bevin's Boutique."

My fingers tremble a bit as I push on the door, ready to go inside and see whether Minerva really will lend a hand. Only, the door won't budge. The lights are on inside the business, but it's locked up.

There's a note on the glass door. GONE NEXT DOOR FOR GLOFFEE. BACK IN 30.

What kind of business closes down for half an hour so the proprietor can get a cup of gloffee? Ugh. Well, maybe the gloffee shop won't be too crowded. I'm not exactly an unknown figure in the supernatural world, so showing my face in a shop that every supernatural person in a one-block radius has to frequent once a day to keep the normies from recognizing them as magical doesn't exactly seem wise, but what choice do I have?

It takes me less than thirty seconds to spot it.

Grand Central Gloffee.

Normies would see it as Grand Central Coffee, but thanks to the horrible smell, they'd all steer clear. All I smell is the wood-char odor of roasting glaffour berries. I haven't really had it often since I don't often go out in public, but it's not a smell you forget. I need to find that Bevin person, and I *really* hope she knows how to contact Minerva.

I brace myself and duck inside, realizing belatedly that wearing my pajamas isn't likely to make the best impression. Luckily, I don't have to interrogate people to find the one named Bevin. No sleuthing is necessary at all.

Because Minerva's sitting on a huge purple couch in the center of the gloffee shop, sipping from a mug the size of a soup bowl. She's laughing and rolling her eyes in the exact same way she used to in school.

"You can't possibly be serious."

A tall blonde woman's nodding vigorously. "Of course I am. You can't go on a second date with someone without introducing him to us first."

"You guys are like goblins, waiting to attack and rob a group of travelers," Minerva says. "The last thing I'd do—" Her eyes shift upward, and the second they lock on mine, she freezes. "Roxana?"

I smile, and surprisingly, it's genuine. "Hey, pal."

When her eyes fly wide, I know she's recognized me. "What are you doing here?" Minerva asks.

"I just couldn't stop thinking about you after we talked the other day. How's life going?" I walk toward the couch. "I'd love to catch up."

Minerva's eyes slide around me and focus on a television screen in the back corner of the shop. I follow her gaze, and realize it's broadcasting something.

My wedding.

Where they've just realized that I'm missing.

I'm officially out of time.

4

XANDER

I can't believe I'm actually standing outside the door of dragona royalty.

Even worse, I won't get to sneak a single peek. I shouldn't be surprised. That's just the kind of luck that I have. I'm literally always in the wrong place at the wrong time—probably the only thing I inherited from my father.

My phone rings, startling me out of my thoughts.

"Hello?"

"What's up with you and ol girl?" Izaak asks. "I didn't see you last night. I guess you spent some quality time with her."

"I'm working right now," I say.

"Ouch. That bad?"

I snort. "What? No, it was fine. Great, even."

"So you didn't hook up." Izaak's voice is flat. "You must've said something that was classic *Xander*."

"That's not very nice," I say. "I say all sorts of things, mostly funny ones, and people love me for it."

Izaak has this way of infusing things, normal things, with some kind of tone that makes them sound dirty. "But did Annabelle *love you*?"

"Her name is *Annelise*, and no. I doubt I'll be seeing her again."

Izaak swears under his breath. "For real, what did you say? Or was it something you did?"

"Nothing," I say. "I swear, I did my best to use that filter you told me I should put on. No jokes, no funny stuff at all."

"And that didn't work? Really?" He sighs. "Then what went wrong?"

I think about how itchy my head was all night. It was bad enough that she asked if I was okay. No need to tell Izaak about that, though. It's too embarrassing. What kind of person gets fleas? A werewolf, that's who.

"Xander." Izaak's voice is sterner than I've ever heard it.

"What?"

"Did she, by chance, leave after going to the bathroom?"

I think back on the sequence of events. . .and, yes. "She came out, asked if we had pets, and then left. How'd you know that?"

I hear the sound of something whamming.

"What was that?"

"You left your flea bath on the counter, man. I told you a million times, you can't do that. You should at least put it in a dandruff shampoo bottle, because that's not hot."

I groan. When Izaak's more clever than I am, things are pretty bleak. "I will," I say. "I swear."

"So, are you at the wedding? Did you see my future wife?" My roommate Izaak likes *all* women, but he's had a crush on Roxana Goldenscales for an epically long time. "I still want that photo."

"They actually stationed me on her hallway, but none of us are supposed to go within a hundred feet of her."

"Oh, man, she's just down the hall?" Izaak's voice pleads with me. "Okay, check this out. Let's say you hear a suspicious sound, smell smoke, forgot your keys, any excuse will do. Make something up. Maybe she'll drop that muscle-headed dragon and hook up with you."

"Yes," I say. "That's what I'm hoping for—if only she sees *me*, in all my practically-lone-wolf glory, she'll throw over her two-hundred-and-fifty-pounds-of-pure-muscle fiancé who is, by the way, a literal prince, and who also scares half the world silly."

"She might," Izaak says. "Think about it. Her whole life, she's been surrounded by giant blocks of testosterone. Maybe she'll like the lighter, fluffier vibes you're throwing down."

"Fluffier?" Is he referring to my wolfy side, or to the fact that I've put on a few pounds?

"Shoot your shot, at least," Izaak says. "Bust a move, man."

"And if I succeed, I'll run away with the world's most wanted bride and live in total bliss for eleven and a half minutes before her dad and her fiancé torture me, kill me, and hang my pelt on the wall," I say. "That's a brilliant plan. Forget acting. You've missed your calling, Bobby Fischer."

"Have you seen her? It would be worth it," Izaak says.

He's such an idiot sometimes. Most times, actually. "I've got to go. The overtime I'm pulling from this gig is going to pay for our new PlayStation, or did you forget why I'm here?"

"Oh, I remember." Izaak loves violent video games as much as any vampire. Maybe more. "I already ordered the new mortal combat. They said you can practically *smell* the blood on this one."

"Just what I always wanted. A blood smell, built right in."

Of course, he doesn't catch my sarcasm. Izaak's a pretty smart guy for a vampire, but he's not someone who looks through the world with as much cynicism as I do. Actually, pretty much no one does. Maybe Britney Spears, or like, Howard Stern, but the majority of the regular people see the world as a happy, shiny place. They never quite fathom how broken things are.

"But if you could get that photo," Izaak says, "*and* the PS3? This might be the best day ever!"

"I'll get right on that."

"Really? You will?" Izaak's voice is so pathetically hopeful that I almost feel bad when I hang up on him.

As the minutes turn into more than an hour, and scads of people leave the room I'm guarding, I begin to wonder how many more support personnel could possibly be in there. Are they really preparing the most beautiful woman in the world to get married? Or are they remodeling a bathroom? When two people carrying bags full of what appear to be hair tools walk out, I can't help myself.

"I didn't realize Ragar was marrying Rapunzel."

"What did you say, mutt?" The tall witch on the right glares at me.

I should drop my eyes and stand still against the wall, but I've always hated how the witches and warlocks act like they're better than the rest of us, just because they have akero blood a hundred generations back. When they act all superior, it's like it short-circuits my brain. "Were there only the two of you, tackling her hair alone? Or are there a dozen more people casting spells on that poor bride-to-be in there?"

The two witches look completely different from one another. One's a curvy, short black woman with an amazing afro. The other is tall and blonde with long hair that falls in waves all the way to her waist. But when they stop in front of me and straighten up, their eyes flashing, they almost look like sisters. The black one purses her lips together, and then snaps, "We made her hair *extraordinary*, and we're the very last artists to leave.

Everyone at that wedding will be talking about her hair for months."

Months? I doubt people will talk about her hair at all, but I'm a little too nervous about how close they're standing to goad them any further. I do what I should have done all along and nod slowly, while backing toward the wall.

"Stupid mongrels, always barking about something."

Every insult flung at a werewolf is some comparison to canines. And yet, people love dogs. You'd think they might get a little more creative.

But then her words penetrate. *Last artists to leave.* If that's true, there wouldn't be anyone in there to stop me from popping in and getting Izaak his one photo.

Except my clear orders. *Stay away from the dragona princess.*

More and more minutes tick by without a single peep.

Maybe she's bored in there.

Or what if someone has flown in from the balcony? She could be in danger. It would be irresponsible of me not to even check.

Of course, if she blabs that I went inside, and I get fired from this job, I could get kicked out of my part-time job with the Manhattan pack, and that would be bad. Wolves need other wolves—we get strange when we're alone. If I get much stranger, no pack in the US will take me in. I need to be welcomed in further, not kicked to the curb.

I sit tight, being smart for once.

That lasts all of three more minutes.

Because then I think about what Izaak would say if I did get a photo. He'd be so shocked and impressed for once. I imagine all the things we could use it for in Photoshop—how many hilarious memes we could make. Wedding jokes. Dragon jokes. The possibilities are limitless, really.

Plus, maybe I'm a little curious too. What does she actually look like? How much is filters? Is she nice? Rude? Childish? How often in my life have I been *this close* to someone so famous?

There's more than twenty minutes until the schedule says they'll be coming for her, and the terrible witches did say they were the last to leave. I listen as carefully as I can —wolves may crave the approval of others to an unhealthy degree, we may have trouble controlling our tempers, and we may find ourselves howling at the moon sometimes, but one thing where we excel is our hearing. Even vampires can't compete with us for sensing noises.

No one else is coming, not anywhere close.

I creep toward the door, my cell phone in one hand, and I tap on it lightly. If she's bored, she'll hear me. If she's busy, she might not even notice the sound.

"Yes?" Even that one word is mellifluous, like her voice is made of carefully crafted wind chimes.

I crack the door and poke my head through, prepared to duck back out if she looks even the slightest bit annoyed. "I'm supposed to check on you every ten minutes, per the orders from Ragar the Ruthless."

She looks more curious than anything else, her shining black hair coiled in an enormous pile on top of her head, her enormous eyes more luminous than the most absurdly drawn comic characters, and her arms more graceful than I could have imagined in a sleeveless white dress. The bodice on her dress is so fitted, it's a wonder she can breathe, right up until the skirt floofs out around her waist, making her look a bit like a broom.

A really hot, really elegant broom.

I should probably say something else, or she'll think I'm an idiot. "Are you alright?"

She's on the balcony, which is what I was worried about. And with that gown, and hair, and her general pull, I doubt she should really be out there, inviting other dragona to land and, I don't know, pillage.

"I'm not sure you're supposed to go out there."

Her eyebrows rise, and she looks a little annoyed. How do I fix that?

"Aren't you worried the wind might ruin your hair?"

"Come in," she says. "Once you're close enough, you'll see that even a hurricane couldn't dislodge a strand of my hair, so don't worry."

She's funny. Now I love her even more. "Now that I know you're alright, I should really go." How do I snap a photo without being creepy?

"Can you help me with something?" she asks.

Um, yes. I would do literally anything she needed. "Your wish is my command." That sounded so horribly pathetic. Do I think I'm a fairy tale prince, stepping out of a Disney cartoon?

"What would a normie do right now, if there was a fire, I mean?"

Fire? She's a dragona—can the females make fire? Is this rhetorical, or is something burning? My sense of smell is nearly as good as my sense of hearing, and I don't smell anything, but. . . "Was there an accident? I heard that female dragona couldn't—"

"No, no, nothing's burning," she says. "But if something *did* catch fire, what would they do? Would they just die?"

Die? She almost sounds like she wants to hear that humans would just—poof, disappear—if there was a fire. I kind of like her perverse line of questioning, but it shows an appalling lack of knowledge about the real world. "Buildings like this have fire escapes." We're on the hundredth floor, though. "Not that I'd be keen on using one from this height, especially on a windy night like this one."

She doesn't look nearly as nervous as I am about the

prospect. "So they'd just have to cling to that little ladder all the way down to the street?"

"I suppose so." I should reassure her. Sometimes people are more nervous than they let on. "Places like this don't typically have fires though, not anymore. And you'd never need to do something like that. I'm sure dozens of dragona would literally fight to fly you down to safety."

"Thank Gabe," she says. "Because I am just *terrified* of heights."

I suddenly feel like I could carry her down myself, if it came to that. "Don't worry. You're safe."

"Yes, yes. Well, thanks for your help." She glances pointedly at the door, and I realize she wants me to leave. The soul-crushing disappointment I feel is ridiculous. Of course a woman about to get married isn't flirting with me. It must be part of the dragona charm I've heard about.

"Right. Good." I've been in here for several moments now, and Izaak's never going to believe me unless I have proof. "This is a strange question, but would you mind if I took a photo?"

She looks at the clock, as if she might not have time for it. Which is crazy. A photo takes two seconds. "With me?"

With her? I had no idea that was even on the table. I can't seem to form any words at the moment, however.

"Uh, sure."

I should try being silent more often. It's the one thing I've never done in my entire life, and look what it's gotten me already! The thought of being *in* the photo doubles my nerves. My hand shakes so much that I almost drop my phone.

"What's your name?" she asks.

"Xander," I say, absurdly proud that I can remember it. "Xander Binnigas."

"Right. Look, I'm happy to take it. I'm not great at many things, but—"

"Oh, I'm sure that's not true." I can't seem to stop smiling at her. She's walked closer and we're within a few feet of one another. Being this close, it feels like I'm drunk, or I don't know. I just know that I never want to leave.

She grabs my phone. "Okay, well, here we go." She snaps the photo so fast that I barely realize what's happened, and then she's shoving my phone back at me. "I better go to the bathroom, if you don't mind. Not much time left before I head down."

The bathroom. Right. She definitely doesn't want me in here for that. That's definitely my cue to go. I can't believe I've been in here this long. Even so, the fear of being caught doesn't kick in until after I've safely exited the door —that's how strong the dragona pull is.

I shake my head once I'm back in the hall. "Amazing." I'm still staring at the photo she took like a complete dope when the honor guard shows up to escort her downstairs.

That's when things really go south, because. . . she's not inside her room.

Roxana Goldenscales has disappeared.

And I'm the last person who saw her.

5

CLARK

Normies are the worst.

They are weak, and whiny, and they have no tolerance for any sort of malady.

Headache? Take it away. Never mind that they stared at a screen for 20 hours straight. Surely their body isn't telling them anything.

Sore back? Eliminate it immediately! Ignore the root cause, which is poor squat form. That's why it keeps coming back.

Can't perform in the bedroom? Medicate the problem! Forget the fact that your diet and exercise are terrible. That's probably not the issue.

I mean, I should be delighted. Normal humans and their refusal to deal with the underlying issues in their lives fund my entire life. But sometimes I get sick of coming up with new spells to deal with the same old issues over and over. Plus, they're always complaining about the side effects of the spells. Unfortunately, that's life. Everything has a cost, even spells.

"Clark." My boss' voice always sets my teeth on edge. It's probably the cumulative effect of years of working for him. He's like a sore on the back of my heel that won't ever go away because he just keeps rubbing and rubbing and rubbing on it.

"Yes?" I plaster a fake smile on my face. "Was the last batch any better?"

Simon Summers—yes, that's his real name—grimaces. "Too strong, according to our testers."

"How can headache medicine be too strong?"

"The recipients reported seeing rainbows and butterflies everywhere after taking it." He chuckles. "Several of them reunited with their exes, went back to old jobs, or renewed contracts and leases, only to realize that it was a terrible mistake after the spell wore off. It didn't just fix their headaches—it made them happy with everything."

I sigh. "Too weak? It's crap. Too strong? Same. No one's ever happy."

"Oh, they were happy. One of them took all his clothes off and ran down six city blocks, covered in nothing but cinnamon powder." He crosses his arms. "He was allergic to cinnamon, too, so those hives." He shudders.

"Fine." I sigh. "I'll lower the amount of toadstool powder and see if that helps."

"That was going to be my suggestion." Simon literally says that every time I recommend anything. It was always his idea first. "Will the next round be ready by morning?"

With only three hours left before the end of the business day, there's no way I could possibly finish the batch tonight, not without staying hours after I'm supposed to finish. But performance bonuses are discretionary, and Simon's the one who determines them. I suppress my groan. "Yes, sir."

The sun has long since set when I finally lock up behind me, but Simon's stupid batch of headache "medicine" is ready for tomorrow's product testing. Which means I won't lose my job, and I really can't afford to, not for the next two years, anyway. I have twenty-four months of alimony to pay, after all. Sometimes it feels like my whole life has just been one unlucky hit after another. I'm so tired that I want to go home and drop face first onto my bed, but that's too depressing.

Plus, I don't actually have a bed.

Carly took all the non-magical furniture in the divorce, since she's the one who picked it out, and that left me with a futon that adjusts its size based on the person sleeping on it, and end tables that collect the television remote and replenish magazines. Of course, since I don't have a television, I don't have any remotes, and since no one reads magazines anymore, that's pretty useless too.

I really need to redecorate, but between the strain of paying alimony and the misery that sets in whenever I contemplate picking furniture to live in my new place alone, I'm still muddling through with my futon and two end tables. It does make me wish we'd sprung for a little more magical stuff. Carly couldn't use it, per se, but most of the magical objects were pretty self-sustaining, even with a normie.

I text my sister. GRAND CENTRAL GLOFEE?

She texts back immediately. YOU BETCHA.

Minerva's such a dork, but that's one of the reasons everyone loves her. I live farther away than the others, but even so, it's only three stops past my apartment and on the same line, so not too inconvenient. At least with as often as I've been going there, I don't have to worry about any humans spotting me casting spells.

Thanks to Harry Potter, even that's not such a big deal anymore. They always assume it was some stunt and write it off as less unlikely than the CGI stuff they see on TV.

Grand Central's not the best gloffee shop in New York, but since Minerva, Xander, and Izaak live upstairs and Bevin lives above her shop next door, it has kind of become our default meeting place. It's so much easier to meet everyone here now that my wife isn't always complaining about the smell. Gloffee smells great to supernaturals, but it smells disgusting to normies. Carly said it smelled like sewage, but I've heard everything from vomit to feces to spoiled milk.

When I push through the door, the smell of roasted glaffour berries envelops me. It reminds me of slightly charred, buttered toast—or maybe that's because of the particular variety I like best, glofficino, made with dragona berries. It's almost impossible to find, but the much less expensive werewolf-berry version's also palatable.

"What's up, fam?" Izaak says. "You look beat. Long day at work?"

I drop into the seat in the middle of the large couch, between Izaak and Bevin. "One of these days I'm going to hit Simon with a stupor spell first thing in the morning and just take the day off." I lift one hand and wave at Gavin, the manager. Since I've ordered the same thing for years, I'm pretty sure he knows what I want.

"Surely he's got charms to prevent that kind of thing." Minerva sips her gloffee from a huge mug—she insists glatté is the best way to drink it, but I swear, no matter what they flavor it with, I can always taste the werewolf when it's made that way.

"Not everyone devotes the proper amount of time and attention to their personal wards and protection," I say. "You'd be surprised how many people can't be bothered to do the bare minimum."

"Some of us can't afford wards and lack the magic to do them ourselves." Bevin coughs. "We have to rely on the generosity of our magical friends to help us." She widens her eyes.

I keep forgetting to reinforce the wards on her shop. "Sorry. I'll definitely come by tonight."

"Speaking of helping friends," Bevin says. "I did hear back about the favor you asked me to do." She's looking at Minerva.

"What favor?" I ask.

Bevin shakes her head. "Private."

"And?" Minerva asks.

"The thing you said you'd give? If you're still sure, that broker will make the trade."

Minerva gulps, but she nods. "Yes. Do it."

"What in the world's going on?" I ask.

Izaak's looking from Bevin to Minerva and back again. "Oh, I think it's pretty clear."

If he's figured something out that I can't, I should just give up. He's not actually dumb, but in our group, he's always the last one to get every joke and the last one to understand, well, everything.

"It's a love potion, right?" Izaak's grin is disgustingly wide.

"A love potion?" I sit up so straight I practically knock poor Gavin over and send my glofficino to the floor.

"Minerva's trying to hook up with this guy in the prosecutor's office," Izaak says. "What's his name again?"

"Ramon, the file guy." Now Bevin's beaming, too.

"It's not a love potion," Minerva says. "It's a favor that will help me make guardian, that's all."

"I need to hear more about this file guy." I take a sip of my drink and set it down on the coffee table, then I fold my arms in a way I hope is menacing. "If you're really into him, I need to meet him, stat."

"What day is it?" Minerva asks.

"Friday," I say.

"Great," she says. "I'll be sure to introduce you. . .never." She rolls her eyes. "Because I don't even like him. Geez."

"Where's Xander?" I ask. He always supports me on

this kind of thing. I can practically hear him making snide comments in the background.

"Oh, I know this one," Izaak says. "He got offered some overtime, and he took it." He's smiling way too broadly for that to be everything he wants to say.

"Please tell me this isn't about the PS3," Minerva says. "You guys do *not* need to waste more time on video games. If you want—"

"Girl, don't take it there," Izaak says.

I have no idea how he gets away with saying things like that. It's either his inherent vampiric charm or maybe the fact that he's black. Either way, if I tried calling Minerva 'girl' and ordering her around, she'd clock me. If I tried it with Bevin, I'd probably lose an arm.

"So it *is* to buy another gaming system." Minerva sets her glatté down, clearly preparing to let him have it.

Bevin gasps, her face fixated on the small television in the corner of the busy gloffee shop.

"What?" Minerva spins around to see what's caught her eye. Bevin's not someone who usually pays much attention to current events.

"It's starting." Bevin sighs with contentment.

"What's starting?" I ask.

"The royal wedding." Minerva has completely forgotten about berating Izaak, which tells me how curious she is.

"The royal—wait, are you talking about your friend's wedding?" My heart has been battered pretty badly lately, so it's not like this kind of thing really matters anymore, but I had a major crush on Minerva's friend Roxana a decade ago. She was the only person who was nice when Minerva got transferred to that magical finishing school.

"It's a bit of a stretch to call her a friend," Minerva says. "She's an acquaintance from my school days."

"You just talked to her the other day," Bevin says. "I couldn't believe you didn't press harder for an invite when you had the chance." She gestures at the screen. "If you had, then you could be one of those shiny, sparkly people on the television right now! One of the magical elite of New York, parading your stuff in front of everyone."

I never figured Bevin would care about stuff like that. After the day I've had, I really don't want to have to watch Roxana Goldenscales marry some overbearing, meathead of a dragon prince. I stand up. "I think it's probably time for me—"

"To what?" Izaak asks. "I know you have a fancy job and a great apartment, but it's not like you have a wife to go home to anymore." He chuckles, and then catches himself. He looks regretful as his eyes meet mine. "Sorry, fam. That's not what I meant."

I did miss a lot of gatherings with my friends back when I was married. Carly was always annoyed when I dragged her here. She didn't love being the only one who couldn't magic the vacuum into cleaning, or drink a little blood to recover from a hangover. In her mind, she was the only one who wasn't special. She hated the difference between us even more when I stayed out late with my magical friends and she got stuck home alone.

Magical misfits, that's what she called our group.

"I tried to be upbeat about it, but I hate being single."

"You wouldn't really want to be locked down," Izaak says. "Lots of women are thirsty these days."

"I desperately wish I was still married," I say.

The door whips open, chilly air blasting through the room, and a stunningly beautiful woman in pink sweatpants jogs into the room. At first I'm distracted by the word "Juicy" in sparkly diamonds across the front of her t-shirt. But when my eyes finally shift, I realize that her face is almost familiar.

I know her.

Hair so deep black that it shines, tumbling in disarray

around her shoulders. Golden eyes that are brighter than any gem. Everything about her is so compelling that I almost don't notice the thorny platinum crown nestled into her hair, glittering with red and black jewels.

"Holy Mother of Dragons," Izaak says. "That's. . .that's *Roxana Goldenscales*."

"What is she doing here?" Bevin splutters. "You can't get married from here! Or wearing that!" She stands up.

"I'm pretty sure she can get married wearing whatever she wants." Izaak shrugs. "Women's rights."

I scowl at him.

"What?" Izaak says. "I support them."

"Roxana," Minerva says. "What in the world are you doing here?" She turns back to look at the television screen on which the wedding march is playing.

"Minerva!" Roxana rushes across the room, staring intently at my sister.

"I totally thought the broadcast was live." Minerva looks disappointed. "Did they film it in advance? Is it all fake?"

"Er, maybe." Roxana glances at the television and cringes. "So I should probably be asking you—you're a witch, right?"

Minerva's eyes go wide.

"Like, could you cast a spell so that all these people who are staring at me right now don't remember I was here?"

My sister would probably kill everyone, or put them into a hundred-year slumber the humans would call a coma, if she even tried something like that. I glance around the room. Maybe because Gavin's a demon-spawn, this isn't the highest powered gloffee shop. I only see two relatively low-level warlocks. One witch. The rest of the people are weres and vampires. There are probably three or four demon-spawn, but not strong ones. I could spell them all, luckily.

"Something like that would require a really talented witch," Minerva says. "There's no way that I could ever—"

"But I can." I stand up. "And the sooner we do it, the easier it'll be."

"It'll be way easier if she's not still standing here," Minerva says. "I'll take her upstairs."

"Good idea." I don't let my eyes linger—she may be the most beautiful woman I've ever seen, but I can't afford, no, Roxana can't afford for me to be distracted right now.

"Wait, what's going on?" Izaak asks. "Why do you need to cast a big spell?"

"If you look at the television, you'll see that people have realized I'm not there, at the very live ceremony they're broadcasting. And any minute, my fiancé's going to realize that I left," Roxana says. "And he's going to be ticked off. Badly."

"A furious dragona prince is bad for everyone," I say.

"Worse than you could possibly imagine," Roxana says.

But I'm not nearly as afraid as I ought to be—instead, I'm strangely excited. That reaction might scare me most of all.

6

BEVIN

Demon-spawn are hotheaded, impulsive, and we generally have terrible instincts. I'm no exception, of course, but after my twin sister ran away at the age of five, my mom's mission became reforming me into something better.

An angelic demon-spawn, as it were.

If something like that's even possible, I'm about as close as it gets. The only reason I'm able to be so good is that I never act rashly. I think things through, and I make the *smart, sensible* choice. I basically live my life constantly thinking, *What Would Jesus Do?* Because the second I go with my own gut feelings, everything falls apart.

My friends are not quite as thoughtful or levelheaded.

Before I can talk any sense into her, Minerva throws an arm around the escaped dragona princess and races for the door. "Do it quick, before anyone leaves." Then she's gone.

"I'll make sure she doesn't need any help." Izaak's out like a shot as well, racing after Minerva and her soon-to-be-infamous friend.

"This just in!" The news broadcaster's screeching. "The security team's saying that Roxana Goldenscales is *missing!*"

Clark's muttering under his breath, and his arms are swinging round and round. He pauses then and glares at me. "Get out, or you'll be caught in the spell."

"I want to be caught," I say. "I don't want anything to do with that mess."

His eyes widen. "But you're Minerva's best friend. If we're helping her, you're bound to see her again."

My lips press together, and I shake my head. "I can't have anything to do with that."

"Bevin, I know you have to be careful—"

"No," I say. "You don't know. You're not demon-spawn. You have no idea what it's like, always being terrified that the smallest infraction, the smallest mistake, might count as a sin, and that I might be registered forever as part demon."

His eyes are sad, but he nods. "At least stand at the door and make sure no one leaves while I finish."

"Fine." As if his words are some kind of challenge, another warlock immediately stands up and walks toward the door. "Sir, you'll have to wait right here for just a moment."

"So your friend can spell my memory?" When the dark-eyed warlock laughs, his belly jiggles. He holds up his hand with a flourish, clearly proud of his signet ring with a flashing, ice-blue stone. "My charm will stop that spell from working on me, anyway, *demon-spawn*."

He must have overheard.

"Maybe everyone else in here's too weak to push against your pal's stun spell, but I'm not."

I grab his wrist and twist his arm. He cries out like a complete coward, but I ignore it. I wrench his topaz ring off and toss it on the ground. He lunges for it, and I kick it, sending it spinning beneath the couch. "Thanks for letting me know you had a charm that would stop the effectiveness of Clark's spell. That'll make things much easier on us." I look around. "Anyone else wish they could keep their memories and be involved in some kind of dragona man, er, woman-hunt that doesn't concern them?"

A dozen wolves on the right side of the shop and nine vampires on the left all shake their heads. The woman who was standing next to the irritating warlock sighs. "I told you we shouldn't have come here. This place stinks of dog."

"Well, be a good girl, and all that will be gone soon." I look over my shoulder. "Clark?"

Clark's still chanting, but he's getting louder. I'm not sure why, but that usually means he's almost done. He throws his hands outward. "Memoria tollunt, ut nihil moveant foeliciter ac nihil sciant."

I close my eyes as the spell washes over me, ready to have the last ten minutes erased from my mind completely.

Everyone else sighs.

They look at one another in a daze. The warlock who was just yelling at me blinks several times. "Why are you holding my wrist?" When the corner of his mouth turns up, I consider clocking him on the nose. I feel like he'd deserve it, 100%.

Just then, the bell to the door jingles, and Xander comes flying through. "Clark! You are never going to believe—"

Clark sinks onto the couch behind him with a sigh.

I cross the room before Xander can start boring us all with some story about his job with the stupid Manhattan wolf pack. "Hey, don't sit yet," I whisper-hiss. "It didn't work on me. Was it because I touched that dumb charm?"

But the warlock who was wearing it has already sat back down with his date, or whoever that witch was, and they're flagging the barista down as if nothing happened.

"I didn't extend it to you," Clark says. "You thought I could cast a spell large enough to wipe the memory of twenty people and not be sophisticated enough to exclude you from it?"

I can't quite help my moan. "But I don't want to know," I say. "What if people show up looking for her? What then?"

Xander sits in the chair across from the sofa. "What are you guys talking about? You did a spell? Why?"

"Can you guys give me a minute? That was a huge spell." Clark braces his forearms on his knees and breathes in and out slowly.

"You wiped everyone's memory?" Xander's clearly still sorting through the stuff we've said since he arrived.

"Geez, are you trying to undo it?" Clark throws one weary hand up, his wand appearing out of the sleeve of his jacket, and he twists it around in a strange configuration. "Aures nostras tege et nos tace."

"Are we safe to talk?" I ask, annoyed that he's still insisting that I know that Roxana Goldenscales is right upstairs. "You shouldn't tell Xander without him wanting to know." I fold my arms across my chest with a huff.

"How could I know if he *wants* to know, without telling him first?" Clark raises one eyebrow. "Geez, you sound so crazy sometimes."

"Tell me what?" Xander's eyes are gleaming now. "I'm the one with big news."

"What is it?" I ask. "May as well hear something interesting."

"The part-time job I had?" He pulls his phone out of his pocket. "It was guarding Roxana Goldenscales before her wedding!" He shoves his phone at us, and there's a photo on the screen of Xander and Roxana. I wouldn't have known what she looked like a week ago, but now I know exactly who she is.

"You're kidding," I say.

"No, and right after I took this photo." Even knowing

Clark warded us, he drops his voice to barely a whisper. "She escaped."

"You don't say." Clark can't contain his smile.

"None of this is funny," I say. "And none of this is cool. Look, when I lived down by Port Authority, begging for food and doing errands for—"

Xander holds up one hand. "Can we go like five minutes without hearing about when you lived on the street?"

"You're on my bad list," I say.

"Oh no. We're on the bad list of a demon-spawn who won't do anything at all wrong for fear of descending. However will we survive?" Clark asks.

"Why aren't you guys more excited about this?" Xander's glaring back and forth between us like a labrador watching a tennis match.

"How about this?" Clark asks. "Follow me upstairs, and I'll show you why."

"Dude, did neither of you hear what I just said? I was the last person to see Roxana Goldenscales!"

"You two are both morons," I say. "But Clark, you're the worst. There's still hope for this one." I pivot and stare at Xander. "Before tonight, had you ever interacted with any dragona?"

Xander blinks.

Clark leans back.

"I'm going to take that as a no."

"My sister was friends with Roxana Goldenscales in high school," Clark says. "I'd met her before today."

"You, a lowly warlock apprentice, met her, a female dragona princess on a sanctioned trip with her friend. But have you ever *worked* with the dragona in an official capacity? The men, I mean?"

Both of them shake their heads.

"Let me tell you this. They are the oldest and the most powerful of the races the akero brought to Earth, and they don't like anyone but other dragona. They are horrible, and the only thing that can possibly make them worse is if one of their precious females is in danger. Capice?"

Clark gulps.

"But I'm sure they'll find her," Xander says. "Within the hour, probably."

"Why are you here, if you were her guard?" I ask.

Xander looks down at his shoes. "I mean, I was her guard, not her prison warden. And it's not like she got injured. She ran away, they think."

"You took a photo with her and they just. . .let you go?"

"I didn't show them the photo, obviously." He huffs. "They said I was no longer needed, and then hundreds of them flew off the balcony. It felt like a tornado."

"Which means they're crawling all over the city, looking for anyone who might have seen a woman in a wedding dress." I glare pointedly at Clark.

"Not in a dress," Xander says. "She left that in the room."

Clark's voice comes out high and a little squeaky. "We should go upstairs."

"But I want a glespresso," Xander says.

"Get it later." Clark stands. "For now, come with me."

"Fine." Xander grumbles, but he lets us haul him out the door and up the stairwell toward his apartment. Once we finally reach his door, instead of letting him go inside, Clark grabs his arm. "This way."

"I still want you to wipe my memory." I block their path.

Xander freezes. "How come neither of you were shocked when I said I'd been guarding Roxana Goldenscales? I mean, it's the celebrity wedding of the year. You didn't think that was cool at all?" He eyes the door suspiciously.

"You know Roxana and Minerva are old friends," Clark says.

"No," Xander says. "Are you. . .?" He shoves his way past both of us, widening the crack in the doorway and freezing, swearing under his breath. "Mother of an ogre, gobsmack me."

"Goblins and ogres aren't real," Roxana says. "Even as sheltered as I am, I know that much."

"What on earth are you doing here?" Xander asks.

"I wasn't sure where else to come—" Roxana cuts off. "Wait." She runs pretty fast, right toward the balcony. "No. How are you here?" Her eyes widen and she claws at the glass door to the balcony. "I can't go back. I can't marry him."

"Why's she running from you?" Minerva asks. "Stop, Roxana, it's fine. He's a friend."

"He was my guard," Roxana says. "He works for my fiancé."

"Not exactly," Xander says. "I work for a werewolf pack your fiancé hired as extra muscle, but when you disappeared, he kind of kicked us all out." He shakes his head. "I still can't believe you're here."

"So they didn't send you? You're not here to take me back?" Her stupidly gorgeous eyes dart all over the apartment, like she expects actual goblins or ogres to jump out and grab her any moment.

"For some reason, my friends are all risking their lives to keep you here," I say. "I'm not sure they realize that, but they are."

Roxana blinks. "Who are you?"

"I'm their lowly demon-spawn friend who thinks this is a terrible plan." I cross my arms. "There must be somewhere else you can go—someone you can impose upon with whom you're actually friends?"

"She is my friend," Minerva says. "At a time in my life

when no one cared about me, and no one would lift a finger to make my life better, she did." She glances at Roxana, the corner of her mouth turning up into a half-smile. "Or more specifically, a fingernail."

Roxana grins back.

She's such a delicate little flower that anything I say is being taken as an attack, when really I'm trying to defend them. "I'm sure you're great," I say. "But the reality is that you are dragona, and your father's a king, and your fiancé's a prince from Russia, and no one's going to stop searching until they find you, which means you're going to have to go back eventually. I'd really rather not be the person sheltering you when you're caught."

"No one helped you after your mother died," Minerva says. "I wish I could go back and change that." Her eyes are kind—they're always kind. It's why she's a terrible cop. "I can't change that, but surely you of all people must see why we should help her."

"Why did you run?" Xander asks. "I mean, has she already answered that?"

"Is your fiancé horrible?" Izaak asks.

"Did he hit you?" Clark asks.

Roxana blinks. "No. I mean, I don't know him, really. I've barely spoken to him."

"Why did you leave?" Minerva asks gently, like she's talking to a baby bird.

Roxana sinks down onto one of Minerva's bright yellow armchairs. "I just realized that I didn't *want* to marry Ragar, and that no one had ever even asked me what I wanted to do. I was informed I'd be marrying him, as if he won some contest and I was the prize." Her eyes are unfocused, her voice soft. Every single guy in the room is staring at her like she hung the moon, and for a vampire and a werewolf, that really means something. "I suppose I shouldn't have run. I didn't think it through—I just, that's my mom's life, and

I've seen it every single day. I guess I just didn't want to *be* a prize for my entire life. It felt like my last chance to avoid it." She stands up. "But I don't want to put any of you at risk. It's my life, and she's right." When she looks at me, her eyes aren't angry or reproachful. They're resigned. "I don't know any of you, and I shouldn't be causing you trouble like this. I'm sorry for coming here." She picks up her bag.

No one stops her.

Minerva glances at me and even opens her mouth, but she doesn't say a word.

Clark scowls, his hands clenching at his sides.

Xander looks frantically from me to Clark to Izaak and back to me.

But no one stops the little princess as she trudges with her heavy duffel bag toward the door I'm standing in front of. I think about what Minerva said. Of all people, of all my friends, I should be the most eager to help her. Only, I'm probably the only one who really understands what it means. The dragona don't follow rules. They don't ask politely. The dragona male who killed my mother. . .I shudder. I can still hear his voice sometimes.

Anyone who would consort with a demon doesn't deserve to live. We used to deal with you properly, but now the akero just hide in the clouds and let vermin wander the Earth. If I don't clean this up, no one will.

I shudder.

If that warlock hadn't stumbled upon us when he did, my sister and I would have died as well.

For the first time, I imagine what it would be like to have my entire life run by someone like that, to be dictated to, to be handed over to another dragona male as some kind of trophy. She may not be aggressive, and she may not have any powers, but that's not my fault.

But.

I do know what it feels like to be the powerless one in a room full of heavy hitters. It must have been a scary thing, to run from everything she knew. She makes it sound like a spur of the moment decision, but it was still a brave decision.

I sigh heavily.

I hate doing this—I hate the risk. I hate the possibility that I might be stuck in some terrible moral quandary, but if I let her walk away, how can I live with that choice? What kind of person would I become? "Don't go."

"Really?" Minerva's more excited than Roxana.

Although, Roxana does stop trudging along, and her head whips towards mine. "What?"

"I don't even live here. If everyone else is willing to take the risk, even as the only person who can really guess what your family might do, I shouldn't get in the way."

"You mean it?" Roxana's eyes really do look like a cartoon puppy. I have no idea how they can be that big and innocent looking.

"It's not my apartment," I say. "And I don't plan to come around often while you're here. But I can tell you that gloffee will only protect you from normies. If you want to evade the other dragona, and they will be searching everywhere, you're going to need some powerful glamour."

"Where will I get that?" Roxana turns toward Minerva hopefully. "You're a witch. Maybe you—"

Clark laughs. "Minerva's a wonderful person, but her glamour is not good."

"Oh." Roxana's shoulders droop. "Well."

"But mine is." Clark's voice is light, breezy. That makes no sense. He's the knight in shining armor here. Why's he acting so—oh.

He likes her.

Clark's annoying at a baseline, but when he has a crush on someone he turns into Yosemite Sam. Ugh. This is going to be really annoying, and from what I can tell, all men are going to act this dopey around her.

"You'll have to come over every single day and cast a new spell," I say. "Her innate magic will wear it down."

"I don't really have any magic," Roxana says.

"Patently untrue," I say. "It may not be the kind of active magic witches and warlocks use, but your charismatic pull is off the charts—and that's why every guy in this room is dying to help you."

"That's why that charm you gave me got me any date to the dance I wanted," Minerva says. "Remember?"

Roxana blinks. "Right. The charm. Never mind that, then," Roxana says. "I don't think I could ask anyone to come over here daily."

"I don't mind," Clark says.

I'll bet he doesn't. He looks absolutely besotted.

"I'm happy to help too," Xander says.

"And me." Izaak saunters toward her. "If there's anything at all I can do, don't hesitate to ask." He lifts one eyebrow and bites his lip.

"Don't," Minerva says. "Izaak, it's her wedding day! A wedding she didn't even want. Leave her alone, please." As if yelling at him wasn't enough, she glares at her brother and Xander as well. "You three are ridiculous. She can't help it, so you'll have to work hard to ignore the pull that just comes along with being who she is. So my first rule is, *none* of you can ask her out or date her or flirt with her. Got it?"

They all start grumbling immediately, as if Minerva's ruining all their hopes and dreams.

"Now, the next line of business is practicing what kind of spell might dampen her allure," Minerva says. "Any ideas?"

"I'll call in sick tomorrow," Clark says. "I can spend all day testing a few different ones."

"Good idea," I say. "You need to make sure it's good before she leaves here."

"Are you not going to tell your bosses?" Roxana's looking pointedly at Xander.

"Me?" His eyes widen. "I would never. I had no idea you hadn't even been *asked* about whether you wanted to get married. That's terrible."

Roxana starts to cry, and that's when I realize I did the right thing. This ridiculous group of idiots would never be able to help her alone. "Alright," I say. "This is what we're going to do."

An hour later, the guest room at Minerva's has been transformed. With donations from everyone, we've managed to put together the basics of what she'll need, and we have a plan in place. I can finally go home without worrying about how they'll manage. They're nice enough, but they barely have enough common sense to fill a maxi pad.

"But tomorrow?" Roxana asks.

"It's likely that for the next few days, there will be constant patrols and flyovers all over the city," I say. "I'd suggest you plan on staying inside for at least a week."

"But then, once things kind of start to calm down?" she asks.

"Assuming we get lucky and nothing leads them to us?" I ask.

"Right," Roxana says. "Then what?"

"Then what?" I look at Minerva. She seems as confused as I am. "Then what do you mean, what?"

"What do you do all day long?" Roxana's genuinely asking. It's not a joke.

"We have jobs," I say. "I run a secondhand magic shop."

"And I'm a paranormal affairs officer," Minerva says. "I work nights. Actually, I need to leave soon or I'll be late. But the good news is that while I'm at work, I can kind of check in on what's going on and what the police will be doing."

"A man on the inside," Clark says.

"A woman," Minerva snaps. "Which is even better."

"Once things calm down," Roxana says, "I'll need to get one of those job thingies, too, I guess?"

What kind of person has never had a job? Oh, right, a dragona princess.

"Uh, yeah," Izaak says. "It's a good plan."

"What do you do?" she asks.

"I'm an actor," he says.

"You're a vampire. . .who's an actor?" Roxana asks. "Doesn't the whole 'normies are terrified of you' thing cause problems?"

She's known him one second and she can sum up his issues in a sentence. I can't help laughing. "Yes. Yes, it's a problem."

"Only for plays," Izaak says. "When I'm filming for television or movies, it's only the crew and the other actors who get scared."

"Only the crew and the other actors?" Roxana's eyebrows lift.

Xander shrugs. "Don't try to understand it. The heart wants what the heart wants."

"I guess," Roxana says, "And now, I'll finally be able to figure out what my heart wants."

In that moment, I really hope she's right.

7

IZAAK

My mother is horrifyingly scary.

I don't mean that in a get-me-a-switch kind of way. I don't even mean that she's got a withering 'mom' look, although she does.

Most of my friends bobbed their heads and commiserated when I complained about my mom—like they totally got it.

Only, they really didn't.

Because my mom's a vampire, and not just any vampire. She's got the vampire job that most vampires aspire to have: assassin.

She spent most of her life teaching her firstborn (that's me) to follow her in that field. She wanted to hand things off to me, right? I mean, she's got eleven kids, and I'm just the first, but she figured there was room for all of us. It's a market with room for expansion, sadly, and the mediocre assassins don't last very long.

But I'm a terrible son and an even worse vampire, and no matter how hard she tried, no matter how scary she was, and no matter how awesome she is at her job, I couldn't ever bring myself to kill anyone. Even when I knew they were really bad people, even when I knew they had it coming to them, I still couldn't do it.

I don't like fear and groveling, for one thing. I don't much care for anger or adrenaline, either. What I really love, what I *long* for, is to make people smile and laugh. Basically, I'm a freak among vampires.

Most of what people believe about vampires is just wrong.

Lots of us love garlic—breadsticks should be their own food group. We don't desiccate, and we are most certainly *not* dead. The whole idea is ridiculous—frankly, it's propaganda put out there by an ingenious freaking werewolf that just stuck.

But one thing *is* true. Unless we're employing our magical ability to draw people to us, we call it our charm, we make humans very, very nervous—scared even. They can sense the predator hiding inside of the human suit.

That's why the whole idea of being an actor is problematic for a vampire. It's not quite as hard for film, but it's downright impossible in stage productions.

Unless you're fine with always being cast as the villain.

"This is good news," my agent Stella says. "I don't know why you'd turn it down. It's a paycheck. Don't you need that?"

"I didn't audition for the bad guy," I say. "And it's not about the money. It's about the image, and you know that if I take *another* role as a villain, I may never get anything else, ever."

"Ed Norton makes a very good living playing the bad guy," she says. "Robert DeNiro. Liam Neeson. Joaquin Phoenix. And they do get the occasional good role, too."

"Even you know," I say. "You just called non-villain roles 'good' ones. No, this is a mountain I'll die on."

"A hill," she says. "It's 'a hill' that you'll die on."

"Whatever." I grunt. "Look, I went there to audition for the lead. Tell them it's that or nothing."

"They said the same thing that everyone says. You're too ominous to play the lead. He's supposed to make people swoon, and you make their palms sweat."

"But if they give me a chance—"

"They already cast Tom Konova."

I growl. "Tom? Again? Why does everyone keep—"

"He's personable, he's charming, and his butt—"

"I do not want to hear about any part of his body," I say. "Certainly not his butt. Look, maybe we can get me an audition where I can do the first few rounds online. Let them get to know me from afar first."

"Before their bodies react to the fact that you could eat them?" Stella sighs.

I thought finding a supernatural agent would help—an old witch too crusty to cast many spells anymore. That plan, like most of Minerva's spells, backfired. She's more resolved than my human agent that I'll never land any heroic roles.

"I think it may be time for you to recognize the reality of your situation, so that you can accept it."

"If I wanted to terrify people, I could've gone into the family business." I fold my arms—and then realize that she can't see it through the phone.

"As an assassin?" Stella still struggles to believe me sometimes. "Isn't that what you said your mother is?"

"One of the top twenty in the country," I say. "She can kill almost anyone with her bare hands."

"Having fangs and claws helps." I can hear the shudder in her voice.

"We don't have claws," I say. "And our fangs don't really look much different than regular teeth. They're just a little sharper and harder than normie's teeth, with a little hole that sucks the blood right up to—"

"Izaak, I can get you another audition for next week, I hope, for the new Reynolds play, but only if you're willing to audition to be the landlord. Did you check out the script?"

"I told you—"

"And I told you that I can't keep turning down roles, here. It would be like a real estate agent putting down offers and backing out. It makes me look bad. You're the villain here, not me."

"I'm *not* a villain," I shout.

Stella hangs up.

"Are you sure about that?" Xander asks, incapable of passing up the chance to make any kind of joke.

When did he come in? I thought he was at work. "Hey, man."

"So, speaking of villains." He gulps. "I paid rent, three days ago, when it was due, but you still haven't paid me your half. And you're three months behind on utilities."

I cringe. "Yeah, my bad."

"I take it the audition last week didn't go well?"

Xander would not like to hear that I got a role. . .and turned it down. "Don't worry." I pull on my jacket. "I was just about to go down and donate at Grand Central. I'll bring that money right up."

"I don't want your blood money," Xander says. "You need that for, like, food and stuff, right?"

My shoulders slump. "I mean, I bet I can go a little more often. Then I'll have extra. It's going to be fine. I'm just in a bit of a slow patch."

"I know it's hard—finding plays and movies that won't film in the early morning is challenging enough. But trying to find a job when you're borderline terrifying to the normies?" Xander shakes his head. "Do you ever wonder if you made a mistake? About wanting to be an actor, I mean?"

"All day every day." It doesn't help that my parents think I've gone insane. And all my friends and family. Except Xander. If I'm losing him, too. . .

"Well," Xander says. "I get it."

"I know you do," I say, "and that's why I can't leave you hanging on rent. I'll be right back."

Grand Central Gloffee's owner loves having a vampire who lives upstairs. "Morning, Gavin," I say.

"It's nine-thirty at night." Gavin shakes his head. "Vampires are whack."

"Potato, potahto," I say.

"You here to donate?"

I nod.

"Give me a minute—I'll meet you around back."

True to his word, Gavin rounds the corner a few moments later, needle and syringe kit in hand. "You're a day late. I was worried the glaffour plants would wither."

"Sorry," I say. "It was a crazy day yesterday."

"Yeah, I still can't believe that dragona's gone. Think she was kidnapped? Or do you think she's dead?" His eyes widen. "Or, wait. Do you know something? I hear your mom's connected."

I laugh. "Mom wouldn't dream of telling me anything, even if she knew. But I think Roxana Goldenscales probably just ran away. Doesn't that make more sense? I mean, who would sign their own death warrant by killing or kidnapping her?"

"If she ran away, someone would have handed her back over for the reward already." Gavin shrugs. "Think about it. If people help her hide, the Russian and American dragona will be out for their heads. Why risk that, when they could just hand her over for ten million dollars right now? What kind of moron wouldn't do that math?"

Ten. Million. Dollars.

I had no idea they were offering a reward, let alone such a huge one.

Roxana must be terrified.

"Alright, same amount as always? One quarter pint?" He opens up the packaging and starts to prep the needle and plunger.

"Uh, do you need more?"

Gavin freezes. "Why?"

"I could use a little extra cash," I say.

"Unfortunately, this is exactly how much I need to feed my vampire-fed glaffour plants." He winces. "I don't really need more."

"Do you happen to know anyone else who might?"

He frowns. "We ran the numbers, Izaak. Remember? This is what you can give weekly without suffering side effects."

"But if I gave a little more, it wouldn't really hurt, right?"

This time, he doesn't just frown. He sets the needle down. "You better not try giving at any other gloffee shops."

"Why not?"

"I knew I should worry. You could pass out, for one. For another, you might have long-term health issues." He shakes his head. "There are other ways to make money. Don't even think about doing that."

"What other ways could I earn money?" I ask.

"You could work here, for one," he says. "We're always looking for—"

"My friends would absolutely love that." I shake my head. "No, I can't mop floors and make gloffee. I just can't."

"Well, if you get to the point where your pride will allow it," he says, "come let me know." He grabs my arm and pushes the needle in, carefully extracting a hundred and seventy five milliliters of blood. "It's too bad you're not dragona."

"Why?" For some reason, even mention of that word makes me nervous right now. I'm not the best at keeping secrets. I'm always worried I've somehow given something away.

"Well, you know what I pay for vampire blood."

"Yeah."

"I pay five times as much for dragona blood."

"What?" I slap the Band-Aid on my arm. "That's discrimination."

"It's the market, my friend. Dragona almost never need money, so they're much harder to find. That's why I rarely have dragona flavors on the menu." He tilts his head. "When I do, they sell out immediately."

"What if I had a friend who wouldn't want anyone to know he was donating, but I could get you some of his dragona blood?" I'm kind of proud of how I remembered to say 'him' both times.

"It has to be fresh, or it'll kill my glaffour plants," Gavin says. "Like, less than an hour old."

"I think I could do that," I say.

"You know a dragona?" His disbelieving smirk annoys me.

"Yessir."

"And you think you could convince him to donate blood to me?" He looks so unbearably smug.

"Maybe." I hope it doesn't matter that it's a female dragona—they can't shift or breathe fire. They're not as strong. But I can't ask. They're so rare, the last thing I'm willing to do is admit I know a female. That would lead Roxana's insane family right to me.

"I would definitely be interested. I'd require authenticity, of course. If it turns out the blood isn't real, I'll never buy from you again."

"Oh, it's real," I say.

"People can definitely taste a difference, so don't even think about trying to sell me werewolf or witch blood that's been spelled, or charmed flame lizard blood."

"People have tried that? Really?"

He frowns.

"You know me better than that."

"People do stupid things when they're desperate," he says. "And you said you needed money."

"I've got good friends," I say. "I'm not desperate, I'm just tired of being strapped. Big difference."

"Well, let me know. I'm very interested in dragona blood, always."

I glance around at his back room, where every single surface is covered with glaffour plants. It takes a bundle of plants to run a successful gloffee house, of course, but I wonder which ones are fed with dragona blood.

"I don't have any dragona plants right now," Gavin says, clearly able to read my thoughts. "But if I get some, and better yet, if I could keep that flavor on the menu?" He whistles. "I could make a killing. I might even be able to compete with The Central Cloak."

That's his nemesis. He and his best friend started it together, but when his friend stole Gavin's boyfriend, they parted paths. I hear there were a lot of spells fired that day.

It doesn't take me long to race upstairs. I bang on the door a little too hard.

But no one answers.

Of course not. Minerva's probably at work, and that means Roxana's alone. She can hardly answer the door for just anyone. "It's me, Izaak," I say. "The super hot one."

"With the dark, smooth skin?" Even her voice is silky.

"That's me," I say. "Women love chocolate."

She's laughing when she opens the door. "What's up?"

"So I was downstairs, giving my monthly blood donation—"

"What?" Her eyes widen like a bloated toadstool.

"At the gloffee shop," I say.

"I thought vampires *drank* blood," she says. "You're saying you *give* blood?" Does she really not know how gloffee works?

"For the glaffour plants," I say.

She blinks.

"Glaffour plants produce glaffour berries." I speak slowly, in case she's just not comprehending me. Maybe English isn't her first language.

"Right." She tilts her head. "I know."

"And when supernaturals eat them, the berries' magical properties keep us disguised from normies. So if a werewolf howls, or bares his fangs, but he's eaten a glaffour berry in the last day, the normie will see what he expects to see instead of what's actually there—the magic from the berries keeps us hidden by altering the normies' brain chemistry or something."

"I'm not stupid," Roxana says. "I know that the akero helped the witches create glaffour plants to protect the creatures they brought."

Then what part baffles her? "I was giving blood," I say. "So they can feed the vampire flavored plants."

The curl of her lip tells me that this is where I lost her.

"Do you really not know that glaffour plants need the blood of a supernatural creature to produce berries? Otherwise, they just look like regular old mint plants."

"Wait, really?"

"If you eat berries made with the blood of your own kind, the berries will be revolting to you. So if I eat vampire-blood-created berries, it tastes like ear wax, for instance."

"Oh, nasty."

"You might taste vomit, if you ate dragona-blood-fed glaffour berries. Or, you know, the gloffee made from them."

"Okay."

"So the gloffee shops need werewolves, mages, and vampires to donate so the patrons have some choices of gloffee that they want to drink."

"That's weird."

"How could you not know that?" I scratch my head. "The type of berry is listed in every gloffee shop. On big signs."

She blinks. "I never go to gloffee shops. I rarely go anywhere that normies might see me. When I drink gloffee at all, it's stuff our chefs bring."

Good Lord. "Well, seeing as your chef isn't here, and you might want to go outside where normies might see you, and you can't use your own glamour since you're not a mage, here's a thought. Gavin, the manager downstairs, mentioned that they can almost never find dragona willing to sell their blood."

She shrugs. "That makes sense. Why would we?" She shudders. "It sounds terrible—donating blood so other people can consume it."

"To be clear, no one drinks the blood. They drink the gloffee made from the glaffour berries that the plant grows because it's fed with your blood."

Her eyes widen. "I'm so sorry—I didn't mean to offend you."

"Oh, you didn't." I can't help my smile. If I got offended every time someone told me that drinking blood was gross, I'd walk around punching everyone on the nose. Daily. "But the point is, since dragona blood's hard to come by, they pay a lot for it."

Her expression is blank. "That's nice."

"Which means, he'd pay a lot for *your* blood."

She frowns. "Why in the world would—"

"I assume you haven't brought a lot of cash with you?"

Roxana gulps.

"And as someone who deals with cashflow problems occasionally, I can relate."

"But it's not like I can walk down there," she says. "If I show my face—"

"Someone will report you," I say. "I'm aware. But wouldn't you like to have money of your own? That you could buy things with online? Or use to pay a delivery guy? Or, I don't know, pay to Minerva to help offset her living costs, now that you're here, sponging off her?"

Her shoulders droop and I almost feel guilty. "I know."

"Is that a yes?"

"I suppose so," she says.

"Great. Well, I'm willing to take your blood and vouch for it, and take, let's say, just half of what Gavin pays."

"Half?" Roxana's eyes narrow. "What kind of idiot do you think I am?"

I had hoped a little bigger than she is, apparently. "Fine," I say. "A third."

"A tenth," she says. "A finder's fee."

"Without me, you'd never have heard of this. And without me, you couldn't sell your blood, since you can't show your face. But I get it. You don't need my help."

"Fine," she says. "A third."

And now, I can make rent. Xander's going to be so pleased.

When I help her draw her blood and then rush it downstairs, I try my hardest not to think about the ten million dollars I could *easily* be getting instead.

8

MINERVA

I love my job.

I've wanted to be a paranormal affairs officer since I was old enough to know what it was. It could have been seeing Dad in his uniform every day. Or maybe it was watching Officers Andretti and Stone lock up demonspawn the first time they descended with such grace and competence. (We don't do that anymore—don't worry!) Or perhaps it was being on the parade floats on Thanksgiving that did it—Dad let me sit on his lap and throw handfuls of candy to people who were cheering us on.

No matter what led me here, I'm living my dream.

But even dreams get a little boring sometimes.

Amber's very sharp elbow wakes me up. "Ouch," I say. "What was that for?" I rub my eyes and glance at my watch. "Forty-one minutes left on our shift. You couldn't have let me sleep through them?"

"Your *friend* called nine times." She points at my phone. "I figured you might want to know, but whatever. It's not like I like her at all."

Why would Bevin call me over and over—*my flame*

lizard egg!! I snatch my phone off the counter so fast that I nearly drop it. Then I call her back.

"Bevin?"

"It's here," she says. "And it's rocking."

"Mother of a wolfcub," I mutter.

"I'll meet you at your place?"

"Yes," I say. "I'm on my way."

Amber laughs.

"I need to go," I say. "I know we're still taking calls, but—"

"I'll cover for you," Amber says. "Good luck."

I shouldn't have told her what I'm trying. If this fails, and it nearly always does with flame lizards, she's just one more person who knows. But Amber loves me, and I trust her, and I'm a talker. I doubt I could have stopped myself if I tried. "Thank you."

I dart out the door right as Peter Freaking Chester and his stupid partner Rufus Moonton are coming through the door. Why are they always early? Don't they have anything else to do?

"You're in a rush, Loosey."

"It's Lucent." I should leave it alone. I should ignore them, but I can't ever seem to do that. "It's hard to remember words when your head's so full of fluff, I know. But try harder, *Jester*."

"It's *Ch*ester." I can't tell whether Rufus doesn't get it, or whether he's intentionally obtuse.

This time, I just keep walking.

"Are you leaving early?" Peter's voice is so loud, there's no way that everyone in the office can't hear him. "That's not the behavior of someone who wants to be considered for a guardian post. Is it?"

The Chief chooses this moment, of course, to poke his head out of his office. "Looks like a good time for a quick meeting."

I suppress my groan. I missed nine calls. That means Bevin has had the flame lizard for at least an hour. And the familiar spell takes hours to prepare. I follow everyone else into the conference room and sit down next to Amber, but my knees are bouncing, and my hands are jittery.

"What in the world is the meeting about?" Amber asks.

"As you all may know," the Chief says, "for more than fifty years, the paranormal affairs department in New York City has taken great pride in partnering diverse teams. A non-magical partner, coupled with a mage. That allows each team to address a variety of different scenarios with insight and compassion. It also means that we are a melting pot, so to speak, of different cultures and views."

Oh, no. These diversity things can drag on forever.

"We've tried our best to accommodate the varying strengths of each supernatural being, including keeping vampires on nights and werewolves on days. But there have been an increasing number of complaints lately that were-wolves never have the chance to do nights."

"And all the fun stuff happens at night," Rufus says.

"We have been listening," the Chief says. "And we've decided to allow partners to apply for temporary rotations —werewolves will be assigned one run of nights, and vampire partnerships will be assigned one run of days per month, on a provisional basis. We'd like to see how the vampires are able to adapt, and whether the werewolves are able to better display their strengths in the busy nighttime hours."

Amber's eyes flash. "But—"

"No buts," the Chief says. "Not until after we've completed a few months and have some hard evidence to back up our positions. Is that clear?"

Normally I might argue a little harder, but I don't have time right now.

"We also may make some partnership changes," the

Chief says. "We come to admire and respect people by understanding them. I firmly believe the unity and cohesiveness of our force suffers when people don't get to know one another very well. For instance, Minerva has only ever been partnered with vampires, and I think her particular issues might—"

"My issues?" I can't keep quiet about that. "My *issues* were resolved," I say. "I have a certificate to prove it."

"Nevertheless," the Chief says. "We're going to mix up some of the partnerships over the coming weeks. Not permanently, but on a provisional basis, as with the shift schedule."

I'm beginning to hate that word, but again, I don't have time to argue. Not today. My stupidly expensive familiar is here, ready to be bonded. That doesn't stop every single idiot on the force from arguing with the Chief, and the minutes keep ticking by, slowly, painfully.

When I finally race out the door, I'm thirty-three minutes late.

And then the subway breaks down.

Every single minute that flies past scrapes its bony, fractured fingers across the bundle of anxiety I have become.

Why does it seem like every part of my life is conspiring to wreck my goals? I finally get home, an hour and a half late, and I race up the stairs. I'm fumbling with my keys when the door swings open.

"You're late." Roxana taps her foot. "That stupid flame lizard is going to pop out any minute."

"The spell!" I push past her and lurch into the family room.

Bevin has arranged blankets—old ones, bless her—on the coffee table, and the little egg is shaking in the center of them.

Every single time I've done the familiar spell in the past, I've taken hours and really focused. There's no time for all that, not if I want any hope of salvaging this. My one hope is that, even when I spent hours on it before, it never worked. Maybe this is fortuitous! If I'm really guilty of overthinking things, I won't have time in this instance.

"You have less than ten minutes," Roxana says. "Look at the striations on that shell. The buckle like that means he's pulling on it with his teeth."

"Ah!" Why can't she say something helpful?

"I brought your spell book," Bevin says.

Generally, she won't even touch magical items she hasn't purchased for her shop, so Bevin really must be worried.

"I can't believe you traded that dumb feather for this stupid rock." She drops my spell book on the coffee table with a thwack.

"You traded an akero feather for this?" Roxana's hand presses to her chest. "Why on earth would you do that?"

"Because I'm a huge idiot," I say. "Now get out of my way so I can try and make it worth the swap."

I flip the book open and start leafing to the right page. "I need glaffour berries," I say. "And goji berries."

"I remember that." Bevin points at a basket of pink and red berries. "And." She scrunches her nose. "I bought ten pounds of raw meat."

Like any good demon-spawn trying not to sin, she's vegetarian. But she bought that for me anyway. "Thank you." I know what a sacrifice it was for her, even though it's not for her to eat.

Roxana hands me a pristine box of new chalk. "Don't want to use the old stuff, not for this, I imagine."

I laugh. With my luck? I almost never risk old chalk. What if a stick gave out halfway through a circle, and I couldn't line things up right again? Luckily, I'm awesome at drawing perfect circles.

Bevin's already shifting the furniture so I can draw my lines around the coffee table. I manage to get both of my concentric containment circles drawn before Roxana starts shouting. "Minerva. Minerva!"

I didn't manage the protection circle, but that only keeps other things out. Should be fine. "It's okay, I'm ready."

Sort of ready.

I wish I had gone over the words another dozen times. I wish I had practiced the hand motions. But at the end of the day, my issues with magic have never been that I wasn't properly prepared. If I knew what my issues were, I'd already have fixed them. I breathe in and out once, then twice, and then I turn toward the egg.

A crack's opening up, bright red light spraying outward from the edges.

I've never seen a dragona egg hatch—I imagine Roxana has—but I've always wondered whether the videos of flame lizard eggs were exaggerated.

Now that I'm watching one, I realize that they weren't.

A blast of heat hits me in the face, enveloping my entire body quickly. Sweat pops out on my forehead and trails down my face, dripping below the collar of my uniform.

"I'm opening a window," Bevin says.

I don't blame her. It's blazing hot, all of a sudden.

"That's fine. It can't leave." At least I finished those containment circles. I need to keep this flame lizard close for long enough to bond it, or I'll have thrown away my most prized possession for no reason.

"Do your spell," Roxana says. "He's coming right now."

If I start it too early, it won't attach. If I wait too long, it won't attach. It's a stupidly delicate balance, and I know she's trying to help, but Roxana isn't a mage. "Got it," I say. "Thanks."

I stare at the eggshell, watching for the moment its eyes lock on mine.

Unfortunately, instead of seeing its eyes when the crack widens, all I see are flames.

"Ah!" I can't help screaming. It's hot. It's blindingly bright. And it's burning my coffee table—and the blankets on top of it.

"Frigida. Tace. Siste flammas. Tace ignem."

The fire, blessedly, winks out. But the flame lizard is now prowling around the edge of the coffee table, looking nowhere near my vicinity.

"Hey there, fireball."

He turns his beautiful, emerald green head toward me slowly, his brilliant jade green eyes flashing. And then he blasts me with fire, again.

"No, no," I say. "Siste flammas. Tace ignem." Luckily, the flames wink out again with minimal damage. I wave my other hand wildly behind me. "Meat. Meat!"

Someone puts the bowl in my hand, and I grab a squishy, slightly cold chunk of it. I extend my hand toward the gorgeous and somewhat angry little creature. "Look, fella. It's food." I smile. "Yum, yum!"

He thanks me for my gesture by roasting my hand like a kabob.

I drop the meat and step back with a shout.

"Just bond the little devil," Bevin says. "Quick."

My hand is throbbing. My whole body aches. And I'm beginning to wonder whether this was all a catastrophic mistake. But I grind out the words. I say them in Latin, but in English, the spell basically reads:

Winged one, flier of the sky, come to me. Be my companion. Be my partner. Love me. Cherish me. Protect me, as I protect you, forever, until the end of days. Never be separate from my side. We are one.

It's a little melodramatic, as familiar spells go, but I'm desperate. I need a strong bond—prior to now, none of my attempts have worked at all.

A loud crash on my patio causes us all to turn toward the wall of windows across the back of my apartment. My arm is throbbing. My head is starting to pound. The little creature I traded my most precious possession for is shrieking, and I have no idea whether this spell worked. I do not have the patience or the time to deal with anything else.

Which, of course, is why an insane pigeon chose this moment to crash headlong into the window of my patio, breaking the glass.

"Uh, Minerva." Bevin sounds even more strung out than I feel.

"What?" I'm a little distracted wondering how much it's going to cost me to repair the glass and replace the charred coffee table. I turn back to see if any of the tiles were scorched.

"Minerva!"

I whip my head up and realize why Bevin's getting upset. The stupid flame lizard's wings have dried, and it's flapping them vigorously. Too vigorously. The wind from its wings is blowing blackened ash and glowing embers from the blankets all over the room, and it's setting tiny fires in every direction.

"Siste flammas! Tace ignem!" Gah, what is with this little devil?

As I'm trying to put out the fires it's still starting, it manages to lift into the air, and fly rapidly away from the coffee table and toward Roxana. Until it collides with the edge of my warded circle. The clanging sound it makes when it hits has all three of us clutching our ears with our hands.

The stupid flame lizard, instead of giving up, flaps and flaps in the other direction, winging toward Bevin. It whams into the magical circle again, this time causing a grinding sound before the horrible clang. My head feels like it might split in two.

That little emerald devil finally lands in the center of the coffee table, and it *shrieks* as loudly as it can. The sound is most certainly going to be heard from all around us.

Roxana's thinking the same thing as I am—her face looks absolutely horrified. "Shut up, you worthless little flying rat." Her shoulders straighten. Her eyes flash. She lifts both her hands and presses them, palm out, toward the center of the circle. "Close your stupid mouth or get out, right now."

The flame lizard stretches to its fullest height, almost twelve inches, and spreads its wings. It shrieks again, this time even more loudly than before, and then it flies straight toward Roxana. I can't tell whether it's drawn to her, or whether it hates her, but this time, instead of a clanging sound when it hits my circle, the entire room is filled with the sound of shattering glass.

And the stupid little beast breaks free.

The force of the spell knocks me backward, right on my butt. My head feels like a shattered gourd. And the lizard circles Roxana once, twice, and then on the third circle, heads for the windows.

More specifically, the broken window.

It doesn't slow down, and that weakened glass does nothing to stop it from flying right outside.

I force myself to my feet and race after it, but by the time I reach the hole, it's gone. I can't see it. I can't hear it.

And most disappointingly, I can't sense it at all.

9

MINERVA

No akero feather.
    No flame lizard.
    No familiar at all.
That's how well my plan worked.

I'm not sure whether the anti-fire spells wore me out, or whether it was the broken circle, or my attempts to bond that maniacal lizard, or whether I'm just tired from being such a monumental failure.

Whatever it is, I don't even bother covering up the hole in the window. I just sweep up the glass, toss it in the trash, peel my uniform off, and climb into bed. At least I don't relive my disaster over and over. Even the bright sunlight streaming down from my window doesn't bother me.

I fall right to sleep.

When I wake up at sunset, I hear a gentle cooing.

At first, my groggy, sleep-infused brain wonders whether Bevin set a white noise machine in my room to make the soothing, gentle sound. It's a considerate, kind, thoughtful notion, and I could totally see Bevin doing that. Not only because she strives to be good in all ways, but also because in spite of my failings, she loves me.

But no white noise machine on Earth pecks you on the nose.

Only birds do that.

I sit up so fast, I nearly fling the pigeon onto the floor. Its eyes widen indignantly, and it puffs up like a ball of fluff. Then it coos, purposefully, as if to say, *what could you be thinking? Watch out, lady. I was trying to sleep.*

Its eyes close again, as if I'm in *its* bed, and not the other way around.

"Hello!" I shout. "Get out, stupid. You don't belong here."

Instead of flying away, like it should, it turns its head toward me slowly, its eyes only half open. "Coo." It closes its eyes again.

This cannot be happening. Maybe it's a bizarre dream. It wouldn't be the first strange thing I've dreamed about —not even the first this week. But even in a dream, there's no way that I can possibly let a pigeon sleep on my bed. It's like having a flying cockroach in my bed. Just, no.

I try to shoo it away, grimacing as my fingers touch its grey and black wings. I tell myself it's a clean pigeon. Those exist, right?

Oh, no. What if it pooped on my bed?

Nothing looks soiled, but that doesn't mean much.

Shooing it away fails spectacularly.

Its head swivels toward me, its little orange eyes blinking open again, and it leans against my palm, like it *trusts* me. "Um, okay, little weirdo. I hate to be the bad guy here, but this is my apartment, and you can't be here."

I pick it up, freaking out inside at how calm it is, and carry it out of my bedroom. Even when I squish it pretty hard to open the door, it doesn't look alarmed. My hands are shaking by the time I open the door and realize it must have come in through the open window. I really should have blocked that off. There's no telling what animals wandered in while I slept the day away.

I'm lucky it wasn't night, or I might have an apartment full of owls and bats. Speaking of the approaching evening, a brisk breeze is blowing through the hole. Instead of shoving the poor little bird back through the broken window, I actually open the door and walk out onto the patio. "You're going to have to stay out here, okay? And don't poop on my patio, or you can't be here either."

When I set it down on the rail, I swear it looks at me as though I've betrayed it.

"Don't give me that look. It's nothing personal. I just can't have a bird sleeping in my house. I'm way too much of a neat freak for that, okay?"

It hops down, fluttering its wings as it lands on the ground, and tries to follow me back through the door.

"No, no." I'm forced to slam the door on its beak. "Ugh, what is your deal?" It glares at me as I cover the broken window with a piece of cardboard and duct tape. "I said!" I'm sure it can't understand me, but I feel like I have to explain myself, for some reason. "I can't have birds in my house! One poop and I'd melt down. You would not want to see that, trust me."

I think about its pathetic little eyes the entire time I'm showering.

But when I step out of the shower, the *last* thing I expect to see resting on top of my clean towel is that stupid pigeon. "How the heck are you in here?"

It tilts its head as if I'm the one who makes no sense.

"I closed the hole. How did you even get in?"

When I shove it off my towel, I find that I can't quite bring myself to dry my clean body off with a bird-towel. I'm forced to use my guest towel, and I hate doing that. It's not the natural order. Besides, what will Roxana use, now?

"Ugh, you! You're messing things up, and I already had a terrible day yesterday."

It starts to coo, and fluffs up, as if it understood what I'm saying. . .and it's trying to comfort me? Oh my Gabriel, if anyone else could hear my thoughts, they'd think I'd gone insane, attributing feelings to a *pigeon.*

"You're the most hated bird in New York. You know that, right?"

Its coo sounds distinctly sad, then. As if I've personally insulted its entire family.

"Look." Is it even the same bird? I don't know how I could possibly know. Maybe a whole flock came in while I was sleeping. Maybe there are twelve of them, poking all over my apartment. The thought gives me the shivers. But after I dry, dress, grab the dumb pigeon again, and emerge from the bathroom—there's no sounds or signs of any other birds, pigeon or otherwise. "Where did you come from?" I ask. "How did you get in?"

"Who are you talking to?" Roxana asks, her eyes wide, and her mouth hanging open. She glances around the apartment, clearly looking for another human being.

"Uh." I tuck the bird behind my back, though I can't think of a single reason why I'd hide it. "No one."

"You were asking *no one* how they got in?"

What's wrong with me? "It's this pigeon." I bring it around to the front, and it's sitting just as docile on my palm as it was before. "It's so strange. It lets me pick it up, and it lets me hold it, and it's totally calm, but it keeps coming inside."

Roxana ducks a little so she can see it better. "A pigeon?"

"It was—" I can't quite bring myself to admit that it was sleeping *by my head* all day. "But I put it outside already, and next thing I know, it's here again, in the bathroom."

"Uh, that might have been my fault."

"What? How?"

"I like the water to be really hot, and that gets things really steamy, so I cracked the window in there. The one that's up really high."

Oh, that makes so much sense. "Alright. Then I'm not going crazy."

"But it must have been awfully hard for it to squeeze through that tiny opening, and why would it do that? Are you sure it's the same bird?"

I pick it up closer, peering at it. "They all look the same. Iridescent head, grey body. Black stripes on their wings and tails. Who knows?"

It coos then, as if I've insulted it deeply.

"I don't even have any idea whether it's a boy or a girl."

It pecks my hand.

"Hey!" I almost drop it. "Did you see that? It's the first sign of aggression."

"I can't believe it didn't do that before. Once, when I was a kid, this blue jay would come and visit me on my patio. It came every day. Once it even sat on my hand, but when I tried to grab it, it pecked the fire out of me and left. It never came back." Roxana scowls at the pigeon. "Birds are evil."

It chitters, then, as if it's yelling at her. I had no idea pigeons could even make that noise.

"I think it's possessed," I say.

"Can pigeons get rabies?" Roxana shudders. "Get rid of it. Quick."

This time, I don't set it gently on the railing. I chuck it through the patio door into mid-air and watch as it flutters away. I feel a little bad for hurling it away from me like that, but what else can I do? It has to learn it can't live here.

"Don't you have to get to work soon?" Roxana asks. "Or are you off work?"

"Right," I say. "Yes, I'm due there in less than thirty

minutes." I straighten my uniform. "I was going to try and clean all this up, but." I glare helplessly at the charred coffee table, the ruined blankets, and the messy chalk circle on the tile.

"I can do it," Roxana says. "I'm not very experienced with cleaning, but I can scrub the floor and put the blankets in trash bags. I wasn't sure whether that's what you wanted?"

"That would be awesome," I say. "Thank you."

"No problem." She frowns. "I'm so sorry about the flame lizard and the disaster—"

"It's fine." I can't think about that now, and I really can't think about how spectacularly I failed after giving up my akero feather. I'll burst into tears before work. "Let's not talk about it, okay?"

"I did tell you they're nasty little beasts," she says. "I guess I should have given more examples."

"Really, it's fine, and I'm fine, and I'd rather never talk about it again."

"Got it," she says. "But how about something to eat?"

Last night, she made me the worst sandwich I've ever eaten in my entire life. "I mostly just drink protein shakes on my way." I edge toward the small pantry at the corner of the kitchen. "I'll just grab—"

"Oh, no, that's not a good enough breakfast, not when you're out there risking life and limb trying to save. . .what exactly do you do? Fight demons?"

I laugh. "Mostly I deal with magical miscreants of all stripes. Zombies, moonstruck weres, domestic violence involving mages or whatnot. It's anyone's guess what problems will be called in."

"Alright, well, you need a healthier breakfast." Her forehead furrows. "Er, dinner."

"I really am—"

"I insist." She hands me a ziplock bag with something squishy inside.

"What is this?"

"You had all that raw meat," she says. "So I meal prepped some burritos."

I don't even want to know how dragona eat meat chunks, and there's no telling what kind of meat Bevin bought for the flame lizard. "Uh huh. Alright, well, thank you so much." I tuck it into my bag and head for the door. I can always buy a bagel on the way to work.

"You're not going to try it?" She bites her lip. "I wanted to make sure you enjoyed it."

"Well, um, right." I'm nearly to the door, so I open it, and then I pull the baggie out of my satchel. "Hm, it sure smells unique."

Her eyebrows rise. "I've never made a burrito before, so I hope I got it right."

"Oh, good." My throat closes off, and my lips twitch, but I manage to stuff it into my mouth and force my teeth down to break off a bite.

Tortillas are meant to be lard, flour, salt, and sometimes a kind of leavening agent. I have no idea what this tortilla was made of, but it tastes eggy. And the meat inside appears not to have been cooked *at all*.

I choke a bit.

"Is it too strong?" She grimaces. "I'm so sorry. It said half a teaspoon of salt, and it'll get more savory as I cook it, but since I wasn't cooking it—"

"Why?" I choke. "Why didn't you cook it?"

"Everyone knows meat is way better when it's fresh, and this was butchered yesterday. It said so on the package."

I spit it back into the baggie. "Roxana." I gag on the acidic and almost metallic taste. "You thought it would be better *raw*?"

She frowns. "It's not? Everyone I know likes their food better raw."

"Other than me, is everyone you know *dragona?*"

Her enormous, bright, round eyes blink slowly. "Yes."

"The rest of the world likes their meat cooked. Preferably, most of the way through."

"Oh." Her shoulders droop. The corners of her insanely full lips turn down. "Well. I'm sorry."

I offer her the remains of the horribly disgusting burrito, and she finally takes it. "I really appreciate the gesture." I push past her and reach into the pantry. If I drink a protein shake fast enough, maybe I can forget how bloody awful that egg-wrap-raw-meat-roll was. Probably not, but it's worth a try.

I open the lid and start chugging, which is why I'm distracted when I step into the hallway and nearly squash the dumb pigeon.

"For the love of howling canids."

It coos and then chitters.

"What are you doing in the hallway? How on earth did you get in here?"

"Is everything okay?" Roxana pokes her head around the door.

"No!" I point at the door. "Don't open it. Don't let that thing in!"

The pigeon chitters again.

"It's possessed," I say. "It's crazy."

"Do you think it laid eggs in here or something?" Roxana asks. "I have never seen a bird try so hard to get inside someone's home in my life."

"I can't figure it out," I say. "But go close that bathroom window, stat."

"Stat?"

"Right away," I clarify.

"Got it." She closes the door.

I race down the hallway, checking over my shoulder. The dumb thing is following me, flutter-hopping as quickly as it can behind me. "Shoo." I wave at it.

It tilts its head and coos.

"I'm a police officer." I straighten my back and square my shoulders. "I will cast a spell on you, rendering you unable to move, if you don't stop following me."

"Minerva?"

Xander's standing in the hallway, and his face looks entirely too amused.

I cross my arms.

"Who ya talking to?"

"That thing." I point at the pigeon.

"The pigeon?" Xander's lip twitches.

"Why is she talking to a pigeon?" Izaak's head pokes out behind Xander's. He's still in his pajamas—we keep similar hours, thanks to my partner and my job.

"It's following me," I say. "I'm not the crazy one. It is." I fold my arms again.

"Okay," Izaak says. "But maybe don't tell anyone at work about this, or they'll never consider you to be a guardian."

"Shut up." My phone rings then, luckily, saving me from any additional jokes. "Hello?"

"Have you been checking your messages?" Amber asks.

"Do I have any?" I've been so distracted by the bird that my whole routine has been knocked off.

"The Chief called me—to make sure we didn't have anything that would interfere with you being interviewed. For that guardian position. I gave him the green light of course, but it's in like twenty minutes. I figured you'd be here early."

I nearly drop my phone. "Oh, no. I'll leave right now."

"Maybe take a cab," she says.

"You think?"

"And maybe less sarcasm." Amber grunts. "Guardians don't like it."

I hang up.

Xander and Izaak are tossing breadcrumbs to the pigeon, but it keeps moving away from them. It won't let them get within two feet of it. "Looks like a normal pigeon to me," Izaak says.

"Actually, it looks dumber than usual. Probably just got trapped in here."

"Hey, don't insult it," I snap. Why am I defending a bird? I have an interview to race toward. "I'm running late. Don't encourage it! I want that thing gone when I get home in the morning."

Izaak looks like he's going to argue with me, but I *so* do not have the time.

I race down the stairs and hail the first cab I can find. Luckily, I have good luck—usually I can't catch a cab to save my life. I reach the precinct about two minutes before my interview is set to start. I'm sweating already, and my hands are shaking, and I haven't practiced a single spell this morning, but at least I'm not late.

And none of them know I just gambled away my entire life savings for a lizard that burned half my house down and escaped.

"Officer Lucent." The Chief's voice isn't super deep, but it's loud, like there's a built-in Bose speaker in his chest. "So glad you could make it." He quirks one eyebrow as if to say, *where the heck have you been?*

I force a laugh. "You know how Fridays go." How Fridays go? What does that even mean? It's like I'm speaking gibberish. I am not off to a good start. Get it together, Lucent.

"Er, well, come right over here," he says. "Apparently, none of the guardians who are on the committee have had food yet. I told them we could go to dinner." He turns toward Amber, who's already standing next to them. "Your partner has been singing your praises. She also said she'll be able to survive without you for a bit if we steal you for this."

"I'm not sure the filing system will survive, but I can muddle through for an hour or two." Amber beams.

I wish she'd shut up about the files. It's not like the guardians are looking for a file clerk.

"You maintain all the files?" A tall man with silver at his temples and bulging muscles that show through his button-down shirt asks.

It's the first time I've looked their direction. "Uh. Yes." Now that I look, there are a lot of them, and just thinking of having to talk to all of them makes my heart race.

There's a tall woman with bright red hair, a short and stocky woman with a close-cut bob, the tall man with silver at his temples, an ancient guy I've never even seen before and at the very back. . .Ricky. My eyes freeze there, unable to shift away from his perfectly sculpted chest and arms, and his too-beautiful-to-be-real face.

"Actually, she's being far too modest," the Chief says. "Our files were embarrassingly bad until Officer Lucent took over."

"That's an undervalued trait," Ricky says. "It shows an attention to detail and a care for the little things that would really help you stand out." He smiles, bright white teeth offset against his beautifully dark skin.

"Uh, thanks." I need to stop saying 'uh' all the time.

"Is Mexican food okay?" the short guardian with the bob asks. Now that I'm looking at her more closely, she's not so much stocky as she is curvy. "I've been craving fajitas."

"Oh, sure," I say. "That's great."

As if leaving the precinct somehow changed my luck, things start looking up. The Chief and the five guardians pepper me with questions. . .and I knock them out of the park.

"Are you okay with sitting on the patio?" the guardian with the greying hair asks.

"Of course," I say. "I love to be outside."

"Another point for this one," the curvy woman says.

"I've heard you work well with your partner." The ancient man hasn't said a word until now. He steeples his hands together. "And that in six years, you've never once requested a new partner or a transfer."

"That's true," I say. "I think it's important to build relationships of trust with the people around me. I always hold up my end of things, and I'm almost never let down by others. They rise to my expectations."

"That's an impressive answer," the grey-templed man says. "But what do you do when they do let you down?"

I shrug. "Lower my expectations for the future?"

The ancient man and the curvy woman both laugh. Laughing at my corny jokes can only mean one thing: they like me. For the next half hour or so, my hopes actually rise. Could this be the group that finally takes a chance on me?

Even without the flame lizard, could this be it?

If so, my dad's up in heaven, smiling down on me right now. I can almost feel his pleasure, his pride.

The waitress brings out a plate of sopapillas and sets them in the middle of the table. "I just wanted to say thank you all for your service. We always give the police free dessert."

"Wow," I say. "This place is a real find."

The curvy woman's smile is broad. "They hooked me the first time I came with these little bites of heaven, and now I'm a regular."

The ancient man hasn't spoken again since asking about my partner. I'm pleased when he opens his mouth.

"I heard from the Chief that you sometimes struggle with spell casting." Until he says that.

"Well, I have in the past, it's true."

"Isn't that why you've applied to become a guardian a dozen times, interviewed for it on six other occasions, and yet, you've never been selected?"

I cough and bring my hand up to cover my face. Unfortunately, that movement knocks my fork and my napkin onto the ground. That gives me a moment to regroup—to think what to say—as I bend over to pick it up. When I straighten, I notice a bird, winging its way toward our table.

A grey pigeon.

It can't possibly be the same one.

There must be more than a million pigeons in New York. Other than a few random white ones, they all look exactly like this one.

But somehow, I know.

It's the same damn bird.

"Officer Lucent?" The Chief widens his eyes at me. "Did you hear what Guardian Holms asked?" He pastes a smile on his face, and it warms my heart that he's trying to help me. "I'm sure you'd like to tell him about the course you recently completed."

"Oh, right, yes, the analysis done by the Institute of Magical Justice found that I was overthinking things in the stress of the moment. We spent months making sure that won't happen anymore, and they recently certified me as proficient—"

"But aren't those classes only for flunkies?" The thin man frowns. "I don't know anyone who ever had to take one."

"Officer Lucent's magical aptitude tests are superb," the Chief says. "And her scores on the entrance exams were perfect. She didn't miss a single question."

"It's rare that an applicant has a full, unlimited recommendation from the Chief," Ricky says. "In fact, I can't think of a time we've considered someone who did. Usually it's the hasty, rash, and otherwise a little reckless officers who want to join us."

"Certainly not the people who organize files." The tall, red-haired woman smiles. "We could probably use a little of that kind of initiative and discipline, honestly."

My heart swells. Are they. . .actually considering me?

"Coo." The pigeon flutters up to the table and lies down next to my right arm, as if it's applying to be a fork here.

"Is that a *pigeon?*" the ancient man asks. "What on earth is it doing on the table?" His eyes slew toward mine, seeking some kind of explanation.

I don't think—I just act. "Who knows?" I sling my hand sideways, jostling it off the table and sending it careening toward the ground.

"Whoa, what was that for?" the Chief asks. "Is it going to be—"

But the pigeon pops its wings out at the last second and veers sharply to the left, flying into the legs of someone sitting a few tables away. It starts chittering immediately and ruffles its way free. Then it immediately launches back for our table, trying to land next to me.

Again.

It must be the same insane bird. Only this time, when I reach out to knock it out of the way, I *feel* how upset it is by my actions.

I feel the bird's feelings.

Inside my head.

That's when I realize what must have happened. The flame lizard broke the circle, and that opened me up. . .flinging my familiar spell outward. And thanks to my time crunch, I never did a spell that kept anything else *out*. That means that technically, it's all my fault.

I bonded a pigeon, and I can't think of a single thing that could possibly look worse.

"Why is that pigeon coming back?" The Chief couldn't possibly sound more confused.

"It's acting. . ." The ancient man turns slowly toward me. "It's acting like it knows you." He pauses. "Have you been here before? Do you feed it a lot?"

The laugh that pours out of my mouth is borderline unhinged. "Knows me? A pigeon?" My laugh kicks it up a notch. "That's insane."

The stupid, moronic pigeon lands on my shoulder.

"Is it. . .your familiar?" the grey-haired man asks.

My laughter has somehow transformed to tears, and I wipe them off, dislodging the stupid bird in the process. It flutters to the ground, but doesn't go far, cooing and strutting around my feet. "Of course not."

"Officer Lucent doesn't have a familiar," the Chief says. "She's never wanted any additional encumberments. No boyfriend. No pets. No familiar. Nothing to distract her from the job."

If I stay here more than another few moments, there's no way they won't realize that this dumb pigeon is bonded to me. I stand up abruptly. "My stomach appears to be upset. I think the tacos might have been a little much for me."

Judging by the looks on their faces, a weak stomach might be worse than a pigeon familiar.

"I'm going to run to the restroom."

The pigeon, of course, follows me conspicuously.

I have no idea what to do. I hide in a stall, staring at the pigeon for more than five minutes. "You."

It coos.

"You can't follow me outside."

It coos again.

Maybe that means it understands. Maybe it'll stay here.

Or maybe cooing means *Go to hell, you crazy lady*. I groan. If it does mean that, I can't even blame it. *I* bonded *it*. It had nothing to do with it. The fact that its brain is smaller than a pea isn't really its fault.

"Are you a boy?"

It pecks me.

"A girl?"

It coos.

I'm going to take that to mean it's a female. "Look. I'm at a job interview, and I need this job. So you must stay in here and stop making me look crazy? Alright?"

Of course, I can't lock it up inside. There's a huge gap above and below the stall. I try telling it to stay several different ways, even promising to come back for it, but the minute I emerge from the stall, it struts out behind me.

And flies up to sit on my shoulder.

Peter Chester has a falcon. He looks pretty cool, waltzing around the office with that feathered predator sitting on his shoulder, ready to attack on his command. Maybe I look cool—maybe I'm over thinking this. I glance in the mirror.

If Peter's falcon looks predatory, awe-inspiring, and noble, my pigeon by comparison looks. . .constipated.

Oh no. What if it poops on my shoulder? I feel like it will do it the second I walk out. I'm in the middle of wrapping my little pigeon in toilet paper as tightly as I can when the door opens.

And the curvy woman walks inside.

"So are you completely crazy? Or is that pigeon actually your familiar?" She looks downright terrified to hear the answer.

I drop the toilet paper and the stupid bird wriggles its way free.

"Why would you bond a pigeon?" It sounds like she's asking me why I crapped my pants.

"Oh, no, I didn't." I sigh, accepting that I've botched yet another interview. "I made the mistake of feeding it a while back," I say. "It's been following me around ever since. If the restaurant finds out it was me, they'll never let me in here again."

"It's nothing personal," she says. "But we can't have people who make mistakes on our team. We need only the very best. The rest of our lives depend on the guardians we choose."

I can't even blame her. I wouldn't hire me either.

10

CLARK

Minerva has always been a magical screw up. She can't seem to consistently master spells, and no one can figure out why. She practices more than anyone I know, but it never seems to help. It plagued her in school, it plagued her on the force, and now, it appears to be spilling out onto her social life.

But she's always been an excellent sister.

She places a huge plate of French toast and a big platter of eggs on the middle of her big kitchen table. "Dig in."

A pigeon warbles from her shoulder.

I can't help laughing about it. "When you said you had an emergency, it never in a million years occurred to me that it might be *this*."

"No wonder it didn't want our breadcrumbs," Xander says. "It had something bigger in mind."

"Food for life." Izaak's smiling.

"Laugh it up," Minerva says. "But I called you all here to *help* me." She lifts the pigeon off her shoulder and sets it on the floor, in front of a little plate—full of tiny chunks of egg and French toast.

"Are you sure it should be eating eggs?" Bevin's face is all twisted up. "I mean, that just seems gross for some reason."

"I looked it up," Minerva says. "Eggs are good for birds, but I agree. It's...strange."

"Isn't it, like, the chicken's baby?" Izaak asks.

Roxana grabs a plate and spears a few pieces of French toast. "Don't chickens lay an egg pretty often?" She frowns. "I think it's more like its period."

"This is such a disgusting conversation," I say.

And yet, in spite of what she just said, all I want to do is pick up Roxana, carry her through the doors onto the patio so we have some privacy, and kiss her. I shake my head to clear it. I'm sure it's just the dragona charm.

"There must be some way I can...I don't know. Eliminate the pigeon, right?" Minerva looks conflicted, even as she says it, her eyes both desperate and soft.

"I know it's cute and this sounds awful, but can't you just kill it?" Xander asks.

"No." I drop my fork. "You cannot kill it. If you kill a familiar..." I shudder. "It's miserable for the mage. Like, months of depression and misery. You don't want to kill it."

"Wait, that happens regardless?" Bevin asks. "Or, like, only if you kill it yourself?"

"You'll be sad if it dies," I say. "But it's way, way worse if you do it yourself. Plus, some people insist you're cursed if you do."

"Cursed?" Minerva's eyes round alarmingly. "I already *feel* cursed. An actual curse would be...I can't deal with that."

"What if I killed it for you?" Izaak leans closer to the pigeon, and it stops eating and peers up at him as if it knows what he's saying.

"That's the same," I say. "If she wants you to do it, and you do it for her, it's the same as if she did it." I shake my head. "No, you're better off buying a cage."

"I'm already the laughingstock of the entire precinct. How much worse will it be if they find out about this?" Minerva groans. "I had no idea that having a familiar could be worse than not having one."

"You need to train it," Roxana says. "Surely if it learned some tricks and stuff, people would think it was cute?"

I sigh. "Unfortunately, that might be worse. Familiars aren't pets. We bond them to help us, to bring something to the table. And having one is also a weak spot—so having one that's easy to kill or injure leaves the mage at risk. That's why people always keep them close."

"Which means having it in a cage at home is a little risky too," Minerva says. "Peter Chester, for instance, could come find it and kill it, and then I'd be miserable—maybe not as bad as killing it myself, but not good."

"Surely no one from the force would do something like that," I say. "But if you were a guardian, for instance, a demon-spawn could use it as a liability."

"There's no risk of that," Minerva snaps. "That ship has sailed. Probably forever."

I hate seeing her so depressed. "Getting a familiar should be a good thing," I say. "I mean, yes, it's not the one you'd hoped for." Or spent her entire life savings on. I don't mention that. She's already thinking it. I still can't believe she was that foolish. I suppose we all do stupid things when we're desperate. "But it's a familiar. Now that you've bonded this one, maybe you can bond another one more easily in the future."

Roxana takes her plate and opens the patio door. She closes her eyes as she stands outside, turning her face upward toward the sun. She's been inside for four days straight, and I'm sure she's starting to go a little stir crazy. Even so, being outside is a risk. There have been constant flyovers from dragona searching for her. All it would take was one glance and. . .

"Should she be out there?" Izaak asks. "Am I the only one who's seen nonstop dragona flyovers since the wedding got called off?"

"No, it's not a good idea," Minerva says.

"Hey, Roxana," Bevin says. "Get your cute butt back indoors."

"I just need a few moments in the sunshine." She sounds so wistful, so forlorn. The patch of golden scales on her cheek glistens in the sunlight.

And in that moment, time seems to slow down. Because there's an ebony dragon flying overhead, slowly. I pull out my wand without thinking and shout, "Veni ad me!"

Luckily, unlike my sister's, my magic never malfunctions.

Roxana flies backward through the open patio door, folding in half as she rockets through the air. Her body knocks the lamp off the end table with a crash and crumples in a heap on the floor at my feet. The black dragon's head whips our direction.

Izaak and Bevin grab their plates and race toward the patio. "What a beautiful day," Bevin gushes.

"It's getting a little bright for me." Izaak yawns and staggers sideways, knocking a patio chair over. "Whoops! Getting a little punchy in the sunlight."

The dragon circles again, staring at them, its dark eyes glittering with malice, but after a few more ominous circles, it flies on.

And we all breathe a huge sigh of relief.

"What were you thinking?" Minerva asks. "It's too hard for you to stay inside when our lives are on the line?"

"It's not like they'd kill you," Roxana says. "They'd just collect me and be gone."

No one argues with her, but none of us believe that.

As if she'd never thought it through, she pauses. "Wait,

do you really think they'd *kill* you? You didn't kidnap me. I ran away."

"But we're helping you stay hidden," Minerva says. "So stop being stupid and don't go outside."

"I'm going crazy in here," Roxana says. "I can't hide in your apartment forever."

"I've been thinking about that," I say. "I'm pretty sure I can come up with a charm spell—mixed with a potion that I'm using glaffour berries for, actually—that would disguise who you really are. Then you could leave, at least for short periods of time."

"What would you make her?" Bevin asks. "Instead of dragona, I mean?"

"She can't be a mage," I say, "since she can't cast spells."

"Or a werewolf," Xander says.

"Why not?" Roxana asks.

"We can smell our kind," he says. "Any other were would know immediately."

"Same with us," Izaak says. "Not the smelling thing, but we can sense one another."

"How can you sense each other?" I ask. "I kind of thought that vampires—"

"We're little alien creatures who pilot the brains of our human hosts," Izaak says. "You really think we can't sense others of our kind?" He rolls his eyes. "I'm not sure how, but when I meet another vampire, I get this little buzzy feeling at the base of my skull."

"Buzzy feeling. Got it." I sigh. "That only leaves one option, unfortunately, since you can't be what you are."

"Ha," Bevin says. "No one wants to be demon-spawn, but here we are. Well, I'm happy to teach you the things you'll need to do in order to be like me."

Roxana looks horrified. "Demon-spawn?"

"It's not all bad," Bevin says. "We can do seances."

"But *I* won't be able to do them," Roxana says. "Remember?"

"Right." Bevin laughs. "Then yes, it's all bad. Everyone hates us, or worse, they distrust us, and police tend to follow us around. Oh, and did I mention that you can't ever do anything bad, or you'll descend and wind up with a demon mark?"

"But then I'd get a cool power." Roxana smiles.

"You aren't actually demon-spawn," I say. "Remember?"

"Right." She shakes her head. "I mean, I know that, obviously."

This might be a terrible idea. Bevin's an awful demon-spawn—she tries her best never to do anything demon-y. Having her teach Roxana feels. . .risky. But as she mentioned earlier, Roxana can't stay hidden in an apartment her entire life, and we don't have any other options. Other than her extreme charisma, which I need to dampen if at all possible with my spell, dragona females don't really have any magic. That means that it's hard for them to pass as any other supernatural creature. . .except a non-descended demon-spawn.

"After work today, I'll start playing with spells. I'm hoping to come up with something that will kind of counteract your dragona charm—"

"You're going to make her look busted?" Izaak's smirk is hard to contain. "Good luck."

"Not ugly," I say. "I'm just going to try to eliminate the magical pull." I clear my throat. "She'll still be uncommonly beautiful and graceful. I can't change that."

Roxana lifts her chin and looks at me with a funny expression on her face I can't read. "Uncommonly beautiful?"

"You do have a mirror in your room, right?" Xander asks.

"Yes, yes, we all know she's gorgeous," Minerva says.

"I'm not sure she knows," Bevin says slowly. "Before you ran away, how much did you get out, Roxana? Didn't Minerva say you were at an all girls school?"

"Magical finishing school, yes," Roxana says. "Most dragona princes don't want their future mate to spend much time with other males."

"So you've been, what, locked in a closet?" Xander asks.

Roxana blinks. "Not a closet, no."

"Did they really keep you locked up?" I ask.

Roxana sits down, as if she's never thought about this before. "I wasn't locked inside, but there were always guards on the outside—who weren't allowed to talk to me. It was for my protection, but. . ."

"You really are like Rapunzel," Xander says. "Only, way less blonde."

"Nothing wrong with being blonde," Bevin says.

"Have you ever been on a date?" I can't help asking. I've been dying to take her out since the first time I met her, back when she and Minerva went to a school dance together. "I mean, how did you find your dates for the finishing school dances, for instance?"

Roxana blushes, and the color makes the golden scales on her neck and jawline really stand out. I'll have to consider that when I'm crafting my spell. Dragona females may not be able to shift, but those dragon scales are a dead giveaway. "My dad would line my dates up. They were tryouts, sort of."

"Tryouts?" Minerva frowns. "You never said anything about that before."

"Dad held these, like, tournaments." Roxana looks at her hands. "The victor would take me to the dance."

"Wait, I knew your dates looked old," Minerva says, "but are you saying that you were taken to the dances by potential suitors—the ones who survived some kind of battle of strength?"

"The dragona like fierce warriors," Roxana says. "They settle everything by battles to the death."

"How did someone win the right to take you to a school dance, then?" Izaak asks, clearly unable to help himself.

Roxana swallows.

"Oh come on, you have to tell us that much," Xander says.

"Well, before my junior prom, Dad had a flight contest," she says. "The fastest flier was allowed to take me."

"That's not so bad," Izaak says. "If I had wings, I bet I could fly pretty fast."

"To make sure they were trying their hardest, the slowest one was executed," Roxana says.

"This takes extreme dating to a new level," Xander says.

"They knew when they entered that one of them would die?" I still can't wrap my brain around it.

"There are twenty males to every female in the dragona world," Minerva says.

"Even so, it doesn't mean they want to die," I say. "Right?"

"Honor's everything," Roxana says. "The person who came in last might have simply committed suicide if Dad hadn't killed him. Execution was actually a much better and nobler way to die."

"I've never felt lucky," Xander says. "Mom and Dad torching their own pack and landing Dad and me as perpetual outcasts in the were world sort of ensured that, but after talking to you, I feel much better about my life."

"Gee, thanks," Roxana says.

"Samesies," Bevin says. "Never been a huge fan of the dragona, not since one of them killed my mom, but at least I wasn't *born* as one myself."

"Glad my terrible life could improve the morale around here," Roxana says.

I always thought being a princess would be great.

Nothing is really what it seems, not in the magical world. "Look, I swear, my top priority, as soon as I'm off work, will be coming up with a spell—" My phone rings.

No one ever calls me, except sometimes my ex, asking for more money. I consider ignoring it, but if she does need help...I swipe to answer. "Yes?"

"Clark." It's Simon Summers. Even over the phone he sets my teeth on edge.

"How great to hear from you before eight a.m."

"Do I sense sarcasm?"

"Not at all, sir. What can I do for you?"

Minerva's making some kind of joke to Xander and they're laughing. Ah, it's her Simon Summers impression. It's not very good, but he's an easy guy to mimic.

"I know that coming to our research lab wasn't your top pick right out of school, although you've excelled here and we've certainly paid you handsomely."

Get to the point, Simon. "Okay..."

"But seeing as you always wanted to be a professor, when my old colleague called to ask if I could recommend someone for a part-time position at the New York Institute of Magic, I thought of you."

I can barely believe what he's saying. The world's most annoying boss *remembered* my dream and is actually doing something to help me? How can this be happening? "That's...amazing."

"Apparently they're in a bit of a bind and need someone ASAP. One of their other professors descended enough that he had to be put down."

I stifle my laugh. It's not at all funny that a demon-spawn professor gained a sixth mark and had to be killed, but I'm a nervous laugher. I've always laughed at the wrong time. "That's terrible."

"But good news for you. Can you make it to an interview in SoHo in thirty minutes? I'll text you the address."

"In thirty minutes?" I can't help my splutter. "Uh. I'm not wearing—I mean, never mind. I'll make it work."

"Listen, I know how much you want this, so I'm going to offer you some friendly advice."

"Okay," I say.

"Be less *Clark* at this interview."

"Less Clark? *I am* Clark."

"Yes," Simon says. "That's exactly my point."

11

ROXANA

The first spell Clark casts turns my skin blue. I mean, it's not *really* blue, but it looks blue to everyone else. It takes almost twenty-four hours for it to fade.

The next morning, when he's about to cast his second attempt, I hold up my hand. "What about Minerva? She's a witch. Maybe she could help?"

Minerva and Clark glance at each other and start laughing. "Trust me. No one wants that."

"Are you worried you'll turn my skin blue?" I lift one eyebrow. "Because that's happened already."

"I'm worried I'll explode your head," Minerva says.

"Oh." I shrug. "Yeah, maybe let's stick with Clark."

Xander breezes through the front door of Minerva's apartment without knocking. I may never get used to how everyone seems to do that. "Morning."

"You're just in time for the fun part," I say.

"Oh, no, you're not blue anymore." He shakes his head, but it's clearly mock sorrow. I've known him long enough to sense that he's queuing up for a joke. "I guess that means your job application to join that Vegas show was declined?"

"The Blue Man Group would be lucky to have her," Clark says.

"Wait." Izaak, predictably, walks through the door next. "Is there something about Roxie that I didn't know?"

"Like what?" I frown.

"Blue *Man* Group," Izaak says. "I doubt they'd take you, even with the blue skin."

"Knock it off," Clark says.

"What about a career as a street performer?" Minerva asks. "I imagine with just a little charm, you could make a killing. Even blue. Or maybe you could change up the colors. Couldn't you, Clark? A nice silver might be fun, maybe for the weekends."

"Unless one of you thinks you can do a better spell that will mask her charm, change her appearance, and dampen any sense or charms that show that she's dragona, then shut up." Clark hands me a glass vial. "Drink this first."

"What is it?" My lip curls at the thought of yesterday's potion, which tasted like feet.

"You'll like it this time," he says.

"Is it something completely different?" I ask.

"No," he says, "but I added grape juice."

Oh good. Grape juice flavored feet.

"Grapes? That's excellent," Xander says. "Did I mention that purple's my favorite color?"

"It's white grape juice." Clark turns to scowl at Xander. "And she's not going to change colors again. I fixed that."

"Out of idle curiosity," Xander says, "how many attempts did it take you to successfully complete your last invention?"

"My last prescription, you mean?" Clark asks. "And if you don't have anything helpful to add, then get out."

"I've never added anything helpful before, and no one has ever kicked me out." Xander sits down at the kitchen table and grabs a muffin off the platter in the center of it.

He pauses, the muffin frozen a few inches away from his open mouth. "Who made these?"

"I did," Minerva says.

"Excellent." He takes a bite.

"I'm a little offended," I say. "My cooking has gotten much better—I didn't even burn the rice yesterday."

"You managed to burn rice with a rice cooker?" Xander asks. "I didn't even know that was possible."

"Burning the bottom gives it a little extra flavor. Besides, I didn't say I'm perfect. I said I'm improving."

"That's like saying Kristen Stewart's acting has gotten *better*," Xander says. "She's still the worst actress to ever play a vampire's emo girlfriend."

"Oh, come on." Izaak shakes his head. "Robert Pattinson was way worse than Kristen Stewart. She just looked the same in every scene. He actually looked constipated. As a vampire and as an actor, I just couldn't be more disappointed."

"Did anyone ever try that, I wonder?" Xander asks.

"Try what?" I ask.

"A bowl of prunes. Maybe that would have transformed the movie."

"That entire film was a disaster," I say. "Sparkly vampires? The only supernatural creatures that sparkle are the golden dragona." I would know.

"The director was a vampire and a narcissist," Clark says.

"Aren't those words interchangeable?" Xander asks.

At first I'm surprised that Izaak doesn't complain—then I realize he probably doesn't know what narcissist means. When Xander wants to get a rise out of him, he really ought to use smaller words.

Bevin actually taps on the door as she walks through. "Everyone decent?"

"Decent, as in a good person?" Xander asks. "Or as in, dressed?"

"Girls live here," I say. "Would she really be worried about us being fully clothed?"

Izaak's smile's wide and wicked. "Uh, you didn't know?"

"Know what?" I ask.

Izaak whispers. "Bevin bats for the other team."

"Oh," I say. "Huh."

"I already know none of you are decent people." Bevin marches through the entry and snags a kitchen chair. "Let's not get ridiculous." She slings her enormous quilted purse onto the floor next to her seat.

Giggles the pigeon flutters down from the top of the fridge and pokes her head inside.

"I knew you'd smell these, you little ragamuffin." Bevin reaches down and pulls a plastic baggie of popcorn out of her bag.

"She's not a wild pigeon," Minerva says. "You can't just toss her scraps."

"Why not?" Bevin frowns. "She wants them."

Based on the way Giggles' head is tilting back and forth, her eye never leaving Bevin's hand, I think she's right.

"Alexa," Minerva says. "Can pigeons eat popcorn?"

A little black cylinder near the knife block starts speaking, practically scaring me to death.

"Popcorn is not toxic to pigeons. However, you should always consult with a veterinarian before providing any type of food to an animal. Also, I found this on the web. Pigeons should not fill up on empty calories such as chunks of bread. Does that answer your question?"

"What the heck is that thing?" I glare at the box.

"Your family can turn into dragons, and you don't know what an 'Alexa' is?" Minerva's smile is smug. "It's a device that. . . Well, it. . ." She coughs. "Someone help me out, here."

"It's, um, like, for shopping and stuff," Clark says.

"For shopping?" I peer at it. "How could you do any shopping on that?"

"You tell it what things you want, and then someone from Amazon brings them to you," Clark says.

"You're all wrong. That's how the government keeps tabs on us," Xander says. "Without it, they'd be unable to spy on all our movements and actions."

My eyes widen. "But. . ."

"It's the normie government," Bevin says. "Don't worry. Most mages aren't forward thinking enough to have one, so they don't check on us very often."

"Those of us with misfiring spells tend to rely on non-magical items more," Minerva says.

"Back to the point," Bevin says, "what exactly are you feeding your little gal here, because she looks hungry."

Minerva crouches and picks up Giggles. "Her bowl is totally full, and it's right over here." Giggles coos and rubs her head on Minerva's hand, right up until Minerva sets her down in front of the bowl again. "See? Plenty of dried peas, mealworms, and dried corn, just like you're supposed to eat." Giggles tries to back away from the bowl, and Minerva shoos her closer again.

"I don't think she wants any of that," Izaak says.

"Can you blame her?" I ask.

"She's just not used to it," Minerva says.

"It looks nasty," Clark says.

"Are you sure she can't have some popcorn?" Bevin asks.

Giggles seems to agree, by the way she's cooing. It's very strange to think about a pigeon understanding any part of what we're saying. But when Minerva tries to usher her toward her food bowl again, she launches upward and lands on top of the fridge. And unless I'm going crazy, she's glaring at Minerva.

"So that's why she was up there all morning," I say. "I actually feel sorry for her."

"It's what's best for her." Minerva looks around, as if she's just noticing how many people are here. "What in the world are you all doing here, anyway? I need to get some sleep."

"This is where we come in the morning," Izaak says. "Isn't it?"

Minerva sighs and pulls some orange juice out of the fridge. She plonks it down next to the muffins. "I should pass around a collection plate to cover the cost of all this food."

"Oh, no you don't," Xander says. "Before Izaak starts paying for anything else, he's got to catch up on his rent. He promised."

"If this spell works," I say, "I'll be getting one of those job things, and then I'll help pay for the food."

I do feel a little bad. I gave her all the money I got from Izaak for donating my blood, but since I have no idea what things cost, I'm guessing it didn't make much of a dent in the things she's paying for on my behalf. I've lived off of someone else my entire life, but for the first time, I'm aware of it, and I don't like the feeling.

"I'll be holding my breath for that," Minerva says.

"Was that a dig at me or at her?" Clark asks.

"Is it mutually exclusive?" Xander asks.

Minerva rolls her eyes.

"Just drink it already," Clark says. "I tried this on several magical objects, and it worked perfectly each time."

"Objects?" I cringe. "Did they drink the potion?"

"Just do it," Clark says.

Izaak rubs his hands together. "This is so fun. It's like being on an episode of *Fear Factor*!"

"*American Gladiators* was better," Xander says.

"I will never understand the two of you," Bevin says. "You're like a joke I can't work out. A loner wolf and a desperate-for-love vampire who live in the same apartment—"

"That makes it sound like a romantic comedy," Xander says.

"Is it?" I ask. "I mean, I just found out that Bevin—"

"We aren't gay," Izaak says.

"Even Xander?" I ask.

After a moment of awkward silence, Minerva asks, "How is *this* like *Fear Factor*?"

"It's just like that," Izaak says. "We have no idea what might happen next! When she drinks that, she could sprout feathers, or, I don't know, start singing." He straightens up. "Ooh, if she starts singing, I call dibs."

"First, they frown on you calling dibs on owning people," Xander says. "And second, why in the world would you want her if she starts singing?"

"With her face and body?" Izaak nods. "My agent would probably give me a cut. Imagine how much people would pay to see her sing."

"No one said she'd sing *well*," Xander says.

Clark stands and throws his hands up in the air. "She's not going to be singing at all."

"You don't know that," Izaak says. "Stop being such a hater."

"I'm going to be late for work if we don't do this right now," Clark says. "All of you, shut up." He points at me. "And you, drink!"

I don't think about what kind of strange toenails or blood or feather mites could be in this nasty concoction. I try not to think about what color it might turn me. I just pour it down my throat and rhythmically swallow. It's not as bad as yesterday's potion, but even the grape juice doesn't cover the taste of stinky burps. "Blech." I gag a bit and wipe my mouth. "Why do all potions have to taste so bad?"

"We work on improving the flavor after we find the right mixture," Clark says. "Pardon me if my groundbreaking spell, that I'm creating for free, isn't delicious and nutritious in the development stage."

I set the glass bottle down on the coffee table. "As long as it doesn't give me a third boob, I guess I'm okay with it."

"A third boob?" Izaak grins. "Let's not be so hasty."

"Ever heard the phrase, 'too much of a good thing?'" Xander asks. "I think that's the photo under the definition."

"Nope," Izaak says. "That's just close-minded werewolf talk. Three is better than two."

"Oh, for the love of Gabriel, just shut up!" Minerva's hands fly into the air, and a second later, both guys are choking.

"*Iterum dico*," Clark says.

And both of them groan in unison. "I thought you said there weren't going to be any more accidental spells," Xander says.

"Don't spells have to be cast in Latin?" I ask.

"No, they do not," Clark says. "The Latin just helps us focus our energy. It's like a wand. We don't have to have them either, but we make fewer mistakes when we're using them."

"I'm sorry." Minerva smirks. "But you kind of deserved it, talking about boobs."

"She brought it up." Izaak glares at me.

"I spent the last twenty-four hours blue," I say. "Anything could happen."

"But it won't." Clark glances at his watch. "Now." He pulls his wand out of the long, thin pocket inside his blazer. "Hanc faeminam dissimula, leporem obvolve. Serva viros pulchritudine sua. Quamdiu nox et dies supremus."

A fuzzy feeling, like my entire body is drinking Sprite, suffuses me, and I shiver a little. This is only the second time in my life that I've been the recipient of a spell, after all. I force myself to glance down at my arm. It looks fine—but then, it looked fine to me yesterday. It was only once I looked into a mirror I saw that I'd turned blue.

I look around the room, waiting for someone to say something. "Do I not look strange?" I finally ask.

Bevin frowns. "You're rail thin with enormous knockers and flawless skin. Your hair shines like the most expensive onyx. Or were you asking about something else I'm supposed to have trouble dealing with?"

I laugh. "I'm the right color?" I smile. "And I have the right number of *arms*?" I glare at Izaak.

"You are exactly the same shade of gorgeous tan you always have been. Your eyes are just as ridiculously sultry." Bevin frowns. "Sorry if that's a disappointment to you."

"Hey, I thought you were gay," I say.

"I'm gay, but I'm also a woman. It's a frustrating conundrum. Around beautiful women, I'm equal parts interested and jealous." She shrugs. "You get it."

Once I think about it, I do.

"It worked," Clark says.

"But what about my scales?" I reach up to rub my cheek. My golden scales always gleam a little too brightly, and they're a dead giveaway that I'm dragona.

Minerva steps closer, blinking.

Xander stands up and cranes his neck.

Izaak mutters, "Mother feather, they're gone."

"I think the next step is to test this out," Clark says. "Now that we don't see anything obvious, it's time to go for a little field trip."

Minerva yawns.

Izaak immediately follows suit.

"The night dwellers should probably call it a day," Xander says. "Or we may have to carry you back upstairs."

"I think my dear friend will want me by her side when she ventures out into the world," Minerva says.

"Yes," I say. "However, will the random people in the world out there accidentally be frozen or zapped if you come along? I feel like being exhausted won't help you make good spell-casting decisions."

"Hey," Minerva says. "I'm upping your rent."

"You should double it," I say. "I may not be an expert, but I know that zero times two. . .is still zero." I snort. I haven't made such an unladylike sound in my entire life. I didn't realize I could.

"I think the spell's working," Xander says. "That sounded like a snort." He chuckles.

"Let's just go," I say.

In spite of their exhaustion during the day—Izaak because vampires are always sleepy when the sun is up, and Minerva because she was working all night—all my friends follow me downstairs. It's a weird thing to have happen. I've had acquaintances my entire life. I've been surrounded by my brothers, by their friends, by loads of guards, and by the other female dragona Mom and Dad deemed worthy. But Minerva was my only friend—someone who spent time with me for no reason at all, except that she wanted to.

And now her circle of friends—a werewolf, a demon-spawn, her mage brother, and a vampire—have become my friends. What a strange group to spend time with. Most supernaturals stick to their own kind, and for good reason. We're too different, and we almost never get along well enough to interact, much less voluntarily pass time.

"Alright," Clark says. "When we leave the stairwell, everyone needs to be on the alert. Watch the people around us for any sign they see something other than. . ." He gestures at me. "This."

"A gorgeous Asian woman in a trendy dress?" Minerva asks.

"You had that dress when we met," Bevin says, "six years ago. Nice try, but I think it's a gorgeous Asian woman in an old dress."

"Shut up," Minerva says.

"You gonna spell me?" Bevin rolls her eyes. "Good luck."

It's strange that Minerva's spells only seem to work when she's not trying.

"I doubt anyone will really pay much attention to Roxana," Xander says. "Well, not any more than they usually would to a gorgeous woman." He looks pointedly at the pigeon on Minerva's shoulder. "They'll all be too busy looking at this."

"Hey, I taught her not to poop," Minerva says. "And look." She shoves through the door leading out of the stairwell and points at the sign on the side entrance to our favorite gloffee shop. "Familiars welcome."

"They didn't realize people would bond pests," Bevin says. "What's next? Cockroaches? Swarms of gnats? Ants?"

Minerva scowls at the rest of us and storms into Grand Central Gloffee.

"She's doing you a favor, you know," Xander whispers. "The more heat she takes for this, the less attention people will pay to the brand new addition to our group."

"We were in the stairwell," I say. "No one else could see us."

"She had to get into character," Xander says. "If she wasn't doing it for you, she'd have left Giggles in the cage upstairs."

I realize he's right, and I start to tear up.

After I wipe my eyes, I march through the door into the gloffee shop. I'm counting my blessings, all five of them. In my lifetime, I've been showered with gemstones. Covered in gold and silver and platinum. I've been pampered and sheltered and protected. I've been admired and gushed over and envied.

But I've never had friends, plural.

Somehow, in the course of one week, I now have five people at my side, all of them willing to risk danger to keep me safe.

"Can I take your order?" A tall man with bright orange hair whips out a pad of paper and a pencil.

"I'd like a gloffee and a pandesal."

"A what?"

"It's a Filipino bread made with light and fluffy yeast," I say.

"We have muffins," he says.

"Are they light and fluffy?"

"Not really," he says.

I glance around. "What's good?"

"The glachiatto is great," Bevin says.

"Try the glafficino," Clark says.

"Or the glespresso," Xander says.

"Don't look at me," Minerva says. "I take mine dark."

"You'll like the glatté," Izaak says.

"A glatté, then," I say. "Since someone thinks *I'll* like it."

"How about, since it's your first time here," the tall man with the bright orange hair says, "I bring you one of each, half off?" He beams. "My name's Gavin. I'm the mage who owns this place."

"I'm Ro—" I choke.

Clark pats me on the back.

"This is my good friend from school," Minerva says. "Rosie."

Gavin glances from Minerva to me and back again, but he doesn't argue or ask any questions. I like him already. "Welcome to the neighborhood, Rosie. I hope to see a lot more of you."

I'm sipping the variety of drinks in front of me, each

of them flavored a little differently—though the glofficino is dragona flavored and it makes me gag—when the door swings open and a tall, broad-shouldered man with black hair and dark clothing strides inside. His eyes are like flint. His jaw looks carved from glass. "Who owns this place?" His voice is deep, and it has a twinge of a Russian accent.

"I do," Gavin says.

"I hear you've got dragona on the menu." The man frowns. "I want to know where you're getting your dragona blood."

Gavin pulls himself up straight. "It's not any of your business. I'm not required to disclose."

The man takes two more steps and stands directly opposite Gavin. He leans forward.

Gavin leans back.

I'm trembling. That man is most definitely dragona, probably one of Ragar's men. I should not be down here right now, and apparently, I should not be donating my blood.

"There's required by law," the man says, "and then there's *required*." He smirks. "Tell me you know the difference."

Minerva stands up, and Giggles fluffs up next to her and sways to catch her balance. She rushes toward the counter, pulling something out of her pocket. "Minerva Lucent, NYPAD officer. Is there a problem here?"

The dark, enormous man turns slowly, a hint of a smile tugging his lips upward. "No, do-gooder. We don't have a *problem*."

"I'm glad to hear it. I thought I might need to ask for your registration and visa," Minerva says.

"How do you know I'm not a citizen?" the man asks.

"Let's call it a hunch." Giggles coos on her shoulder.

"The police here use pigeons as their familiars?" He

laughs, and the sound sends chills up my spine. "Very intimidating."

"Listen, buddy, we don't have to intimidate." Clark stands, too. "It's like a big, burly man like you wearing black. It's unnecessary. You could wear pink, and people would still know you were more likely to flame them than to talk. We have the spellpower to back up our rules. Minerva Lucent is one of the most powerful casters on the force. Why else would she have a pigeon as her familiar?"

The man ignores Minerva and Clark, focusing only on Gavin. "I'll be back soon, and I expect you to be ready to tell me where your dragona blood comes from." He doesn't even glance my way, thanks to Gavin, Minerva and Clark.

"It looks like the disguise worked," Clark says.

"He didn't immediately sense her," Minerva says, "but I'm not sure we're out of the woods yet." She glances over her shoulder at the door.

"Those dragona are terrible," Bevin says. "No offense."

"None taken," I say. "I'm not sure I knew quite how awful we were until I left."

"Don't say 'we,'" Clark hisses.

"Can I suggest you find a job, when you get to that point, where you're not interacting with supernaturals all the time?" Bevin asks.

"Yeah, I second that," Minerva says. "I can't be here all the time."

"Shining angel Gabriel, I guess that's something I have to think about now," I say.

It should feel overwhelming. It should feel scary, especially with that dragona showing up to threaten people for information he might use to find me.

But it doesn't. For the first time in my life, I feel like I'm not alone. And it feels like I might be able to make choices for myself.

They're both pretty good feelings.

12

XANDER

My mom caused my dad to get kicked out of his wolf pack.

Or more to the point, I did.

Werewolves aren't supposed to marry normies, of course. Aside from the expected cultural disconnect, there's also no way to know what kind of children such a union will produce.

Not that my parents got married.

They ignored all the common-knowledge rules prescribing interspecies mingling. They didn't pay much attention to birth control either, apparently, and lucky me —I was born a wolf. When I shifted into a wolf cub in the hospital bassinet, Mom wrapped me in a blanket and fled the premises. She dropped me at Dad's door in a dog carrier and sped off.

That's when they kicked him out of his pack for breaking the rules. I mean, I get that they didn't plan any of it, but their disregard of everything has made my life really suck.

My kids, if I ever had any, would be wildcards—some normie, some wolf. If I married a normie, I'd have a twenty-five percent chance of my kid going furry. If I married a were, it would be the same odds, but the other direction.

My genetics were ruined on the very day I was conceived.

To make matters more complicated, wolves come in four varieties: shredders, rangers, nurturers, and innovators. Innovators come up with new ideas. They organize and manage and teach. That's what I wish I was. Nurturers care for others, they fix problems, and they smooth over the rough things. Rangers explore and test and scout. Any of those would be fine. Even as a halfie, I'd be alright if I were an innovator, a ranger, or a nurturer. Someone would have taken me in.

Shredders, of course, are the worst of the lot. They do just what their name implies—they fight. Given my luck, it's no shock that *I* was born a shredder.

Most wolves *want* to be shredders. They change quickly, they're stronger, and they heal the fastest. They're also the only type of wolf that can be born with the ability to become an alpha. It's rare—maybe one in fifty or seventy shredders can even be alphas. And only alphas can start packs, but even if I *was* an alpha, it wouldn't help me a bit.

No one would join a pack with a halfie alpha.

It didn't take long for me to realize that the cons of being a shredder far outweigh the pros. There are two ways for wolves to join a pack. You're born into one, or you fight your way in. You'd think that being what I am would help—but it means that I bring out the worst in every other wolf simply by existing. I'm not strong enough to snarl my way to the top, and no one wants me around. That makes fighting my way into an existing pack as impossible as the 'being born in' route.

Thanks to my spotty genetics, I'll never be able to start my own pack, either. No wolf in her right mind would mate with a half-breed. Which is why I've been living as a third party contractor—an outside-edges fringe member of the Manhattan pack. It can't last. It won't be a permanent solution.

But I hoped I might be able to find some kind of loophole through which I could squeeze. So far, no luck.

"Three, two, one, *go*."

The instinct to fight when the alpha shouts 'go' is so ingrained by now that I don't even think. I just shift. Muscles melt and reform. Bones snap. Sinews stretch. Fur sprouts. Fangs lengthen.

And I howl like the deranged dog that I am.

"Come on, Cliff, get him."

"Go, go, go, Cliff. Destroy him!"

"Rip his halfie throat out!"

No one ever cheers for me.

Cliff lunges at me, his teeth snapping far too close to my jugular. I race around the edge of the ring to clear myself some space. Cliff's bigger than I am. He's probably tougher than I am. That's precisely the point, of course. No one ever thinks I might actually win.

Being beaten so that I remember my place—that's the reason for my daily 'training.'

Cliff chases me for a bit, until he gets tired of it. Then he leaps across the ring and snaps at me—only this time, his teeth clamp down on my hind leg. Pain radiates through me, and this would likely be the beginning of the end for any other wolf in the pack.

But this is my one strength. I've dealt with so much pain my entire life that I barely notice it. I can take a beating better than any other wolf in New York. Maybe in the whole US. Instead of blacking out or whimpering or begging, I feign collapse.

The second he releases my leg, I pivot on it and take my shot. I sink my teeth into Cliff's shoulder. Blood floods into my mouth. His whimpering hits my system like a shot of some kind of illegal stimulant. I push harder then, dragging him across the mat, leaving a trail of blood behind us. I'm not even sure whether it's his or mine. I shake my head and press down harder.

In spite of all the odds stacked against me, I might win. For once, I might defeat him—

A surge, no, more of a flex shoots through me. Like a hammer to a tuning rod, or an electric current hurtling down a live wire, my entire body shakes, and I release Cliff involuntarily. Before I have time to regroup, he's on me. His teeth slam closed on my front paw, and he shakes like a terrier would shake a rat.

It takes him another few moments, and two more shocks from the alpha, but eventually, Cliff gets what he came for. A kill shot to my throat.

Only the intervention of the same alpha who kept me from getting close to winning keeps me from dying. Because the thing about being in a pack—the same thing that can kill you can also keep you alive.

He heals Cliff first, leaving me to slowly bleed out, becoming colder and colder and colder. This might be it, honestly. Maybe they're ticked about the photo of Roxana on my phone. Maybe the dragona demanded I die as punishment for talking to her just before she went missing. It's not like the pack would argue—or that they'd even do me the courtesy of telling me I was being disposed of beforehand.

They don't owe a non-pack member anything.

But just as spots shoot across my vision, relief finally floods through my body, a cessation of pain, and then a return of movement, all courtesy of Lo Ren Fang.

"Better, halfie," Cliff groans. "That was actually the best I've ever seen you manage."

"Thanks." I cough, blood spraying the mat even as my wounds heal.

"Now that you've completed training for the day, we need to talk to you." Lo Ren Fang doesn't wait to make sure I heard him. He turns and marches out.

"You better hurry," Cliff says.

He's actually being pretty helpful—encouraging even. I'm nothing more than extra muscle. I can't ever make the pack alpha wait. It still hurts to move. It's agonizing, really, since Lo Ren would only use enough energy to keep me from being in mortal peril. He'll expect me to heal the rest myself, slowly, using my own reserves. Even so, I shove myself up to my feet and pull on my pants. I stumble across the mat, climb out of the ring, and head out through the door Lo Ren Fang just left.

He's waiting in the next room.

"We gave you that apartment on the edges of our territory as a show of good faith," Rylan says. Lo Ren's second in command also happens to be his mate, and usually she calms him down. But today? She looks ticked.

"I'm grateful for it," I say, sure to quickly return my eyes to my bloodstained, bare feet.

"You've been working with us for two years now without incident," Rylan continues. "We thought you knew your place."

Two years of just enough interaction with a pack to keep the madness at bay, to keep from fraying. "I am," I say. "More grateful than you probably know."

"But you took that selfie with the princess," Lo Ren says. "And I specifically told you not to communicate with her in any way." His hands clench into fists, the veins in his forearms popping. His voice is growly when he says, "I told you not to go near her."

Rylan curls her manicured fingers around his forearm, and he visibly relaxes—the power of a mate. "If he hadn't done that, we'd have no idea what kind of time window we were looking at. The dragona might be accusing us of stealing her away, or any number of other things. Worse things."

"He broke my order," Lo Ren says.

"Which he can only do because you haven't made him part of the pack." Her gentle reminder isn't as kind as it seems. She wants me gone—always has. She sees third party contractors as a major liability.

"I should cut him loose," Lo Ren says.

Rylan smiles. "Yes, you should."

Lo Ren's head snaps her direction.

"But not until this danger is past, and the dragona aren't angry with us. They don't know he's not part of the pack—"

Lo Ren starts pacing. "They told us that perimeter security was the only important thing. They said—"

Rylan grabs Lo Ren's wrists and snaps them downward in a possessive show of force. "Listen to me, love. We can't display any weakness to them. You know that, so for now, we conceal this. . ." Her lip curls. "This mistake." She sighs. "After this is over, you can terminate him."

I wish I thought they were talking about firing me.

Although firing me might be worse than killing me. Without any wolves to associate with, I'd become increasingly more twitchy, paranoid, and unstable. Eventually, I'd either attack someone I couldn't defeat, or I'd take my own life. "Is there anything I can do to help?"

"Did Roxana say anything to you, when you went in to talk to her in clear violation of protocol?" Rylan releases Lo Ren and turns to face me. She doesn't act like she just told him to terminate me. She doesn't act like I could hear a single thing they were saying. "Did she give you any indication she wanted to run or that she was afraid of anything?"

My brain races ahead. I need to look like I'm helping them, but I can't give Roxana's location away. If I was part of the pack, they'd already know what I know—they'd be able to compel it out of me.

Ironically, only my third party status is keeping Roxana safe.

I finally decide I can share some of what we discussed without harming her. "She asked me about the fire escape."

Lo Ren swears.

"You didn't think that might be relevant?" Rylan asks.

"She merely asked if normies would die if there was a fire in the building," I say. "I explained there was a fire escape they could take if they had to." I pause. "I honestly didn't know anyone in New York City wouldn't already know about the existence of fire escapes."

"Of course not," Lo Ren says. "And you'd never suspect a princess of running away. We didn't either."

"They still maintain she was kidnapped," Rylan says.

"It's the only option that keeps them from looking monstrous—that Ragar especially," Lo Ren says. "But there's no sign of struggle, and she clearly went down the fire escape—the last thing we're doing is telling them that we gave her the idea." He glares at me. "Not a word about that, clear?"

I nod.

"I know one way he wouldn't be able to share what he said." Rylan's lips compress into a flat line.

Lo Ren glares at her.

It may be the first time he's ever done something for me. It's not much, but telling his wife she can't kill me with a look is better than ignoring her.

They grill me for another half hour, but eventually they give up and drag me with them to the all-pack meeting. Wolves may long for companionship, but two hundred and thirty-four wolves shoved into one giant room is not a comfortable occurrence. If we didn't have such a strong alpha, it wouldn't even be possible.

Even Lo Ren looks like the strain is wearing on him. "I won't keep you all here very long," he says. "But I need to make something clear. The Manhattan Pack has a lot of plans, and we have made a lot of progress in the past few years, but everything is on hold until we can help the dragona locate Roxana Goldenscales. As you know, female dragona are already rare, but the daughter of their leader for North America, and the fiancée of the leader of all of Russian dragona? She was lost on our watch, and we have to be instrumental in reclaiming her."

"Or there will be repercussions," Rylan says.

Lo Ren's scary, but his mate might be scarier.

"Whoever helps us locate her will be richly rewarded," Lo Ren says. "If you're not in pack leadership, it would land you a spot. If you're already a leader, you'd get special training from me."

"Whatever your situation, we'll take immediate action to improve it," Rylan says. "If we can find her and bring her back, the dragona will be very, very pleased."

A strange situation.

A dire need.

It feels very much like a loophole.

But is it the loophole I've been searching for?

I've spent the past twelve years trying to find a pack that would take me in. I've begged, I've cheated, and I've fought countless times. I don't hate my life as a werewolf enforcer, but it's hardly the life I'd have chosen, and I never belong anywhere. The longing gives me the courage to raise my hand. I can't imagine betraying one of my friends, but Roxana is new.

I barely know her.

"What about non-pack members? What if one of us located her?"

Rylan's smile this time is sly. "If someone *like you* was able to recapture Roxana Goldenscales, well, that would be a big enough miracle to get you official membership in the pack, halfie."

13

IZAAK

I'm a high school dropout. Or at least, I think that's still what they call you when you're expelled. My dad, being a normie, was pretty worried at first. For nonmagical people, being a high school dropout is bad. Really bad, I guess.

My mom just laughed. "Saves me money on the tuition."

But Dad insisted I enroll in public school after that—human school.

I figured Mom would save me from it, but she didn't. She just shrugged. "Who knows? You might learn something useful. Most of our hits are on normies."

At the age of fifteen, for the first time in my life, I packed up a backpack, drank three containers of silver nitrate—Red Bull for vampires—so I wouldn't fall asleep in my first class, and marched through the front doors of the local high school. For the first fifteen years of my life, people had immediately judged me based on just one thing: the fact that I'm a vampire. Hiding who I am and what I can do didn't seem too exciting, but I was kind of jazzed to just be Izaak for once.

Only, that didn't happen.

No, for the first time in my life, I wasn't a vampire. . . but I was a black kid. I mean, I've always been black, right? But it just wasn't as important as having retractable fangs.

But for normies?

It totally is.

On that first day of school, with the silver nitrate still pumping through my body like a combination of the fear of almost getting hit by a crazy NY cabbie and the cold sweat that you get that first time you cut your own hair, I tromped my way through wide, unfamiliar hallways. The white kids shifted out of my way as I walked past them. Some ducked their heads. Some of them glared. A lot of them just looked away from me uncomfortably.

The difference between us was palpable.

Black kids, on the other hand, fell into two categories. Some bobbed their heads, subtly welcoming me as a brother without knowing me at all. But a few of them inexplicably hated me on sight. It was one of the strangest experiences I've ever had. Magical people like or dislike you based on your species, based on your abilities, or based on your family. But here, in normie high school, they liked or disliked you based on the color of your skin.

Even when you remove the magical powers from the equation, I suppose people are still people. We still shove others into a box so that our brains can make sense of what they are. It's only the names written on those boxes that change. The way we reduce people to just one obvious thing? That's apparently universal.

Friend. Enemy.

Black. White.

Ally. Threat.

Vampire. Werewolf. Mage. Demon-spawn.

I made one real friend that semester. His name was Dmitrius—D for short. Instead of a non-committal head bob, he smiled at me. He asked my name. He never knew

I was a vampire, and he didn't need to know. He helped me catch up on math—not much of a priority for me before then. He laughed at my stupid jokes, and made fun of me for my really bad ones. He couldn't believe how many siblings I had, but thought it was cool since he was an only child. He made that semester of high school bearable.

He taught me that friends make life worthwhile.

But other than D, I hated normie high school even worse than magical school. That's the only reason I agreed to train with my mom—so she'd let me drop out a second time. That was my biggest mistake, because training with my mother was horrible. Truly, deeply miserable. It's also when I discovered that I'm not cut out to do what she does. Deep down in the fiber of my being, I despise the idea of ending someone's life. I would wake up in the middle of the day in a cold sweat, panicked at the thought that someone's death might be my fault.

My family, or more specifically, my mother, will never understand wanting to be an actor. Vampires are exceptional at many things, but making people smile? Making them laugh?

That's definitely not on the list.

"But Clive, you lied to me," Xander says, in a cringy, falsetto voice.

"It wasn't a lie." I gulp and swallow. "I did it to save you."

"Save me?" Xander's falsetto keeps making me laugh, and this is not a funny scene.

"If I had told the truth, if I had told you that I loved you," I say, "you would have run, and even though the Valdez family wanted you dead. . ." I pause. "I can't live without you."

"Oh, Clive," Xander coos.

When I step toward him, he backs up, flinging his

hands in the air. "Whoa, whoa, whoa. I said I'd run lines. I didn't say you could practice your blocking with me."

"That's the part I always mess up," I say.

"Because whatever girl you're reading opposite of always panics." Xander laughs. "She can sense the vampire coming to eat her."

"Right." I drop the script onto the end table. "You gonna help me or not?"

Xander tries to suppress his laughter, but not very well. "Just turn on the old vampire charm?"

I sigh. "You think I haven't tried that?"

"What?" Xander collapses into one of the lounge chairs next to the end table.

"It's either on or off, and when it's on, it's too strong," I say. "The last time I did that, the lead actress practically attacked me. She forgot her lines, she forgot her own name. She just wanted to suck on my face."

"Is that all she wanted to—"

I kick his chair. "Listen, I need to figure out how to control that fear response in the same way I can control the charm, okay? You said you'd help."

"How can I?" He shrugs. "Your fear thing doesn't work on me. I don't feel it, ever."

"I need a normie to help me," I say. "Is that what you're saying?"

"Maybe," he says. "But a half-human isn't working."

"Stop playing," I say. "You're not half anything. You're all Xander."

"Speaking of half humans." Xander sighs. "What would you be willing to do to land the part of your dreams?"

I pause. "What?"

"Like, how far would you go?"

"You mean, would I kill someone?" Most vampires kill as their job. It makes getting little sips of blood here and there easy, and for most of them, it's exhilarating. It should be in my blood—my mom's been the most famous assassin in upstate New York for decades. I sigh. "I couldn't do it for a living, as you know. The family business wasn't for me. But if it would get me the part of my dreams?" I shrug. "Maybe."

"You'd *kill* someone to get the part you want?"

"I'm a vampire, dude. Killing people isn't the same moral quandary for us that it is for you. Remember? If someone has a hit taken out on them, someone's going to take it. It might as well be one of us."

"Except that you don't do that," Xander says.

He's right. In theory, I get it, but the half dozen times I've tried, when I was right next to the person, even knowing they were terrible people, even knowing what kinds of things they'd done, I couldn't bring myself to do it.

I'm a vampire who can't kill, but I still scare all the cute little humans without even trying.

Clearly, I'm broken.

Maybe Clark's stupid ex had one thing right. "We kind of are magical misfits."

"A half-were. A demon-spawn determined to be good. A mage who married a human and couldn't even pull that off. A witch who can't reliably cast and bonded a pigeon. A vampire who wants to make people smile. And now a dragona on the run, making us risk everything so she can, what? Make a killing selling her blood to gloffee shops?"

"You can't really think that's why she busted out," I say. "She said that guy's a real jerk and her parents didn't care."

He frowns.

"What do you really want to hear?"

Xander kicks the coffee table with his toe. "I'm not sure."

I sit down on the armchair next to him. "What's up, man? You're not usually this...confused."

"Let's say your agent called, and she—"

"Wait, did she call?" I look around, as if she might be hiding somewhere, which is really stupid. "Because I really would be perfect for that role as Jacques. I'm one-sixteenth French. Did you remind her of that?"

"There's no way you're French," Xander says.

"My aunt says that when she—"

"This isn't about your crazy agent." Xander huffs. "But if she called and offered you a part, and to get it, you had to betray a friend. . .would you do it?"

"Like, betray a friend how?" I feel uneasy for some reason, like Xander's about to confess something terrible. "What did you do, exactly?"

He leans his head against the back of the chair, closes his eyes, and sighs.

"Xander."

I've known him for almost three years. It's not a long time, really, but it feels like I've known him longer. "Even after three years," I say. "I'm still grateful you let me stay with you. I know I'm not super reliable on my rent, but I paid this month, and I have this new gig thanks to Roxana, and between her blood and mine, I should be able to pay you every month."

"It's not about you," Xander says. "Obviously."

"Then. . .who?"

He runs his hand through this hair, leaving the ends sticking up all over. "It's Roxana. If I hand her over to them, I could get a permanent spot in the pack."

Just as he's making his declaration, the door to our apartment opens, and Bevin walks inside. Xander and I turn toward her slowly, and her eyes are so wide, there's no way she didn't hear.

"If you turn her in to whom?" she asks.

Xander gulps again. "To my bosses," he says. "They'd hand her over to the dragona. To her own parents! It's not like they'd kill her or anything."

"Right," Bevin says. "They'll just force her to marry that brute she doesn't even know, and keep her in a room for the rest of her life, popping out tiny dragon eggs so that he can have loads of dragon overlord sons."

"I thought you didn't want her to stay with Minerva at all," Xander says. "You said you wouldn't go along with it."

Bevin marches toward us, her eyes practically shooting sparks. "She's my friend now. And for the record, I was wrong—she was always Minerva's friend. Minerva, who has always been our friend. And now we've known her for weeks already. Do you really think that turning her in—sending her back to her horrible family and that marriage she didn't want, is the right thing to do?"

"I barely know her," Xander whispers.

"And you want to join a pack. No, you *need* to join a pack. I know you do." Bevin crouches in front of him. "But is this really how you want to do it?"

"I'm running out of time," he whispers.

Bevin's eyes are sad, but they don't waver. "Your pack's losing patience?"

The pain's clear on his face. The longing. But even stronger than longing is the guilt. "They are."

"Will they kick you out?"

He shrugs.

"Let's say you do it," I say.

Bevin straightens immediately, her eyes flashing.

I hold out my hand and raise my voice. "Let's say he *did* turn her in." I ignore Bevin and turn toward my very best friend. "You'd join the pack permanently."

He nods.

"You'd have a place, finally, a pack, finally. But would you be able to live with yourself?" The Xander I know couldn't. He mocks and jokes and kids around all the time—mostly to keep himself safe. But he also cares about his friends, and like Bevin said, I think he cares about Roxana, even if we haven't known her long.

The word sounds practically ripped out of him. "No."

"You asked Izaak because you wanted him to tell you it was fine," Bevin says. "But that's how you know it's not."

He runs his hands through his too-long hair again, but instead of smoothing it, the tufts pointing every which way seem to worsen. "I know."

"You do," I say. "And I get why you wanted to do it, but I'm with Bevin. You can't."

"Fine," he says. "Fine!" He stands up and shoots out the door.

"How do you do it?" I ask.

Bevin stands up. "Do what?"

"How do you *always* do the right thing?" I pick up my script. "I feel like I spend most of my life not knowing what to do." And right now, I wish I could turn Roxana over *for* Xander, so he could live with himself and finally have a place. I wish I could make the tough call so he didn't have to.

Roxana's face would haunt me. I'd lose sleep over whether she was okay. But there are friends, and then there are *friends*, and Xander's my *friend*.

Bevin laughs. "I never should have been born," she says. "If my mom hadn't been such a crazy mess, she'd never have summoned a demon, and she'd never have had twins. Heaven knows, she was such a drug addict that my sister and I would never have come out healthy if we hadn't been half-demon."

"But you're the best person I know," I say. "You don't eat animals, or wear them either. You give free seances all the time to people who miss their departed family members. You don't lie or cheat or steal. You volunteer at that normie food kitchen, and you're always doing do-gooder-ly things like helping people across the street and loaning money you can't afford to lose."

She laughs, but her voice is sad. "I'm afraid, Izaak, all the time."

"Afraid?" Bevin's the least scared person I've ever met, or that's how it seems. "But you're so brave."

"Being brave and being scared go hand in hand. You aren't brave if you aren't scared. You're just naive."

Huh. I'd never thought of it like that. A lot of people discount Bevin as random and kind of off-the-wall. They miss out on the real Bevin. She's pretty balanced for someone who's one-half pure evil.

"I'm half-demon," she says as if she can read my thoughts. "And that half of me is always clamoring to escape. It promises me things sometimes with whispers in the dark. It tells me what powers I would gain and what strength I could have. I could gain just a few marks, just descend a few levels, and life would be so much easier, so much better."

"But you don't do it," I say. "Why not?"

She grabs my wrist. "For the same reason you and I are going to go find Xander right this moment."

"Why?"

"It's the right thing to do," she says. "And the only thing that keeps me from being a demon is the same thing that keeps you from being one."

"But I'm not—"

"We're all a little demonic," she says. "And we're all a little angelic. Why do you think the daimoni and the akero can have children with humans?" Her mouth quirks upward. "Because we're all a little of both, deep down. And I have to weigh each action I take and be sure the choice I make is the angelic one."

"But sometimes, are you unsure?"

Bevin inhales, her nostrils flaring, her eyes welling with

tears. "Every single day." She sniffles. "But not about this one. At first, I thought I should have nothing to do with Roxana. I thought I couldn't be put in a position where I might be forced to lie to save her."

"That's why you didn't want to get involved."

"Now that I know her, I see that more than most of the other people I've ever met, she really needs our help. She may look like she has everything, but she was as lonely in her own way as Xander would be without us. She needed friends—and being a friend is more important than the possibility that I may have to lie."

I think about her words all the way downstairs. It's not hard to find Xander. He's stewing over a cup of glatté, which is pretty much the opposite of his normal glespresso, when we walk inside. Minerva's next to him, laughing at something he said.

"But aren't all of you guys half-breeds?" she asks.

"Huh?" Xander frowns.

"It's always ticked me off that they won't let you join their stupid club," Minerva says. "When the akero brought the werewolves here, there were only a few dozen left, right?"

Xander tilts his head. "I guess."

"You're telling me they didn't have kids with the humans?" Minerva snorts. "If you think about it, every single supernatural group that lives here is a half-breed. The vampires mix with humans all the time. All mages are the children of akero and humans, and I'm positive the wolves expanded their failing numbers that way, too. That means that while your average werewolf may not have human blood in his or her last few generations, it's there. They're just being snobby brats."

"Xander," Bevin says. "Are you alright?"

Minerva pats his hand. "He's fine. Those stupid bullies

he's working with are always so bigoted, but it's nothing a little perspective and a huge glatté can't fix."

So he didn't tell her about wanting to betray Roxana. That's probably good. It means the fact that he even considered it embarrasses him.

I'm taking the first sip of my gloffee when Clark walks in the door with Roxana on his arm. She's beaming, and there's no sign of golden scales on her face or cheek. I don't feel any kind of strange pull toward her, either.

She's still drop-dead gorgeous, of course, and she looks almost the same, but the differences are subtle and effective. Her hair doesn't quite gleam. Her smile is merely nice, not blindingly brilliant. Her voice, when she speaks, doesn't tug at me, pulling me toward her, forcing me to worship her.

"I think we got it just right," she says. "Or at least, we've been walking around Central Park for an hour, and no one has even looked at us sideways."

"Well," Clark says. "I'm not sure that's true. You're still breathtakingly beautiful."

She laughs, but this time the trilling sound doesn't make me want to crawl on my hands and knees toward her and beg her to kiss me. "It's definite progress," I say. "Nice work, Clark."

"Thank you," he says. "It's a complicated spell, combined with a finicky potion, but I think if she takes it daily—"

"I can't thank you enough for this," Roxana says, staring at Clark, her hand wrapped around the bend of his elbow. "You're my hero." When she smiles, her dimple comes out to play.

"No, that's, I mean—"

I've never seen Clark stammer like that. "Oh no," I say. "Are you sure it's still working?"

Minerva glares at me and shakes her head. "Hush."

That's when it hits me. Clark, even without her glamour pulling him toward her, *likes* Roxana. Of course he does. She's beautiful, she's fragile, and she's needy. That's like Clark's kryptonite. And he has to go over there every single day to cast a spell on her so she'll be safe.

Wow, this is going to get interesting. Or awkward. Knowing Clark, probably awkward.

The front door to the gloffee shop opens with a bang. Two huge dragona stride through—their broad shoulders, all black clothing, slicked back hair, and flashing red eyes making it clear they're Russian dragona. They scan the room.

I stand up, as does Xander, all of us prepared to block them from grabbing Roxana.

What no one was prepared to defend against was them leaping halfway across the room to snatch Bevin's arms. "Bevin Bahar, we have reason to believe you know something about the whereabouts of Roxana Goldenscales."

"Let me go." Bevin's eyes are frantic. "You must have the wrong person."

I notice she doesn't lie—she never says she knows nothing. I wonder what happens if she does lie. Would a simple lie be enough for her to descend?

"Let her go," I say. "She hasn't done anything."

"No one cares what you think, bloodsucker." The taller of the two dragona spits.

"She's my friend." Clark steps away from Roxana, moving to block their view of her. "You can't force her to go anywhere."

"Yeah, let her go." Xander crosses his arms and glares at them.

The shorter of the two enormous dragona laughs. "Did we forget to mention that the NYPAD officers assigned to our case are right outside? We're not here without the proper support." He grins, sharp white teeth gleaming ominously. "We came with the full approval of the local law."

"It's fine," Bevin says. "Truly. I'll be just fine."

"Unless she's hiding something," the tall dragona says with an evil grin. "Then we'll rip her limb from limb."

Bevin slams her elbow into his face, probably breaking his nose, judging from the sound he makes and the blood that sprays all over the floor. "You can try, thug." She walks toward the door. "Let's go—I'll answer your questions, even though you've been unbelievably rude."

About that descending thing. . . I guess we're about to find out what happens if she lies. Because it doesn't look like Bevin's going to tell them anything about Roxana.

And I thought Xander was the one to watch.

14

BEVIN

Most normies know about seven of the deadly sins: pride, greed, lechery, anger, gluttony, envy, and sloth. They don't seem to know that each sin is embodied by a very specific daimon. Very few of them know that those daimoni are real, and that they're hovering around the metaphysical edges of Earth, kept away only by the wards established by the akero.

The daimon Rahab has, true to form, disguised his existence with pretty high success. Almost no one knows about the daimon of destruction. It would work against his purposes for people to know he's out there—tearing things down whenever he can.

There's no way for me to know, but I think he's my dad. Mom wasn't that subtle, and the names she wrote on our birth certificates were Bevin and Soki Bahar.

Rahab backwards.

Coincidence? Maybe.

Or, not.

Demon-spawn only descend when they commit a major sin, each of which corresponds with a particular daimon's nature. A vital part of chaos is deception, and the sin that always plagues me is a burning desire to lie.

The day I met Minerva, I *really* wanted to lie.

I mean, I really, really wanted to lie.

The years I spent saving, the months I'd labored to make my little shop perfect, were all about to go down in flames because a freaking cop moved in above the shop next to me, and she poked her nose into everything. I'd done everything right—except they don't give business licenses to demon-spawn who aren't registered.

"You're saying I needed to procure a business license from the NYPAD *before* I opened my doors?" I asked.

"Of course you did," she said. "All demon-spawn are required to declare themselves and fill out the proper forms in order to—"

That's when my brain just quit listening. *All demon-spawn.* Not all supernaturals. Not all werewolves. Not all mages. No, only demon-spawn are required to register before they can open a business in the supernatural world.

Because everyone just assumes that we're inherently bad.

It was on the tip of my tongue to tell her that I did it, that I'd already applied for a license, and I was just waiting for the paperwork to reach me in the mail. The second she stepped out, I'd make a single call, and I'd have forged documents on the way. My twin's pretty useless, but she's a whiz with forgeries.

But that's what held me back.

I am not my twin. Bevin is not Soki. And I vowed then as I had vowed many times before to never be like her. The split second when I thought about lying—I still remember it perfectly. The terror. The adrenaline. The lie that rose readily to my lips, and the words I spoke instead.

"I didn't get it," I admitted. "I didn't realize I should have, but I'm also morally opposed to the NYPAD forcing demon-spawn to do things they don't make any other groups do."

Minerva's sweet little girl-next-door face collapsed. "It does feel pretty unfair."

Her partner, a tall, frightening vampire pushed through the door at that moment. "So? Did she get it?" She tapped her foot.

"She's on the up and up," Minerva said, surprising me. "Those reports were wrong." She shoved a blank form at me on her way out the door. Only one line had been filled out. The date I began my shop was listed as the present day.

If I had written that down, it would have been a lie, but since she wrote it. . .

As hard as it was, as much as I risked, I didn't lie to Minerva that day. I told the truth through gritted teeth, and that formed the basis of a very long-term relationship that has blessed my life in many ways. Demon-spawn aren't usually optimistic, but I am. I feel like most things in my life, even the bad ones, happened for a reason. Usually, if I have the fortitude to see things through, that reason will become clear. If I stay strong, if I hold to the right, I will come out the other side the better for it.

I think back to that day, that one moment, over and over while the dragona beat me. Most supernaturals are made to withstand torture.

I am not.

Other than my ability to see through the glamour that disguises supernatural creatures from humans, and my ability to reach out beyond the boundaries of Earth and past the point of death, I'm essentially a normie. Even so, I can't answer their pointed questions, not without harming Roxana or lying outright.

"I'll ask you for the last time, you worthless sack of demon-sperm." The dragona kicks me. "Do you know anything about the whereabouts of Roxana Goldenscales?"

That one question, I can actually answer. "I don't know where Roxana Goldenscales is." I mutter the words, "right now" under my breath. I wipe my mouth—my hand comes away slick with blood.

He crouches next to me, his eyes practically glinting. "Have you seen her since the wedding?" When he speaks, his spittle sprays me, and I discover the rumors are correct. Their saliva does feel like acid on my face.

"There was no wedding." I close my mouth and press my bloody and battered lips together.

That earns me a few more kicks.

"She's got to be close to this pathetic wretch," the taller, smarter of the dragona says. "If she won't talk, someone else she knows will."

And that's when I realize what I probably should have known all along. If I don't say anything, if I won't tell a lie, they'll continue to plague everyone I know. They'll beat Minerva, and Clark, Izaak, and Xander. Eventually they'll kill one of us, or they'll find Roxana. Keeping my mouth shut will have done none of us any good.

I'm finally stuck.

"Yes," I say.

The barrage of kicks finally stops, and the dragona take a collective step back. "Yes. . .what?"

"I did call her," I say. "Like you thought. I had a client who wanted a flame lizard egg."

"Okay." The tall one grabs a piece of paper. "Who was that client?"

"Does it matter?" I shrug. "Someone told me she would have a lead on one, but she didn't know anything. In fact, she yelled at me for bothering her."

The tall one crouches down near me. "Why did your client want a flame lizard egg?"

Sorry, Minerva. The best lies are almost true. "She's a witch, but she's a weak and erratic one," I say. "She's a member of the NYPAD, and she wanted to look stronger. She thought bonding a flame lizard would help her do that."

"You called Roxana about that?" He squints at me.

"I sure did," I say. "And then I called a dozen other places—no, probably two dozen. I'll show you my phone records. I finally located an egg, but it didn't help. The thing practically burned down my client's apartment trying to escape after it hatched."

The two dragona laugh. "Nasty little buggers," the short one says. "Serves her right for trying to keep a dragon-kin as a pet."

"Regardless, I think that answers what you wanted to know."

"Not entirely. Did you hear from her again?" the tall one asks, narrowing his eyes at me. "Roxana, I mean."

"I didn't," I say. "I never heard from her again."

And that's it. A complete and total lie. A violation of the law of creation and order and transformation, the goodness that counteracts Rahab's evil. I've taken a step away from the akero who parallels Rahab—Azriel—and I've run headlong toward Rahab.

I expect the demon mark to appear right away. Certainly, descending will be a dead giveaway that I wasn't being truthful. Was that what held me back from the beginning? The assumption that as soon as I lied, it would be obvious?

It doesn't happen.

In fact, nothing at all happens.

I show the two dragona out with a sigh of relief. They stop at my door and point one finger at me. "You, do *not* leave the country. We may be back."

"Thanks for that," I say. "I was totally attracted to you two, but now? All my hot and heavy thoughts are gone."

His jaw drops right before I slam the door in his face.

I'm sure my friends are worried, but it takes me almost half an hour to clean up in the shower, examining every inch of my body for any sign of a demon mark without finding any. It takes another twenty minutes to apply enough makeup to the visible bruising that I think I'll be able to convince them that I'm fine. Luckily, with the cool autumn weather, no one will think much of the fact that I'm wearing dark jeans and a long-sleeved turtleneck.

By the time I limp downstairs and fifty feet down to Grand Central Gloffee, they're all gone. I don't freak out, though. I slowly hobble-shuffle my way up to the third floor, and that's where I find them.

They're all at Minerva's, of course.

"Bevin!" Minerva yanks me toward her and hugs me tightly.

I do my best not to cry or whimper at the contact.

Oblivious, Minerva wraps her hands around me and squeezes even more. "Thank Gabriel you're alright."

"Are you really okay?" Izaak asks. "We've been freaking out over here."

"Minerva was about to call the cavalry," Clark says. "And I was telling her to do it."

If they called the police, that would mean more attention, and Roxana might be caught. "Don't do that," I say. "Bringing the NYPAD here is the only thing that might be worse than being knocked around by some idiotic dragona."

"Are you really alright?" Xander tilts his head, clearly examining me for injuries. "They didn't hurt you?"

"No," I say. "I'm totally fine, and I didn't give Roxana away either."

"How did you keep that secret?" Minerva's shoulders

droop and her eyes widen. "Wait, did you have to *lie*?" As if the possibility's just occurring to her, she frantically looks me up and down.

At first, I can't figure out why. Then it hits me. She's searching for my mark.

I think about confessing that I lied and somehow the mark never came, but then they'll worry. I'm already freaking out, wondering whether the mark and the power that comes with it is a delayed reaction.

"No way. I told the truth, and I'm completely fine." I force a smile.

"You told them the truth?" Clark asks. "How?"

"I was careful with my words, saying things like, 'I spoke to Roxana on the phone, but—'"

"So that's why they found you." Minerva bangs the front of her forehead. "It's all my fault."

"No," I say. "It's not your fault. I could've walked away. I could've stuck to my initial insistence that I wasn't getting involved."

"But they left, with just a few vague non-answers?" Xander asks.

"Really?" Minerva asks. "They did? I can hardly believe it."

I should tell them the truth. I should fess up. But for years I've told Minerva that I'd never do *anything* to endanger myself, and the whole world by extension. Now, looking into her earnest face, I can't bring myself to disappoint her.

Could I have put them off? Could I have gotten out of that without lying? I may never know. But what I was afraid of never happened. I lied, and I didn't descend. So I do it just one more time.

"It's true," I say. "No lying from me, and as you can see, I'm completely fine."

Apparently lying to your closest friend is different.

Power pulses through me in that moment, hurling my arms and legs backward, flinging my body outward. And then, just as quickly, it's gone, and I collapse on the floor.

There's a terrible ripping sound next, and a pain tears through my backside, like someone stabbed me. . .and a bright red, forked tail whips around and stops, hovering just beside my face.

Xander swears under his breath.

Clark's jaw drops and he starts to stammer.

Izaak drops down to his knee beside me. "Bevin."

Minerva's face is sadder than I've ever seen it. "So you did lie."

That's the face I lied to avoid, and look where that got me. "At least it comes with a power, right?"

Minerva's laughter's a little unhinged. "Like, buy a tail, get a demonic power free?"

"Something like that," I say.

Minerva walks over to the desk that's shoved against the windows to the patio, and pulls out a zip tie. She hasn't even reached my side yet when a magical blast knocks the door down.

"Demon-spawn, we know you've descended."

Guardians pour into the room. Not one, not three. Not even five. Nine of them form a semicircle around me. I suppose the tail *is* sort of a dead giveaway that I'm the one they're here to nab. "Hello."

Minerva holds out the zip ties, but before she can put them on, the guardians have frozen me, flipped me on my belly, bound my hands, and gagged me. "You'll be taken down to headquarters immediately. You'll be licensed as demon-spawn. Your powers will be tested and registered. You have a right to remain silent. You have a right to humane treatment. You have a right to a lawyer. But if this is your sixth mark, you will be weighed, evaluated, and eliminated."

"It's not," Minerva says. "It's her first."

One of the guardians, a tall, muscly guy with dark hair, startles. "Officer Lucent?"

"Oh," Minerva says. "Hey Ricky."

"What are you doing here?"

Ah, so that's Ricky. Not the best circumstances, but I finally know what Minerva's hot guardian guy looks like. His voice is nice, too. Fluid, confident, and smooth. "Did you reach the scene before we did?"

Minerva shakes her head sadly. "The demon-spawn you've bound and trussed like a pig is my best friend. That's how I know it's her first mark." Even when it's hard for her to say, even when it may hurt her chances at getting the job she wants, Minerva always tells the truth. If I'd been a little more like her instead of worrying what she'd think of me, I might not be in this mess.

"And you were here when she got it?" he asks.

Minerva sighs.

She's probably thinking what I'm thinking. If we tell them how I got it, and what the mark is, it will lead them in a direct line back to Roxana. Their job may be stopping demon-spawn from descending, but they're still cops.

Where the heck is Roxana, anyway? I crane my neck, but shoved against the floor as I am, I don't exactly have the best view of the room.

"Are you going to keep her like that?" Minerva crouches beside me. "She has rights, you know."

She's buying some time to think of a story that won't get Roxana caught. Smart, Minerva. Smart. Her hands circle my upper arm, and she helps me sit up. It's not exactly comfortable, with torn pants, a tail underneath me for the first time, and my arms tied behind my back, not to mention the bruises and misery from the dragona.

But at least I'm not facedown on the floor.

"You want to be a guardian," Ricky says, "and your best friend's demon-spawn?" It clearly makes him uneasy.

"Demon-spawn aren't evil," Minerva snaps. "Bevin's amazing."

"But she did just descend," he says.

Another guardian, a short, curvy woman with a bob, whips out a notepad. "You didn't answer the question. Were you here? Did you see what crime she committed to descend?"

Minerva shoots to her feet, squaring her shoulders and facing off against the short bob guardian. "I didn't." She crosses her arms. "And not all descents result from *crimes*. Just *sins*."

Ricky cocks his head sideways. "Huh?"

"A few moments before I arrived," Minerva says, "two dragona goons showed up and shoved her and beat her and attacked her. You'll find the evidence of it on her body, and you could certainly ask the customers in the Grand Central Gloffee downstairs. They'll confirm it, too."

"I'm sorry you were mistreated," the bob-haired guardian says. "But how's that a sin?"

Minerva's lips compress. "Maybe you don't get mad about anything, but being beaten makes me pretty angry."

"Oh." The guardian frowns. "But surely—"

"The dragona are fine," Minerva says. "Being attacked by a livid, but still un-descended, demon-spawn isn't much of a danger to two male dragona. They flew out the window the second her mark showed up." She points at my thrashing tail.

The guardians sigh and groan and shuffle and mumble. Minerva lets them have it for shoving me to the ground. She reads off lists and lists of laws I've never heard.

But mostly, she gives them a hard time about insisting on taking me down to the station to be tested and prodded and detained. "Why?" she asks. "She's not arguing. She's the victim, and I'm willing to vouch for her."

"It's protocol," Ricky says.

"She can't even speak," Minerva says. "She's been gagged for half an hour, after being beaten and abused. She needs medical care and rest. She's demon-spawn, but she's still a person."

Good Gabe, I love her.

"Fine, ungag her," Ricky says. "Let's see if their stories line up."

For the first time in my life, I realize that I can lie my ass off, and no one will ever know. I fill in some details to Minerva's story, and eventually, after making me do quite a bit of paperwork, the guardians agree that I can simply fill out an extra form and submit it once my power shows up. I'm so relieved when they leave that I collapse in a heap on the ground.

"Are you alright?" Minerva's by my side already, but Izaak and Clark and Xander crowd around just as quickly, their heads peering down at me with nearly identical concerned expressions.

Once I'm sure they're gone, I ask the question that has been burning me up. "Where's Roxana?"

"She had an interview," Clark says. "I brought her to the gloffee shop to make sure everything was perfect before she went."

"An interview?" My side aches. My face is throbbing. My mouth is dry. But I'm still nervous.

"You seem scared, but don't be. It was just with a normie pharmacy. I figured she needed a job somewhere that she'd never see supernaturals, and that was what came to mind."

"It was the only place where any of us had connections that wasn't crawling with vampires, and werewolves, and dragona," Minerva says. "It seemed like a good plan."

"Thank Gabriel for that," I say. "Not to insult your spell, Clark, but that was a lot of mages."

He offers me his hand.

I take it.

"I agree," Clark says. "Roxana argued with us and complained when we packed her out the door. She didn't want to leave while you were with those guys, but we insisted she put some space between herself and them. I'm really glad she left when she did."

Yeah, if they caught her anyway? That would suck.

Two weeks ago, I'd have said that descending was the worst thing that could happen to me. But now that it has, I realize that I'm still me. A little darker, perhaps, but a little stronger too. Or you know, I will be, if I ever figure out what my power is.

A knock at the door startles us all, but when Minerva answers, it's Roxana, beaming from ear to ear. "I got the job!"

"As a pharmacist?" Izaak asks.

"I'm qualified for nothing," she says. "Of course not as a pharmacist. But I'm a pharmacy clerk!"

"Still great," Izaak says, high-fiving her.

"Right?"

As she beams at me, I decide it was worth it. I open my arms wide, and she steps toward me. When my arms wrap around her for a hug, I think about how much my life has changed since she came in to it. Everything I thought was scariest in the world happened—and I'm still me. Roxana inadvertently caused all those things, but I don't blame her. I'm glad she's growing and learning and living a real life.

Now if we could just get rid of those stupid dragona so she could truly be free.

As my arms tighten on her, my anger at the dragona increases. It's really their fault I descended, not Roxana's.

The anger inside me shifts a little bit, into a bizarre kind of fizzy, sparky feeling.

She squeezes me back, and it frigging hurts. I forgot about all my bruises. Probably as a reaction to the pain, I *zap* Roxana.

Not on purpose! It just happened.

She leaps away and yelps. "What was that?"

"I think I discovered my power," I say.

"What?" Xander looks between the two of us.

"She shocked me," Roxana says.

"Cool," Izaak says. "Do me next!"

I can't help my laughter. I finally descend, in spite of my best efforts not to, and I finally get a real demon power. My sister's first power was that of foresight—to see into the future. Her second was firepower, literally. She can torch most anything.

Me? I get the power of. . .static electricity. A power that could literally be defeated with a handful of Bounce sheets. Why does that not even surprise me?

15

MINERVA

I never, ever, should have traded my akero feather for a flame lizard egg. I'd heard over and over what disasters they were. I knew my odds of bonding one were low. But it never occurred to me that it might be anything more than a huge waste.

The second my fingers touch the goopy spot on the side of my head, I scream. "Giggles!"

In a zillion years, I never considered I might wake up with pigeon poop in my hair because I lost my priceless angelic feather. You'd think the smell would have alerted me, but apparently I grew accustomed to it while sleeping.

She flies away immediately, taking up her second favorite spot in my room at the top of my bookcase, where she can see me, but I can't reach her. Although I leave my window open at all times, she never seems to take the hint and fly away.

"We've talked and talked about this," I say. "I told you that if you did this one more time, I'd lock you in there overnight." I point at the huge cage that has taken up the spot in my room that used to be occupied with a cute ladder stack bookcase. Now those books are stuffed in the bottom of my closet to make way for a poop machine that coos too much.

"You've given me no choice," I say. "You're going in there."

She tilts her head, and even though birds can't frown, I swear she manages it. "Coo."

"No, I don't care what you say. The window was open. You should have gone outside to do this." I gesture at my head, my finger getting a little too close and shifting it. A wave of poo-smell hits me. "Ugh, this is so nasty."

I grab some clothes and yank the door open, pausing to glare at Giggles one last time.

She makes a warbling sound, and I swear, it feels like she's saying, "Flame lizards poop, too."

"Not on my head! They'd be smart enough to go *outside!*"

Although, strictly speaking, I'm not sure that's true. Since I didn't bond a flame lizard, I can't really speak to what they would do. But it stands to reason that a pigeon would be way dumber than a temperamental but majestic creature like the flame lizard.

While I'm showering, some of my anger ebbs away. I mean, it's not like I wasn't going to shower either way. I didn't see anything on my sheets, but I was supposed to wash them tomorrow anyway. Is there really anything wrong with having sheets that are clean one day sooner?

Why am I making excuses for that stupid rat with wings? Why?

It must be the infuriating familiar bond, manipulating my feelings. Or it could be her apologetic feelings traveling down the bond. Either way, it's messed up. If I can't hold on to my righteous indignation, who am I?

By the time I exit the bathroom, Roxana has come home from work, and she's chatting with Giggles at the table. "You don't say." Roxana smiles.

"She can't actually talk."

"Obviously." Roxana offers her a piece of toast. "But it kind of *feels* like she can. Does that sound crazy?"

Clearly not to me, since I was talking to her before Roxana came in, but I'm not about to admit it. I roll my eyes instead. Giggles flies toward my shoulder, probably assuming that all is forgiven, right as the door opens.

Xander and Izaak are walking in when I block Giggles from landing, a quick flip of my hand knocking her away and sending her careening toward the wood floor.

"Wow, you're mean," Izaak says. "That poor little bird just wants love."

"She pooped in my hair," I say flatly.

"Yep, slap her hard." Xander air kicks.

"For a member of the premier Manhattan Pack, you're not very good at that," Izaak says. "Guess you didn't have to kick anything during the interview."

"Wolves don't do a lot of kicking," Xander says. "And most of our fighting is done in animal form."

Roxana tilts her head a bit. "I would like to see that one day."

"A wolf fight?" Izaak leans against the counter. "Or any fight? Because I'm not a bad fighter myself." He lifts his eyebrows.

"Dear Gabriel," I say. "I thought you were past that."

"Sorry," Izaak says. "Flirting's a bit of a reflex."

"Occupational hazard for an actor, probably," Roxana says. "This job thing really sucks. So far, I'm learning to try and read terrible handwriting and to ignore people who yell at me, which seems to be most everyone."

"Sounds like the job's going well," Xander says. "You're complaining almost as much as the rest of us."

"Growing up, Mom told me that there weren't any stupid questions," Roxana says. "But it only took me a day working at a normie pharmacy to realize *that* was a lie."

"Before you think that it's all humans who are the problem," I say, "think again. Yesterday I had to restrain a werewolf who wouldn't stop peeing on fire hydrants."

Xander scowls. "When you're a wolf, it's hard to restrain yourself. And I've seen plenty of dogs—"

"He was in human form." I shake my head. "Supernatural or not, there are more stupid people than smart ones in the world."

"Whoa," Xander says, "you're the one who finally stopped Charlie?"

I blink. "You know him?"

"I heard someone arrested him, but they didn't say for what, and it didn't occur to me it might've been you." Xander laughs. "I would've paid good money to watch that."

"I can probably pull the footage from our dash cam," I say. "But don't say I never give you anything."

"That would be the best birthday present ever," Xander says.

"Wait," Izaak says. "You said *my* present last year was the best ever."

"Uh, yeah." Xander looks at me and widens his eyes. "It would be the second best present ever. The tooth filing kit was definitely the best."

"I never see you using it." Izaak crosses his arms.

"That's only because you're sleeping all day, buddy," Xander says.

Roxana frowns. "Vampires' teeth never stop growing, but what would a werewolf do with a tooth filing—"

"So how's your boss?" Xander asks. "Cool person? Terrible?" He sits down across from her. "Tell me all about it."

Roxana tilts her head, as if she can't quite figure out why he cut her off. "He's not bad, but he is not a fan of me."

"Why not?" I know Xander was just trying to change

the subject, but I'm actually interested. Roxana hasn't said a word about this to me.

"He's always yelling at me for counting out the wrong number of pills." Roxana tosses her last bit of toast to Giggles, who's happily strutting around on the ground at her feet.

"For...counting out the *wrong* number of pills?" Xander asks. "Did I hear that right?"

"Yeah, he gets, like, *really* mad about it. Today, he was all, 'Rosanne, if you give them thirty-five Vicodin instead of twenty-five *one more time*' and then he just stops talking, like that's a complete sentence."

"So you changed your name for work?" Xander asks.

"Duh," Roxana says. "Seemed like the smart thing to do."

Xander's eyes bulge and he looks at me. "But Rosanne—"

"Wait, you're giving people the wrong number of medicine?" I ask. "I feel like dispensing the right quantity is kind of an important part of your job."

"Geez, you sound just like him. Only he also says, 'I have to fill out a report every time you give them more.'" Roxana glances at the clock. "Isn't being on time a big part of your job?"

I swear under my breath. "Stupid pigeon makes me late every day." I groan. "I haven't even pulled my sheets off the bed yet."

"Don't worry," Roxana says. "I have a huge pile of clothes I need to wash. I can wash your sheets, too."

"Out of curiosity, have you ever washed your own clothes before?" Xander asks.

Roxana blinks. "Well, not exactly."

"What've you been wearing the past few weeks?" Izaak asks.

"I brought quite a few things," she says. "But I've

borrowed some of Minerva's, and I spent all the money I haven't given to Minerva on new stuff. Did you know that people sell clothes like *right* on the street and in little shops all up and down basically every part of the city?"

"Did you know that the Earth orbits the sun?" Xander asks.

"It does?" Roxana shrugs. "So many things to learn that they never even taught me in school."

Xander's still spluttering when I snag Giggles. She turns her head toward me and coos, and I almost feel bad. Almost. But once, after a fit of guilt last week, I left her in the apartment loose and she found her way to my shoulder a block away from the precinct. I was late for work that night, since I had to hoof it back home and lock her up.

It's awfully hard to keep people from realizing you have a pigeon as a familiar when she escapes and follows you around like a dog.

If dogs sat on your shoulder and cooed.

It's almost as hard to ignore the look Giggles gives me when I lock her in the cage.

"Listen, I know you want to come with me. The thing is, I'm a paranormal affairs officer. That's like being a police officer, but even harder. We deal with drunken vampires and werewolves who exhibit themselves in public."

Giggles bumps my finger with her head and rubs it back and forth.

"That's not all we do. We also handle fights between different species, and misfired spells. We encounter summoned demons sometimes, and domestic disputes—do you have any idea how messy all of that can get when the people we're dealing with have fangs and wands and claws?" I sigh. "I would take you if I could, but keeping you here is really what's best for you. My job is not a safe place for a pigeon."

"You're talking to it too," Roxana accuses. "You must

feel the same thing as me." She walks closer to the cage. "You are the smartest pigeon in the world. You'd be such a good familiar, if mean old Minerva would just give you a chance."

"I can't give her a chance." I huff as I lock the cage. "If she shows up at the office, any hope I had of becoming a guardian is gone forever."

"Are you sure you're not just worried that they'll all laugh at you?" She arches one perfect eyebrow.

"They already laugh at me," I say. "Not much has changed since high school."

Her face softens. "People are stupid. Did you hear what I said earlier?"

Roxana may not be great at math, and she may not be the best at picking up when people are mocking her either, but she's a caring person. She really does want me to be happy. "If I could just master my magic a little better, I might have a chance the next time they're looking for a guardian."

"I thought your interview went well." She reaches through the cage and strokes the side of Giggles' face.

"It went well, right up until they caught me trying to tie Giggles up with toilet paper in the bathroom."

"So they've already chosen the new guardian?"

I shake my head. "But it won't be me. I'm sure of that."

"I think your problem is less about Giggles and more that you're trying to be like other people instead of embracing your real strengths."

"Unless they're looking for an A-rated organizer for their file room, they aren't likely to care much about my real strengths." I grab my wand off my nightstand and stuff it into the slim pocket sewn into my uniform.

"Their job is dealing with demon-spawn, and they all hate them. How can they register and log and interface with a threat to our Earth security when all they do is threaten them? They need someone like you, someone who cares about the people you're working with." She folds her arms under her perfect chest and huffs.

I wish anyone else I knew thought like she did. "Look, I gotta go. Can you check on her before you go to bed?"

Roxana nods. "Of course."

Clark's just walking through the door as I'm leaving. "Did you train that bird to stay put?" He beams.

I shake my head. "I had to lock her up again."

His brow furrows. "Basic familiar training involves you commanding them to do things like stay and come to you. You need to work harder or you could end up with—"

I'm about done hearing all the ways I'm unsuitable with everything magical. "Got it. I'll work on it in the morning." The door slams a little too hard when I leave, but maybe they'll finally get the message. Their constant suggestions aren't helping me.

They're annoying me.

It's not like most familiars have the same brainpower as mine has. Giggles seems to have two brain cells most days —and they're usually fighting.

I know something's wrong the moment I walk through the door at work. My first clue is that Rufus and Peter are leaning against my desk, harassing Amber. The harassment is normal, but staying late isn't. They're usually the first people out the door. Typically we only see them at the end of our shift.

"Is it buy one goon, get one free night?" I ask. "Because if so, I want to know who bought the first one. We're going to have words."

Amber's lips are compressed tightly.

"Oh, we just wanted to congratulate you," Peter says. "On staying alive to suck a little longer."

My heart falls. I told Roxana I knew I wouldn't make guardian this time, but I guess part of that was a lie, because hearing him gloat that I wasn't chosen hurts. "Who did they take?"

"I'm sorry it wasn't you this time," a deep voice from across the room says.

It takes all my self-control, but I manage to turn around slowly.

I've known Hudson Leclair since kindergarten. Since puberty, looking at him has always hurt my eyes. But today, out of his uniform and wearing plainclothes? It's a little like staring at the sun.

"I didn't know you even applied," I say.

He shrugs his broad shoulders. "I didn't mean to, not for another year or two at least, but at the last minute, I changed my mind."

"Why?" Peter asks. It's strange to hear him speak without his signature nastiness. Apparently he saves all that for me.

"A friend of mine is demon-spawn, and he just descended," Hudson says. "I figured the guardians need a few among their ranks who ask questions first and shoot later."

Be still my heart. "I agree." If I wasn't going to be chosen, at least they're getting someone great. Someone who cares about the people he's out there monitoring.

"It's really too bad they haven't seen your potential yet," Hudson says. "When I get up there, I'll be sure to put in a good word."

"A good word?" Peter laughs. "About Lucent?"

"She's smart, she's hard-working, and she's brave." Hudson crosses his arms, causing the lean muscles in his arms to ripple. "Actually, my problem will be only saying a few good things. I'll probably annoy them with my recommendations."

My disappointment over not being selected is changing to sadness that Hudson's leaving. I had no idea he thought so highly of me. I'd have stalked him a little more if I knew.

Too late for that—he's heading over to guardian headquarters.

And now I have even more reasons to want that promotion.

"You haven't been here long," Peter says. "Clearly you haven't spent much time with Minerva. She's rash, unpredictable, and flaky, and I haven't even started talking about the unreliability of her magic yet."

"If you like her at all, then don't recommend her," Rufus says. "She's so incompetent at what she does that you'd be signing her death warrant if you did."

Amber's fangs glimmer as she bares her teeth. "You stinking sack of dog sh—"

I grab her wrist. "I can handle this myself." I'm done letting them bully and insult me. "I'll challenge you to a duel, Peter, if you're so sure that I'm incompetent."

"A duel?" Peter's laugh is loud, obnoxious, and bright. "You must be kidding me. What are we, middle schoolers?"

I step closer. "Are you afraid of me?"

"Why should I be scared of you?" He snarls.

"Because you're all talk and no spell," I say. "You spend a lot of time berating me for misfired spells, but I looked it up last week. You've cast fewer spells this year than anyone else on the force." I step even closer. "I wonder why that is."

"Shut your mouth, Lucent," he says. "Before I close it for you."

"That would require a spell," I say. "And I'm not at all sure that you—"

The falcon on his shoulder launches toward me so quickly that I don't even have time to think of the words to a spell, much less recite them. But before it can reach my face with its extended claws, something grey and small collides with it, knocking it off course.

It's another bird.

Giggles.

The terrifying falcon and my pigeon slam into the ground—I feel the force of the landing in my own shoulder. The falcon's claws are much sharper, and its talons dig deeply into Giggles' plump side. Its beak is open and it's shrieking, and I realize it's about to *bite* my little girl.

I act without thinking. "Duratus," I shout, my wand extended.

Not only does the falcon go utterly still instantaneously, but the ground around the two birds is coated with bright blue frost.

Technically, that's a misfire.

A freeze spell shouldn't literally freeze everything. It should merely stun the intended victim. Looking at the horrible little falcon, utterly blue and coated with ice, I'm not sure whether it will pull through.

The Chief's door opens. "Lucent," he bellows.

Everyone in the precinct was already watching, but this is worse. Because there's literally only one defense for what I just did, and it's going to out my secret.

"I had no choice, sir," I say.

He quirks one bushy eyebrow. "No choice but to literally *freeze* Chester's familiar?"

I inhale deeply, and then exhale slowly. "That's right. It was attacking *my* familiar, Giggles." My pigeon stands up and shakes herself, fluffing up to maximum volume. One drip of blood, then another, falls to the ground. But as if she's not injured at all, she launches herself, very ungracefully, toward my shoulder. She doesn't quite get the height she needs and she hits the side of my desk on the way, knocking a pencil sharpener and a stack of folders onto the floor.

But finally, her wings flapping wildly, she reaches my shoulder, her claws digging into my side so she can pull herself up to the top of my body. She fluffs up again and then coos into the deadly silence surrounding us.

The idiot actually looks proud of herself.

Amber groans.

"You're saying that the *pigeon* you're holding, the one we saw in the Mexican restaurant before, is actually your familiar?" Even the Chief can't hide his disgust.

I swallow. "That's right."

"You'd better come talk to me."

His office isn't far, barely a dozen feet away, but it feels like I'm walking two miles, with all the eyes on me. I know what they're all thinking. I didn't imagine I could drag my reputation further down than it already was, but here we are.

After I walk past him, the Chief slams the door. He points at a chair. "Sit."

I do, Giggles preening herself as the Chief circles to take his own seat.

"What on earth were you thinking, bringing that creature here?"

Actually, until this very moment, I hadn't considered how she got here. "I locked her in a cage," I say. "I've been doing it every day."

"I knew she was your familiar," he says. "But I pretended I didn't for your sake. I honestly thought you were smart enough to keep it hidden."

I can barely believe what I'm hearing. "So that's why I didn't get the guardian spot?"

He laughs. "Oh, Minerva, what am I supposed to do with you?"

I'm confused. "I know it looks bad, having a pigeon as a familiar and all, but if that was the reason, why did it take them so long to make up their minds?"

The Chief stands up and braces his hands, palms down, against his desk. "Minerva Lucent, the pigeon isn't the problem. Your misfiring spells aren't the problem either. They're symptoms of the real problem."

I stare at him, dumbfounded. What does that mean, symptoms of the problem?

"Do you really not know? What was your father thinking, keeping this from you?" He runs one hand through his thinning hair. "You should pull your own file. Maybe you can figure out what the rest of us already know." He leans forward again. "And give up on this idiotic dream. You, Minerva Lucent, will never be a guardian. You're lucky to be able to cast spells *at all*."

No matter how much I press, he doesn't say anything else. He keeps insisting he's keeping quiet for *my dad*, which is crazy. Dad never mentioned anything about a secret, and he was as frustrated as anyone else about my spell-casting misfires.

Since Giggles is with me today, I notice a lot of my co-workers eyeing me strangely, but Amber never misses a beat. "Let's go," she says. "We have criminals and idiots to help."

We catch a few strange cases during my shift that serve to distract me pretty well, but by the end of the night, I still can't shake the Chief's words.

"Time to do paperwork?" Amber asks.

I don't argue, because I've had an idea. "I think, instead of going through things here at my desk, I might work better back in the file room."

Amber frowns. "You're sick of people staring? Just tell me who and I'll—"

"It's really not that," I say. "But there is a window out there, and Giggles could duck out and stretch her wings if she needs to." I bandaged up her wound, and familiars can draw energy from their mages to heal, but even so, she's been pretty miserable. It's not an unbelievable lie.

Amber hates most everyone, but after watching tiny,

weak Giggles spring in front of that falcon, my partner loves her. "Alright, but I'll be right here if you need me." She bares her fangs and hisses. "You have more than a brave little pigeon to watch your back."

I can't help but laugh. "I'm sure we'll be just fine."

The second I'm alone with the files, I drop the stack I'm supposed to be working on and rummage around through the hard copy files. . .until I find my own. I've been running through possible scenarios. Could I have suffered some childhood trauma I repressed? Could I have had some kind of surgery that impacted the part of my amygdala that controls aptitude for spells? Or maybe in my dedication ceremony, a priest said the wrong word?

Unfortunately, when I open my file. . .most of it is redacted.

Why?

Why would it be redacted? What in the world is going on? What does the Chief know? What did Dad hide from me? I'm about to shove it back into place with disgust when I notice one very strange word.

Where it should list my parents' names, the slot for my mother is redacted, like most of the file, but the space for my father's name is not.

There, on that line, it clearly reads: Mario Leehack.

My mother's maiden name is Melina Blitz, and my dad is Holden Lucent. I've known that all my life. Holden and Melina Lucent are my parents.

Or are they?

Of all the many, many circumstances I imagined, I didn't even consider that I might be adopted. But how on earth would that impact my ability to cast spells?

As much as I dread having dinner with my mother, I call her right away. "Mom?"

"Yes, Minerva. How are you?"

"I think we need to talk."

16

CLARK

I won the Innovation for Mages award in seventh grade, and I got to meet the wizard who inspired the character of Dumbledore for the Harry Potter books that normie wrote.

Alvin Brilliantus is the single most gifted spell caster in all of America.

It still annoys every mage in the United States that the normie who stole his identity set the whole thing in England. As if. Then, to make matters worse, she took his last name—Brilliantus—and turned it into a veiled insult. Dumb-ledore.

She completely missed the connection between mage surnames and light. We're all descended from angels, lady. We all have last names that are in some way affiliated with light, the sun, brilliance, or divinity.

Back when I won the award, I was offered a choice. I could eat dinner with Alvin Brilliantus, or I could accept a huge scholarship for my future education. With a father who was a chief of police, I should definitely have taken the scholarship.

I chose to meet my hero instead.

And it was absolutely the right call.

I've wanted to be a Professor at the New York Institute of Magic ever since that day. The fact that the most gifted mage of our generation chose to teach has been a lifelong inspiration for me.

The prestige, the exciting atmosphere of magical partnership and innovation, and the status that being a professor affords are only occurring to me now. The benefits are good and the pay isn't bad, even for an adjunct professor, and the colleagues I would surround myself with could help me develop the ideas that are always rocketing around in my brain. On top of everything else, the beautifully manicured grounds are a serene and peaceful place in the middle of New York's chaos and entropy.

Or at least, they usually are.

A frisbee whizzes by my head, nearly clocking me on the temple, and a giddy werewolf bounds past and leaps straight up into the air two feet away, its teeth snapping down onto the plastic toy and cleaving it in two chunks.

"That was amazing, Nolan," a brunette with bushy eyebrows says.

She's clearly also a werewolf. If the eyebrows and the arm hair hadn't clued me in, the sappy and disturbing way she's staring at that dog, as if she wants to both eat and kiss him, would have. That's a pretty clear sign that they're mates.

Watching them makes me feel bad for Xander. The mating process with werewolves is a big deal. In fact, once they meet someone and start to develop feelings, it's almost impossible to walk away. After they fall in love and the mating bond settles, that's it. They're locked down for life.

It sounds a little creepy to me, but it's every wolf's dream, and Xander's probably never going to find that.

I wonder whether dragon shifters have anything similar, and then I check myself. The last thing I need to be doing is spending every waking moment thinking about Roxana. I did enough of that my first few years of college. In fact, it's her fault I married a normie in the first place. I was sneaking out of the dorms to try and visit Roxana under the guise of seeing my sister Minerva when I met Carly.

I'm not delusional enough to truly blame Roxana, of course. Mages don't have mates in the same way that werewolves do, and I'm the one who fell so hard for a normie. I won't be caught again—from now on, I'm dating another mage or no one at all.

Lately, it's been no one at all.

I wonder whether it's a good sign that they're bringing me on campus for a second interview. It can't be a bad thing, right? I push past a few throngs of students evacuating the arcane arts building and force the heavy wooden doors open. Professor Jonas is waiting in the lobby when I arrive.

"Clark Lucent." His smile is warm, his eyes bright.

"Nice to see you again," I say.

We make small talk as we walk to the elevator and then as we wait to reach the eighth floor, where his office is located.

"It was your paper on the ethics of spell casting on humans that drew my eye," he says. "We have plenty of powerful mages on staff, as I'm sure you know, but there aren't enough of us thinking about the ramifications of what we do."

I hate that my heart falls just a bit, hearing that it was my analytical and ethical studies that drew him to me. I suppose that's better than nothing, but I was hoping he'd been impressed by my inventions or my new potions. "My interest is probably because of my failed marriage to a normie," I admit, "but those things are important to consider. After all, the reason mages exist at all was so that we could keep the world safe from the threat of the daimoni."

"So true," Professor Jonas says. "The akero may not often be among us, but their guiding principles and rules must never be forgotten. We are servants, not masters, at the end of the day."

Most mages don't like to think about that at all. It makes me uneasy too, but if we all ignore everything that makes us uneasy, the world will be a terrible place. No one can grow without challenging their existing worldview. "I couldn't agree more." No matter how hard it is to stomach.

"You know, it wasn't merely me who was impressed. I recorded your first interview and replayed it for the rest of the department. They all agreed with me—you're our top pick."

My hopes soar.

"The reason we invited you here was to discuss the details of what we'd have in mind. The class load, the pay, the benefits for an adjunct professor, and how you can make it work without interrupting your current job and lifestyle overmuch."

I can barely believe what I'm hearing. "That's, well, it's amazing."

We spend the next hour touring around the Ethics of Magic department, and then looking at the small room that will be *my office*. It's hard for me to believe it's happening.

"Do you see the possibility of this position growing?" I ask. "Obviously you won't need more than one course on the ethics of magic use, but I'd be delighted to teach other things."

"Actually, I'm pushing the dean to make this a requirement of graduation. Your reach could expand dramatically, and quite soon. But even if that doesn't happen, I see plenty of opportunities as you meet more of our faculty for you to expand in other ways. And of course, the speed at which you're able to publish will greatly impact the pace and magnitude of your success."

The worst thing about academia is the absolute demand for publishing articles and books and research papers. I suppress my groan. "I really appreciate your support."

He gestures for the door. "Now that you've seen your future office, shall we head to mine? I have some paperwork we'll need to get filled out right away." Once we reach his desk, he rummages around for what feels like forever before brandishing a stack of paper at me.

"I already filled out the application for employment online," I say.

"These are the required releases and legal mumbo jumbo so that we can complete your background check."

I freeze. "My. . .what?"

"As I'm sure you already know, our most generous donors are the dragona—the bulk of our endowment for this particular institution came from them. They're always the most celebrated of our students who major in business, and alumnus from that department keep the lights on." He shakes the papers at me.

I reluctantly take them from him, scanning the basic information listed. Right there on line eight is a request for me to list my friends and family. "But do they really suspect me of. . .what? Like, being friends with insurgents? Demon-spawn?" I can't help thinking about Bevin. Would they take issue with her?

"Trust me, Clark. There's nothing to worry about. Even if you have a few demon-spawn friends, or even some normie pals as a throwback from your marriage, it's fine. None of that's a crime." He smiles reassuringly. "Just fill this out and you can go."

But it's not as simple as he makes it sound. "What happens when I do fill all this out?"

He shrugs. "They'll arrange a time to interview your

family, as well as their roommates and friends. Once they've done their due diligence, that's it. My wife and friends said it took less than an hour of their time, so don't feel too bad about it."

We'd have to lie about and then hide Roxana. What if it goes wrong? What if she's caught because of me? As much as I want this job, I can't risk exposing her.

Right?

Mother feathers. It's starting to feel like it was a huge mistake to hide her.

Until I think about the life she'd be living right now if we had turned her away. She'd be stuck on house arrest with a man who dominates everything about her. She'd have no say of her own. She'd be miserable.

Having to pass on a job opportunity for now and having to go by her place every morning to spell her doesn't feel like such a big imposition, not when I think about what a difference it makes for her.

Freedom. A life.

"Actually," I say, "I have a meeting at work that starts soon. Can I take these forms and fill them out and get them back to you tomorrow?" That gives me some time to tell him that something has come up, and I won't be able to work here, without it being immediately apparent it has to do with the background check. Something like that, when they're already on high alert over a missing dragona princess, might set them after us anyway.

"Of course," Professor Jonas says. "Yes, yes. You do that. Just email it all to me later."

As I walk off campus and hike back to my car, I start thinking of all the reasons it's not a good time for me to pick up an extra job right now, anyway.

Not that I really believe any of them.

We really need to start working on an exit strategy for Roxana. Living her life in hiding isn't much better than living under the thumb of that stupid Russian prince. How can we get her free from the dragona overlords so she can live her life as she chooses? Like, really live it as she chooses? In the open.

As if all the thinking I've been doing about her summoned her somehow, Roxana pings me. DOES YOUR APARTMENT HAVE A LAUNDRY ROOM?

Why's she asking me about a laundry room? Then it hits me. Minerva said theirs was being refurbished. Roxana probably has a lot of dirty clothes.

I'VE NEVER DONE LAUNDRY, AND IT'S PILED UP PRETTY HIGH.

I hate how excited I am at the thought of spending time with her, but a little healthy self-loathing doesn't slow my fingers down. They fly over the keys to text her back. NEED HELP?

THAT WOULD BE AMAZING!

MEET ME AT MY BUILDING IN 45 MINUTES. I'LL BRING THE DETERGENT.

Thanks to a delay on the subway, I'm barely reaching my apartment building 45 minutes later. I have no time to change clothes, let alone tidy up my place, and this is Roxana's first time coming over.

She's arriving just as I am—by cab. I can't believe she called a taxi—to do her laundry. I can't even blame her. As she unloads her clothing on the curb, I can see why. She has four big bags full of clothing.

"Wow, I think I'd have just called a laundry service," I say.

She slaps her forehead. "That's an option?" She groans. "Why doesn't anyone tell me this stuff?"

I laugh. "Here, I'll help." I swing the two biggest bags over my shoulder and march toward the door.

Roxana just looks at the other two, making no effort to pick them up herself.

"Uh, are you coming?" I ask.

"Oh." She sighs. "I guess you can't carry them all?"

"Did you ask to use my building so I'd help you do laundry? Or so you'd have a free pack mule?" I lean over and grab one more bag, barely lifting all three. Surely she can bring one herself.

My doorman yanks the glass door open as we approach and waves us through. "Mr. Lucent."

"Hey, Ralph."

"You came at a good time. There's hardly anyone doing laundry." He beams at me. He may be demon-spawn, but like Bevin, he's one of the great ones.

"Thanks." I pause occasionally to make sure Roxana's still following me, and she is, albeit slowly, dragging her single bag along the ground.

"Oh my word, how much farther is it?"

"Just through those doors." I point. Once we're through, I set her bags on the ground and point at the stairwell in the back. "I'm going to head upstairs really quick and grab my clothing and my detergent. Do you want a book or something?"

"A book?" She blinks. "Do you wash those too?"

I laugh. "Uh, no."

She sighs. "You meant so that you have something to do while your clothes are washing, right?"

I smile. "Yeah, that's what I meant."

"Do you have any books that aren't about spells? Because I won't get anything out of those."

"Of course I do." But part of me wonders whether she'll really like any of my books. They tend to focus on things like spell craft, potions, ethics of magic, and mage politics. Even the ones that don't usually feature mage protagonists. "I'm sure I can find something."

She looks even less sure than I sound, but she doesn't argue. "Or maybe you could just, you know, talk to me."

Talk to her? That sounds. . .nice. The more time I spend with her, the more I like her—I know she's not using her charm on me, but sometimes it feels like she is. With her, it honestly might be more like an innate magic.

She literally can't keep guys from falling in love with her.

It doesn't hurt that she's the most gorgeous woman I've ever seen. She's wearing mismatched sweatpants and a ratty t-shirt right now, and I bet if she posted a photo, she could sell them on eBay for a fortune. Her hair, in a messy bun on top of her head, looks like it was artfully and carefully placed the way it is. Her lips are full, her eyes luminous, and her cheeks dramatic.

Just as I reach the door to the stairwell, a tall vampire offers her laundry detergent. "Did you forget yours?" He grins, his bright white incisors flashing. "Please, take mine."

Oh, heck no. "Actually," I say, "I was just going up to get mine for her."

"But mine's already here." His dark hair falls forward across his eyes. "Jacques Ferrar," he says. "You must be new to the building."

I practically race back to her side. "She doesn't even live in this building." I hate how my voice squeaks when I get agitated. I force myself to swallow. "She's here with me—my girlfriend. I'll go get some detergent and I'll be right back."

Roxana turns toward me slowly, her eyes widening. "Your—what?"

I sling an arm around her shoulders. "That's right. We're going steady." *Steady?* What's wrong with me? Am I the lead in a 1950s Grease-esque sitcom? Should I be slicking my hair back and rolling up my jeans?

"You're going steady?" The vampire looks ready to rip my throat open.

"Um, sure. Yeah. This warlock is my boyfriend. I'm

planning to just wait here dutifully for him to fetch me some detergent." She's one second away from flinging my arm off and reading me the riot act, I can tell.

I lean down and whisper in her ear. "The fewer people who get close to you, the fewer who can learn who you *really* are."

She stiffens. "He'd better hurry, though. I'm losing my patience."

At that, I nearly sprint upstairs. I grab my laundry basket without thinking and throw detergent and fabric softener on top. I dump a fistful of change into my pocket for the machine with a broken credit card swiper, and race back down.

I'm breathing heavily when I reach the laundry room, but I'm glad I sprinted. In the four and a half minutes I've been gone, she's gained a witch, and a demon-spawn admirer, too.

"I can't believe you can handle working at a pharmacy," the witch is saying. She keeps touching Roxana's arm and laughing, and I want to slap her. I've never wanted to slap a girl before, but here we are.

"Hey sweetheart," I wheeze. "I'm back."

"You really shouldn't leave this one alone," the demon-spawn man says. "I just might steal her."

Roxana's laughter is like bubbling silk. "Oh, stop."

"Never," he says. "I look forward to seeing you often, and I make no promises about behaving when I do."

"My brother's with the NYPAD." The witch frowns. "If you can't behave, I'll be sure to invite him over to deal with it."

"Alright," Roxana says. "Let's not have any of you snapping at one another. We're all friends, right?"

Just a few words, and suddenly they're all pretending to like one another. Definitely innate magic at work. I need to get her clothing washed and get her out of here before someone else figures out why they're all obsessing over the same person.

For a short period of time, it's probably fine. They'll attribute it to her incomparable figure, her dazzling smile, or her silky hair. But if they have long enough to think about it, they may figure out why she's so compelling.

Especially if that witch is usually straight.

Or if the wizard who just showed up and is offering her dryer sheets, who's wearing a fabulous purple suit, is usually gay. Those are often the people who realize something is off the quickest.

"Hey, actually, I forgot to grab a book," I say. "Let's get your wash started, and we can hang out upstairs. I'm sure one of your new friends would be happy to keep an eye on your clothes for us." I glance around. No one volunteers, as if they realize that doing so would be surrendering their time with her.

"Really?" Roxana clasps her hands together enthusiastically. "If you could, that would be amazing."

"I'd be happy to," the witch says.

"Of course I will," the vampire offers.

"No one would dare cross me," the demon-spawn says.

"Let me," the wizard says. "I'll even spell them beforehand to make sure the stains all come out."

"You can do that?" Roxana asks.

"No need," I say. "Her boyfriend's a warlock, remember?" I whip out my wand. "Come over here." I point at the back row of machines, all four of which are empty. I dump my clothes into one without watching.

"Uh." Roxana clears her throat.

I glance down.

The witch is laughing. The wizard starts laughing a second later. The vampire stifles his laugh, which is at least polite.

A pair of my bright green underwear has fallen out and

is lying on the floor. Which would probably be fine, except for two things. Number one, there are dinosaurs on it. That's a little embarrassing. And number two?

Skidmarks.

I don't think I've had skidmarks on my underwear since elementary school, but here we are. I whisk my wrist. "Ascende et vade in." The undies fly up and into the washer.

Roxana turns away quickly, and picks up one of her bags. She's not allowed to empty it into a washer herself, of course, and within moments, her four admirers have stepped up to place all her clothes carefully into empty washers. A few pairs of her underwear also fall out in the process, but seeing as they're lacy pink bras and matching g-strings, no one laughs.

I suppose it's as close to changing the topic from my epic embarrassment as we could get.

And it's not like I care what any of these random people think about my underwear. Or what Roxana thinks. She's not a witch, after all, and I'm not going to date *anyone* but a witch. It's the one thing I'm absolutely sure of.

Of course, like everyone else, the more time I spend with Roxana, the harder it is to hold onto that resolve.

17

ROXANA

I went from being a bird in a golden cage...to being a nuisance to everyone around me. At least when I was in the cage, I didn't feel guilty about it. Now it feels like my existence makes life harder for everyone I care about.

Never having had a job before, I never realized how unsuited I was to, well, to everything.

I can't count out meds with regularity.

I can't manage the label machine.

The computer's a devil sent to make my life into a nightmare.

Stocking shelves has proven more complicated than I imagined it could be. None of these bottles are labeled in a sensible way. If it said, "Headache elixir?" Totally fine. I could nail that. But the humans seem to only want bottles that say long and complicated, nonsensical words. Like Acetaminophen. Or if it said, "heart attack remedy," okay. But Clopidogrel? Who knows what that means? "Give this to manics," I could remember. But Zyprexa? It means nothing!

It's not really my fault I gave them Zivox instead. I

mean, they sound the same. And if they'd had an infection instead of hallucinations, that Zivox would totally have helped.

Why can't normies just accept the truth? Why do they need the fancy and confusing names? There's really only one place I'm able to work without ruining everything, and only because the normies seem to expect complete incompetence here.

"Here's your prescription." I hold out my hand to the customer who told my co-worker over and over that he's been waiting for more than half an hour. (Even though I saw with my own eyes that he arrived fourteen minutes ago.) "Thanks for your patience."

The portly gentleman smiles at me. "Look at that smile. I'd wait a lot longer than thirty minutes to see that again."

"Uh. Okay, well, now your wait is over." I shake my extended hand. "If you have any questions about this, you can speak to the pharmacist over there."

"Oh, I didn't come here to talk to the pharmacist." He takes the prescription, his hand brushing my fingers. "Did you know—I didn't even need this refilled."

I pause. "You didn't? Then why are you here?"

"I wanted to see you," he says. "I haven't been able to stop thinking about you since I picked up my blood pressure meds last week."

Grabe, not again. "Uh, well, that's nice." I gesture to the line behind him. "But I have a lot more patients—"

"Can you send someone to help me back here?" A surly-sounding warlock in the back is unloading a new shipment of meds. I wonder whether the humans realize that the most amazing medicines they take are really potions and spells.

As if insulin and Viagra and Adderall are really made by humans. Valium? That one really makes me laugh. It's obviously a calming spell, through and through.

"Rosanne," my boss bellows. "You can at least lift things, right?"

He appears to be impervious to my charm, which is just fine with me. I'd rather have him yell at me than start stalking me. "Yessir."

"Great. Delivery guy says he needs a hand."

I yank my hand away from the overeager customer and sprint for the back of the pharmacy. I didn't even know Clark was coming today. When I get there, there isn't much to do. I look around blankly. "Uh, what exactly did you—"

The warlock, who is most certainly *not* Clark, grins. "You looked like you could use a break."

"Oh."

He has a nice smile. It's broad, and not at all condescending like most of the warlocks I've met in my life. His eyes are a startlingly bright blue, but they aren't overly intense, like most dragona. "If I was wrong, please, by all means, return."

I sit on a large box. "Not at all. I feel like I haven't sat down since I started working here."

"Maybe I should fill in for Clark's deliveries more often," he says.

"Why are you here?" Clark got me the job—he knows the manager because he delivers all the potions and spelled pills here.

"He had a big meeting today, so I'm filling in." He's not as tall as Clark, but he's still pretty tall, at least six inches taller than I am. His hair is so blonde it nearly glistens. None of that's quite as shocking as the square cut of his jaw, and the perfectly straight line of his shiny, white teeth.

This guy could be a model on a magazine, easily. What in the world is he doing delivering pharmaceuticals? "Well thanks for calling me back here. . .for no reason."

"Any time." He salutes—which should be weird, but instead, it feels just right. Casual. Like he's not afraid to make fun of himself. "I'd better run grab the last dolly of stuff." He points his thumb backward over his shoulder.

"Of course." I stand up and start rummaging through the parcels he's dropped off. "Did you bring everything on the reorder list? Because we're almost out of Viagra—that's a big mover."

"I sure did. It's in that one." He points at the box on the bottom. Of course it's on the bottom. I use a sharp fingernail—dragona fingernails require diamond chip files to wear them down—and slice the box on top open. I start pulling out the individual items and stacking them on the right shelves. By the time the mage has brought in the last load of things, I've almost reached the Viagra box.

Of course, I've also created quite a large pile of empty boxes that I'll have to deal with.

"No chance you guys want to take these back, huh?" I point at them by bobbing my head toward the corner.

He tilts his head. "Did you just point with your mouth?"

I think about it. "My mom always does that."

"It's cute." His lips are compressed, but kind of shaking, like he's trying not to laugh.

"Will you take the boxes or not?"

He shakes his head. "We don't reuse packaging. Seems wasteful, I know. Maybe I can talk to someone about it."

"Good idea." But until then, I slice the bottoms of the boxes open too and collapse them all. I'm a little bit proud of myself for learning to do all the routine things. The first day it took me half an hour to do what I can do in under three minutes now. "Thanks again."

I'm walking toward the back door, ready to chuck the boxes into the trash when I hear a sound. A scritchy-scritchy-scratching sound—it must be a rat in the dumpster. I drop the boxes and shout, and flames burst from my hands, igniting the pile of cardboard boxes I just dropped.

Female dragona are practically useless. Other than our

charm and our super strong fingernails—which makes for toenails that are insanely hard to clip—we have no magical powers at all.

Except for one that most people forget about.

We shoot sparks from our fingers, but not at useful times, like if we were angry, or if we wanted to harm someone. No, our sparks only fly when we're startled or scared. Which means they're more of a hazard than a power. Just like right now.

"Douse ignis!" The warlock doesn't miss a beat, putting out the fledgling flames before I can even go for the fire extinguisher.

"Oh wow," I say. "I have no idea how that could have—"

The mage takes my wrist. His hands are large and warm. "Clark said you're demon-spawn, but that was a lie." He sniffs the air, like a bloodhound. "You don't *smell* like a dragon." He glances down at his wrist, staring straight at the dull black rock in a charm, probably. "This isn't flashing red."

I swallow.

"But you're dragona." His voice is soft, but very, very clear. "Who cast the spell to nullify your scent?" The corner of his mouth turns up. "It's someone very gifted, to fool my charm *and* my nose."

I open my mouth to protest, but what can I say? I'm not a mage, obviously. I can't work any spells. I'm clearly not a werewolf or a vampire. What does that leave?

"Don't be afraid. You're clearly hiding—" His eyes widen. "A remarkable beauty and you looked so familiar. You're Ro—"

I wrench my arm away and clench my hands into fists at my sides.

"I would never reveal who or where you are to anyone," he says. "I swear."

"*Bastilan!*" My heart's racing, my pulse pounding loudly in my ears. "Why should I believe anything you say?"

"Tagalog. I knew it." He beams. "Whoever it is, they also did a great job disguising your scales." He's staring at my face, peering directly at my neck and cheeks. If he's been watching the television at all, he'd know that's where mine show the most clearly. "You have a powerful mage on your side, and you're working. . ." His jaw drops. "Wait, is *Clark* the mage who's been helping you?"

I press my lips together, my mind racing a million miles a minute. There must be some way out of this. It's not only me who would get in trouble. If he turns me in, he could get Clark fired, or maybe even attacked by my dad. If I just—

"I had no idea he was that talented." He sighs. "I suppose I should have known. Wait, did the manager say your name is *Rosanne*? That's your version of hiding?" His lips twist and his eyes sparkle.

"I'm at a human pharmacy," I say. "What supernaturals. . ." Other than the wizard deliveryman. Why did I come back here? Why didn't I ignore him and head right back in to man the sales counter? I'm such an idiot.

"The last thing I would ever do is rat you out."

I want it to be true, but it seems too lucky. "The bounty's enormous," I say. "Who wouldn't want that kind of money?"

He laughs, and it sounds sincere. "The one thing in the entire world I don't need more of is money."

Okay, that's odd. "Everyone likes money."

"I like it," he admits, "but I have plenty already. Let me take you to dinner, and I'll tell you all the reasons why you can trust me."

"Or you'll call my dad on the way, and by the time we reach the restaurant, they'll be waiting for me. Along with your huge bounty."

He laughs again. "Call Clark if you want. Ask him if Lincoln from work cares about what he gets paid. Ask him if I look like someone who struggles."

He seems awfully sure of himself. "What kind of person doesn't want *millions* of dollars?"

"Actually, don't call Clark. He knows I'm rich, but he doesn't know the half of it." He taps his lip.

"Look, just go, and I'll hope for the best." And I'll run like a demon's on my tail the second he's gone.

"No, you won't hope for anything. You look panicked."

"I'm not panicked," I lie.

"You are. I could get in real trouble for telling you this, but. . ." He waves his hand through the air, and everything about him goes fuzzy. Then it comes back into focus. He was blonde before, but now it's a little darker—streaks of deep gold shooting through his whitish-blonde strands. And where his hair was short and clean cut at a first, almost a military style, it's now long and wavy. A golden strand shifts and falls down across his left eye. "I disguise myself for work too."

My eyes widen and I search for scales. But no, he's casting spells. He's a wizard for sure—so then, why would he hide?

"You don't recognize me?"

I study him more closely. His teeth are still straight and white, but the nearly unbearable perfection is gone. His nose is a bit crooked, and one tooth is turned slightly. He has a sprinkling of freckles across his nose. Instead of making him look worse, the humanity makes him look better somehow, as if he's a real person, not a statue carved of marble. And he's taller—at least two inches taller than he was. Maybe taller than Clark, now.

Even so, I have no idea who he is.

"I'm sorry, should I know you?" I shrug. "I don't watch much TV. Are you an actor?"

He sighs. "This is a little embarrassing. I recognized you, but you don't know me."

"Didn't you say you're friends with Clark?" I ask. "I mean, I've known his sister for a long time, but—"

"I'm Lionel Sol," he says.

As if that's all I need to hear. Is his name famous, for some reason? I wrack my brain, but I haven't heard of any singers or actors named—then it hits me—*Sol*. That's the name of the leader of the Illuminae, the most powerful mage organization on Earth.

He smiles, clearly noting my recognition.

"My dad's Orion Sol, the Grand Chancellor of the Illuminae."

They're probably the only group in North America that has more money—and power—than my father. And they have direct contact with and the blessing of the akero. "Oh."

"If you did watch television, you'd know that Dad and I don't see eye to eye, but he hasn't ever cut me off. I have plenty of money, and if Dad knew about you, which he certainly won't from me, he'd be wanting to use you himself, not hand you over to someone else."

I swallow. "Okay."

"Your next question is, what in the world am I doing working with Clark at Spellcraft, right?"

I can't even argue. He's right. "And also, why disguise who you are?"

He reaches underneath his shirt and fishes out a badge. He brandishes at me. "I do work there, as Lincoln Star. Look right here."

His badge really does say Lincoln Star, underneath a very official logo and the words 'Spellcraft R&D Team Member.'

"It's so cliche. I've told Dad that a hundred times. Making his successor start at the bottom and work his way up?" He rolls his eyes. "I mean, I hide who I am, because otherwise it won't work at all. Everyone would defer to me and I'd learn nothing new."

"Looks like you're learning a lot, delivering human pharma," I say.

He rolls his eyes. "We only deliver to a half dozen places, because they run all our experimental protocols. It's easier to just bring everything they need at once."

"Experimental? Clark didn't tell me he got me a job at a guinea pig store."

Lionel laughs. "Well, that's what this is. I mean, it's a regular pharmacy, but it also handles all the clinical trial participants for the new spells we work up."

"Well, if you're really not going to hand me over to my parents, I better get inside and get back to work. It may look like grunt work to you, but I need this job, and in case you couldn't tell earlier, I'm not very good at it."

"When are you off for the day?" He leans against the wall, the spitting image of a spoiled rich boy.

I shake my head. "Not a good idea. Two famous people in hiding going to dinner? If they don't catch me, they could easily spot you, and that would be worse for both of us."

"I disagree," he says. "I've been hiding for years, and I could probably cast even better spells to keep you hidden than Clark does."

"You may be handsome, but you're clearly not too bright," I say. "No means no."

I head for the door back into the main pharmacy.

He grabs my arm just before I push through it. "Hold on, now. Even if you don't want to go to dinner, you shouldn't turn down my offer of help. In addition to being rich, I really am one of the most talented casters in New York."

I shake him off and fold my arms underneath my chest.

"Why would I need you to spell me? Clark's spells are working just fine."

"Having a fall back option's always a good idea. What if Clark gets sick? What if you fight?" He leans a bit closer, a glint in his eyes. "Plus, if I come up with a better disguise, you could work somewhere much better than this. You could start *living* again."

"Clark's already working on—"

"Having me to help him will only benefit you," he says. "Why not let us put our heads together? We could get you free even sooner."

"None of that has anything to do with you taking me to dinner," I say. "So why did you start by asking me out?"

He shrugs. "That's my price." He grins. "If you want my help, you'll have to let me buy you food."

He's charming. He's handsome. He's rich.

Most girls would go nuts.

I'm not like most girls.

And this feels too much like Ragar, forcing my hand. If he had been in the same situation as Lionel here, I could totally see him bargaining with me for something I *need*—in exchange for something he wants. Like dating him, or loving him, or serving him. But that's not noble. It's manipulative, and I walked away from that for a reason.

"I'm not interested," I say. "Domineering men piss me off."

This time, he doesn't stop me on my way back into the pharmacy, and I hope I didn't overplay my hand. Rich guys are unpredictable, and with my charm restrained by Clark's spell, there's no way to be sure he won't get angry and hand me over to Ragar or my parents.

I can't decide which would be worse.

I'm sure that by now, they're both good and royally hacked off. The news reports have shifted and instead of angry threats directed at whomever stole me, they're now focused on an empathetic message indicating their desperation for my safe and happy return.

Mom has clearly realized that I left on my own, and I won't be coming home anytime soon.

They're now trying to convince me that I *want* to come back, and that they aren't mad. I'm not stupid enough to believe any of that is true. Being kidnapped would be my only saving grace at this point. If Dad's positive that I ran away, he'll never forgive me for the embarrassment I put him through. He might even manufacture an enemy just to eradicate them—nothing could be worse than people hearing that his own daughter ran away from him.

I was nervous when I thought Lionel was gone, but when he circles around and enters from the front, a smile on his face, a paper script in his hand, irritation pulses through me. "What are you doing?"

"Getting a prescription filled," he says. "What does it look like?"

I lean closer and hiss. "You can't just magic up a prescription."

He leans in as well, his eyes sparkling again. "I can't? Because I just did."

"Go away." I cross my arms.

"I'm not domineering," he says, "I promise. It's just that you need more encouragement than a normal girl would, thanks to your situation."

He has the overconfidence that's common with most rich men. "Listen," I say. "I appreciate your offer of help, I really do. I also appreciate that you're not going to claim the bounty, but I still don't want to go out with anyone right now. Am I being clear?"

He rocks back on his heels. "I just met the most beautiful woman alive, the most alluring, and also as it turns out, the most interesting. But no matter how many times I ask you out or offer to help, you turn me down."

"Do you think I'll go out with you just because you complimented me?" I ask.

"You're ugly, fat, and boring." The corner of his mouth twitches.

I cock one hip and drop my hand on it. "Insults won't help you, either."

"Fine," he says. "Message received. But I have a feeling this won't be the last time we meet, and I never give up without a fight."

Reminding me more and more of Ragar every minute.

"Not, like an actual fight," he says. "Though—not to brag—I haven't ever been bested in a duel."

"Rosanne," my boss shouts. "Car line is piling up."

"I've got to go," I say.

"See you around." Lionel winks as I walk away from him.

Part of me, a very small part, is a little disappointed now that he finally listened. Ironically, I kind of like him for doing what I asked, but now that I've shut him down, I really doubt I'll see him again.

What's wrong with my brain?

I manage to survive the last hour of work, and then I'm finally ready to go home. I don't like my job, and I don't particularly like being sore and achy and dirty at the end of the day, but I do like the feeling I have after doing something instead of sitting around.

Today's my first payday, and I discover that I absolutely love the feeling of someone giving me money for the work I've done, until I look in the envelope and realize it's even less money than I got for donating blood. Ugh. How is hard work so undervalued?

I'm just walking out the door when my phone rings. "Hello?"

"Roxana? You're off work, right?" Minerva sounds

strung out. Like the time Holcott turned her down for the homecoming dance.

"I'm headed home." I think about telling her I met a mage, but I figure she probably doesn't need anything else to worry about right now. Clark will spread the news soon enough, I imagine.

"Thank Gabe. My mom's coming over soon, and Clark's headed over, but it's my *mom*. I need more of a buffer."

"What's going on?" I ask. "Why's she coming over?" Minerva doesn't *hate* her mother, but she would never invite her to visit. She turns into a twirling mess whenever her mother calls. I can only imagine an in-person visit will send her over the edge.

"I invited her."

"Why would you do that?" I really can't think of a single reason.

"It's been a long day," Minerva says. "But. . .I have to ask her something. Something big." She pauses.

I think about how I might pry the information loose.

Before I can say anything at all, she blurts out, "I really need you there. Having other people around when I ask her is the only way I can be sure of whether she's telling the truth."

"The truth about what?" I still have no idea why she's so panicked.

"I don't know anything right now, but if my hunch is right, it could change everything."

18

BEVIN

Mark Twain said, "Everyone is a moon and has a dark side which he doesn't show to anyone."

Or something like that.

It's not like I'm an English teacher who memorizes dumb stuff normally, but that moon comparison stuck with me even after I dropped out of school and ended up living in an alley. I wish I didn't have a dark side. I wish I was all light and summer skies.

I wish I wasn't demon-spawn.

But I am, and my dark side threatens to consume me every single day. My dark side is held at bay by only a tiny sliver of goodness.

Some demon-spawn, like my twin sister Soki, crave that darkness from the moment they're born. She never turned toward the light. She never decried the evil cravings that tempted her—no, she embraced them. I can barely stand to spend any time with her, and it's not because I'm so disgusted by the choices she's made.

It's because they *call* to me.

Even thinking about Soki makes me burn for what she has. The last I heard, my twin had descended four levels.

She's actively planning to descend the other four, so that she can Descend and bring about the prophesied war to end all wars. Most of the demon-spawn I've met want to be the one who cracks the world in half. They look forward to hastening the war that will eventually destroy everything.

"Bevin?" Xander waves at me. The way he's looking at me convinces me it's not his first time saying my name. "You alright?"

I wave him off. "Fine, fine. Just contemplating the end of the world as we know it, and how likely I am to be the one who causes it. You know, typical weekend stuff."

"Okay." He glances sideways at Izaak, who looks just as shell-shocked.

"Looks like your adjustment to the descent is going well," Izaak says.

"How about you?" I ask. "Made any humans scream in horror and run away today?"

He scowls. "I haven't done that in weeks."

We're a pathetic bunch. "Why can't you just assassinate people like your mother always wanted?" I ask.

"Says the demon-spawn vegetarian who's the treasurer of a recycling club." Xander smirks. "And apparently, who is also. . .just coming from the laundromat?" He leans toward me, plucks a sock from the side of my skirt, and tosses it onto my lap.

"That happens a lot, now. Stupid static cling."

"Could there be a worse power?" Xander asks.

"Not that I can think of." I sigh and sink deeper into the tired couch. "Thought much more about handing the dragon in to get a place in the pack?"

Xander looks around like I just made a sexist joke and he expects us to be attacked. "Lower your voice, geez." He frowns. "And stop whipping your tail around."

I hate my stupid tail. "This thing's worse than the static shock. I can't wear pants, for one, and for a second, I can't sit in most normal chairs." I groan. "And when I get upset, or happy, or, well, anything, it gets all agitated."

Izaak eyes my tail appreciatively. "You don't say."

"Stop." I kick him.

"Ow," he says. "What was that for?"

"You know what it was for," I say. "You dirty pervert."

"I'm not the one with the twitching tail." He wiggles his eyebrows.

"Is the waiter ever coming?" I wave my arm around like a lunatic.

"Hey," Xander says. "This is the first time you've ever needed gloffee, right?"

"Did I mention how much I hate this tail?" I sigh. "It's expensive to buy this stuff, and gloffee tastes disgusting, and now I have to drink it every single day, or humans will notice that I have a red demon tail."

"Are you mad at her?" Izaak asks.

"Roxana?" I ask.

"No, Mother Teresa," Xander says. "Yes, Roxana. The one who caused you to lie, and consequently, to descend."

I shake my head. "She didn't force me to lie. She's the victim. It's not fair to get angry at her for a choice I made."

"But if you were mad," Izaak says, "Xander would be helping you by handing her over."

Xander rolls his eyes. "Shut up about it. I already decided."

The waiter finally shows. He's new, and he's the twitchiest werewolf I've ever seen. He bats at something near his face, like he's standing in a cloud of gnats, although it's nothing I can see. "What do you want?" He glances from Xander to Izaak and back to me quickly. He blinks twice. Then he looks around at the guys again.

"You really don't like gloffee?" Izaak asks, politely trying to ignore our waiter's tics. "You must not have tried the right kind yet."

"I've tried the gloffiato and the glaffucino."

"What about a glatté, a gloffee au lait, or a glespresso?" Xander asks.

"We'll try a glatté, a gloffee au lait, and a glespresso," Izaak says. "One of each, in werewolf, vampire, and dragona."

"Dragona?" Xander raises one eyebrow. "Who's paying for this?"

"You are, of course," Izaak says. "You were just saying last night that you never got Bevin anything for her birthday last month."

"You didn't get her anything either," Xander says.

"Not true," Izaak says.

"Giving her a cup full of good intentions does not count," Xander says.

"It does," I say. "And he did give me that."

"I'll get you a cup of water, too," Xander says. "If that's really—"

"It wasn't a cup of water." Izaak frowns. "It was clearly—"

"So do you really want all those gloffees?" The werewolf waiter sniffs the air like he smells something terrible. Then he swipes at his nose. "Or not?" His right eye blinks repeatedly. I wonder whether it's hard for Xander to watch, a wolf who's clearly on his way to being a fray—a wolf without a pack who's going insane from the isolation.

Xander sighs and waves him off. "Yes, yes, bring them over. We'll drink whatever she doesn't like."

"And you'll be up all night," I say. But I wonder whether he'll be up all night anyway, worrying about the future that looms ahead of him if he can't find a pack.

"I'm already up all night." Izaak winks. "Vampire, remember?"

"So, tell me about your new play," Xander says. "You

were really excited when you told me a few days ago, but I've barely seen you since then."

"It starts next week. They agreed to hold rehearsal from four in the afternoon until ten at night, which is a real coup for me."

"Because you might not sleep through all of it?" I ask. "Like the last one?"

Izaak's grin is sheepish, which is a strange look on a vampire. "Exactly."

"I guess drinking that pot of super shot gloffee didn't really help?" Xander asks.

"For a few hours," Izaak says. "But after that?" He shrugs.

"And what's your role?" I ask.

"You are looking at Claudio," Izaak says.

"Who the heck is Claudio?" Xander asks. "Is this a Latin play?"

Izaak frowns. "No, Claudio's the king. He marries the queen, Ger. . .Ger something."

"Ger*trude?*" Xander asks.

"What am I missing?" I ask.

"Is the play you're doing called *Hamlet*, by chance?" Xander asks.

"Yes!" Izaak's whole face lights up. "How did you know that?"

"It's probably the most famous play of all time," I say. "Even I've heard of it, and I dropped out of school at the age of eleven."

"To live in a van, down by the river," Xander says. "We all know."

"Not a van," I say. "Although that sounds nice, compared to—"

"Nope," Xander says. "No time for an encore of that one. I'm too busy taking this beautiful moment in." He turns back toward Izaak. "You're doing *Shakespeare?*"

"No, that hot director's definitely not called Shakespeare."

"Oh. My. Gabe," Xander says. "But you said you weren't doing villains anymore."

"Did you hear me?" Izaak asks. "I'm the *king*."

"Yeah, the king who killed the original king and married the mourning wife," Xander says. "Hamlet's the hero, and you are most definitely the villain if you're Clau*dius*. You should probably try and remember that there's no Clau*dio*."

"Claude, Claudius, Clyde, whatever." Izaak blinks. "I need to call my agent."

Xander sighs.

Luckily, the waiter shows up with our tray of a million gloffees, or his brain might have exploded. I've learned with Izaak to just smile and nod. He works stuff out himself, given enough time. His strength has never been in complicated method acting. He's relaxed, and manly, and chill, and that's more than enough for most things.

I do agree with Xander on this one. Shakespeare and Izaak? Doomed to be a disaster.

After a lot of blowing, and adding of sugar packets, and sipping, and hemming, and hawing, I determine that the best of all my drink options is the dragona gloffee au lait, which is, coincidentally, very nearly the most expensive drink on the menu.

Of course I like the thing that costs more than everything else. Ugh.

"You're not in love with the vampire ones?" Xander can barely control his smirk. "Could that have anything to do with your familiarity with the donor?" He coughs.

"Hey, I happen to know that this is made with some grade A vampire-fed glaffour berries." Izaak frowns. "They should put my face on there. It would probably sell way more gloffee. I'll mention it to Gavin."

"I better head back to the shop," I say. "I have a seance

in. . ." I glance at my watch. "Three minutes?" I leap to my feet. "Gotta run."

Luckily, my shop's only forty feet away. I toss some bills on the coffee table and sprint for the exit, nearly knocking Clark over. "Sorry, sorry."

"Whoa, there. Where's the finish line?"

I don't have time for his lame jokes today. I force a smile. "Yeah, I was going pretty fast. Well, see you later."

Turns out, I could've been a lot more polite to Clark, because my client's more than forty minutes late. And when she shows up, it's not a real client at all. It's my twin sister, who actually looks nothing like me. No one ever seems to realize that not all twins are identical. They're always shocked that we look completely different.

I try slamming the door closed on Soki, but she lifts one hand, flames dancing across her fingers, and I cave.

"Oh, just come in," I say.

She flicks her right hand and the door flings open—that's new. She pushes past me with a crooked smile on her face. Her skin's olive, and her hair falls in a shiny waterfall of ebony down her back, interrupted only by the tiny blood-red horns poking up from either side of her head.

Once you get past the differences, you can see that our face and body shapes are similar, and her eyes are almost the same color as mine, too. They're an icy blue to my deep sea azure, but unlike mine, hers practically glow with pure evil.

"What do you want?" I ask.

"I heard a rumor." Soki tilts her head and scans me, head to toe. "And it seems like it's true." Her eyes stop when they reach the tip of my red tail. "This is a sight I've been longing to see for a very long time."

"Shut up," I say.

"What sin was it?" Her mouth dangles open, her eyes searching my face.

I put one hand on my hip. "You weren't invited in, and I want you to leave."

"Your self-righteous little wards won't work anymore," she says, "not now that you've descended." Her smirk is infuriating.

"But I can still call the police," I say. "Or do you think they'll find that you've registered each of your descensions like a good little demon-spawn?"

She knocks a lamp to the floor, not even batting an eye when it shatters.

"Hey," I say. "That was spelled to provide calming energy to an entire room."

Her hand whips toward a vase that keeps flowers fresh for weeks on end.

"What do you want?" I ask. "Because I want you to leave, and I'd prefer my shop was not shattered and destroyed when you do."

Her hand freezes in mid air. "I want to know what your new power is, and I want to know what you did to get it."

"It's none of your business," I say.

And she smashes the vase against the wall, damaging the drywall with the same violent act.

I grit my teeth. "I had a buyer for that."

"That's so distressing to me." Her voice is completely flat. "I wonder about this ugly statue." Her hand shifts again, her index and middle fingers prepared to wreak even more telekinetic havoc. Her new power sucks.

"I can zap people," I say. "Want me to show you?"

Her hand drops to her side. "Zap people?"

"It feels like static electricity, mostly," I say. "Only it can be a little stronger when I'm upset."

"Good girl," she says.

I want to slap her. Or zap her. I bet it would really hurt in this moment.

"Now just confirm how you got it, and I'll be on my way."

"I lied," I say.

She rolls her eyes. "Please. That's not a major sin, or I'd have descended when I was four."

I hate her for making me admit this aloud. "I lied. . .to my best friend."

Soki beams from ear to ear. "That's very interesting."

"Why's that so interesting?" I ask.

She taps her lip. "Ah, Rahab."

"What?"

"Rahab must be very pleased right now, that you've stepped back from your friends." Her lip curls just a bit farther, because we've both always suspected he was our father.

Shame rolls through me—my sister knows, now. I couldn't even be honest with my closest friends, with my best mates. Bonds of family and friendship are all that keep demon-spawn *human,* that keep us caring what we do and say and how we act. If I'm willing to tax those connections, what meaningful bonds are left? It was my separation from them that caused this. I should have known. I'm actually grateful to Soki for sharing that insight with me.

Not that she'd thank me for hearing it.

I wonder if that was her first descent. Did she also lie to someone who mattered to her? Is that what gave her the flame power? The only thing that stops me from asking her is my absolute confidence that she'll never tell me the truth. She'd lie just to spite me, and then she'd revel in it.

My sister's finally heading for the door.

I breathe a sigh of relief.

Of course, before actually exiting, she turns and looks over her shoulder. "So what's your plan?"

"My what?"

She huffs. "You've descended, which you never wanted

to do, but now that it's happened, how are you going to descend again?" When I don't answer, she scowls. "It's harder than it looks. Trust me."

"I will not be descending again." As I say the words, a part of me is sad. It's nice having a power, and I'm even getting used to the tail. It's helpful being able to snag things that are out of reach and skirts are growing on me.

But I am who I am, and I won't let my personality, my soul, be subsumed by darkness, no matter how tempting that thought may be. I shove thoughts of power and safety and strength away.

"I mean it," I say. "I won't make a mistake like that again."

"Oh, please," she says. "It's not that simple. The more you use your power, the more power you'll want to use. And the more you want to use it, the more creative your rationalization will become. The only path for us is to descend." She shrugs. "You're one of us now, finally."

I don't accept her premise, that once you've made a mistake, you're doomed. But I'm happy to know that using my power will make things harder. "Thanks for the tip."

"When you come to your senses, call me."

"Oh, I don't mean about that. I meant, thanks for warning me against using my powers."

Soki's hands clench into fists, and her eyes flash almost white. "I didn't mean—you are so annoying."

"Again, thanks."

"You denied who you were for a long time, but *we're demon-spawn*. We can live for millennia. It's never going to work for you to ignore your innate self."

"I disagree," I say. "My innate self is half human, and humans have struggled to do what's right for thousands of years."

"Struggled and failed." She crosses her arms. "By the

way, why did you lie to your precious little mates? The ones you love more than your own sister?"

I don't want to talk about Roxana—even mentioning her would put her in grave danger. Although I usually avoid lying in general, lies are a better option with my sister. "Minerva has a boyfriend," I say. "And he's kind of a drag, and because of his stupid actions, we're all stuck lying. I told her I didn't mind doing it, but clearly I did."

"I'll give you one more piece of advice, although I'm sure you'll ignore it." She leans closer, her beautiful face as earnest as I've ever seen it. "If you really don't want to descend, and I'm saying this strictly as your sister, not as one demon-spawn to another, stay away from that guy. Stay away from anything that causes misery, or confuses you, or upsets you. Being around someone like that will lead you right down where you don't want to go."

She heads for the exit, stopping in the doorway.

"Of course, I hope you ignore that bit of advice, because speaking from experience, you should join us." Her smile darkens her entire face. "The water's warm."

19

XANDER

I'm not a very athletic guy, especially for a werewolf. Once though, when I was a kid, I got first place in the obstacle course on field day. I was so proud of winning that my cheeks hurt from beaming.

Only, then someone noticed that I had cut off one corner of the race, skipping the monkey bars. It wasn't like I did it on purpose, and it wasn't like I ever expected to win, but after winning, it hurt really bad to have them take that blue ribbon away.

This is kind of like that.

I'd kind of reconciled myself to never having a real pack, to always being on the fringe, but when I heard I could join the Manhattan pack. . .and then I decided not to turn Roxana over? It's like that blue ribbon, only way, way worse. I've been aching inside ever since I made up my mind, and not in a good way.

"Feel like being a wingman?" I ask.

Izaak smiles. He's always up for going with me when I hit a bar. I don't have to ask him twice. Vampires can't get drunk unless they feed on someone who's also drunk or high, and I've never seen Izaak do that, so it's not about the buzz. No, for him, it's about watching the normies and mimicking what they do. It's about studying their mannerisms, their thoughts and feelings while they're uninhibited. It's about increasing his odds of being a successful actor.

He's a weird dude.

But he's a pretty decent wingman, with his inhuman speed and strength, and his complete sobriety. Even if I pick a fight, even if I act like an idiot, he always gets me home safe and in one piece.

"You're a what?" the gorgeous blonde next to me asks.

"Look." Am I slurring my words? I think I might be slurring. "Most of the things that normies believe about werewolves are ridiculous. For instance, silver bullets will kill us, but only because any bullet would kill us. I mean, we do heal fast, but pump us full of enough shots, and we'll still die. I think a werewolf made that up—I mean, at least if they use silver bullets, when they pull them out of our corpses, it'll cover the funeral costs, you know?"

"The corpses?" The blonde blinks, her voice a little shrill. "Why would someone shoot you?"

"You mean, other than, like, the obvious?" I lean a little closer. "Because we can shift into a wolf?"

She laughs. "Does this whole gag work for you very often?"

"No." I shake my head. "No, it does not."

She giggles. "Tell me more. What else do we humans think about you werewolves that's absurd?"

"Well, we don't *have* to shift on a full moon. Or, like, any time, really."

"You don't?"

I shake my head and the room spins.

"What about shifting? Can you show me?"

I scoff. "It hurts to shift, you know. I don't just *do* it. It's not a parlor trick."

"Excuse me for wanting some proof." She stands up and

grabs her purse. "This feels weirder and weirder the more you talk about it. I can't tell if you're being funny or if you're actually nuts."

"Oh, fine. I mean, it does hurt to shift, but I'm pretty fast now." I'm definitely slurring my words. "And the faster you get, the less it hurts. Like ripping a Band-Aid off."

"Alright, big dog." Izaak wraps a big, strong arm around my shoulders. "I think it's time for us to head home."

The blonde looks from Izaak to me and back again. "Wait, are you *gay*?"

Izaak snorts. "As if he could get someone like me. No. I'm his roommate."

"Oh," she says. "That makes more sense."

"Right?" Izaak cocks his head sideways. "I need to get him home, but maybe you leave me your number."

"Okay." The blonde who was just mocking me giggles.

"Hey." I shove Izaak away. "I'm not ready to go yet."

"I think you are." He grabs my arm and marches me out the front door before I can even mount a defense.

He didn't even wait for the blonde's phone number. "But what about the girl? She wanted to give me her number." I think she did. I'm pretty sure.

"Wrong again. She wanted to give *me* her number."

I whip out my phone. "There's someone I need to call. Definitely someone I should call."

Izaak yanks the phone out of my hand. "Nope. I knew that was why you wanted to go for a drink, and it's also why I said yes to going with you."

"Why?" I frown. He's not making any sense.

"You came here specifically to get drunk, so that if you called your boss and handed Roxana over, it wouldn't be on you. You could claim you were drunk and you didn't mean to do it."

That sounds cowardly.

He's probably right. "It's not a terrible idea." I fumble around for my phone again.

"I have your phone, idiot." Izaak shakes his head. "I took it away already, remember?"

"I do not, in fact, remember that."

Izaak grabs my arm and drags me to a bench. He shoves me down onto it.

I shiver—is it cold?

"You didn't even bring a jacket." Izaak sounds disgusted.

"You could give me yours."

He's wearing a nice, black leather coat. It looks warm. "I'm not about to put myself out for your stupidity."

"Oh, come on."

"No. I won't reward your diabolical."

I try to decipher what he just said. "Have you been reading my word of the day from the calendar in the kitchen?"

"I can't agree or contradunct what you've said." He grins like he's proud.

Normally I have no trouble following Izaak logic, but drunk, I struggle a bit. "Do you mean contradict?"

Izaak frowns.

"Before you use those words, maybe go over the context with me first."

"Shut up," Izaak says.

"Just hand me my phone and we'll call it even."

Izaak slides my phone into his jacket pocket. "Even for what?"

"For all the things we aren't even for!" Why is he being so obnoxious?

"Instead of letting you become a villain, I'm going to tell you a story." He presses one finger to my forehead and shoves me backward until my back is leaning against the bench. "A story I've never told anyone."

Even annoyed and drunk and cold, he's caught my attention. "Never told anyone?"

"That's right. But first, how much do you know about vampire anatomy?"

This feels like it's going somewhere bad. "Are you hungry?" I slide away from him.

His hand's just a blur when he grabs me and yanks me back. "Don't be an idiot. I know that's hard for you right now." He sighs. "Listen, vampires aren't really human—which I'm sure you know. When the akero brought us to Earth, we didn't handle the transition very well. We're quite small, actually, and we ended up having to sort of *climb* into human bodies."

"What?"

"They didn't teach you this at school?" Izaak frowns.

"I'm pretty sure I'd remember that you're wearing a human skin suit if anyone had taught me that."

"No, it's not like that. The difference between a human and a vampire is that the vampire is a smallish creature that inhabits a human host."

I can't prevent the look of horror that comes over my face.

"I should clarify. That was when we first came—millennia ago. Now the vampires who came here have integrated with humans, and they're inseparable. I was born exactly as I am now, but if you cut my body open, you'd find a sort of glossy golden octopus thing that inhabits my brain, instead of the depressing looking grey matter that humans have."

"I'm very, very positive that we never learned this in school."

Izaak scrunches up his nose. "It's possible that I've just told you something I wasn't meant to share. I went to an all vampire school in elementary, so. . ."

"This is a really strange story so far."

"Right. Well, for wolves, you guys can marry a human, but you can't find a human *mate*, right? That bond that you value so highly isn't possible, except with another werewolf."

I nod.

"For us, it's different. Vampires can marry humans and even have children with them. My mom was born a vampire—and my dad's a human. They've been happily married for thirty-one years."

"Congratulations?" I ask.

"It's messier for me—if I were to marry a human, but I won't bore you with that right now. The point of this story is that humans are drawn to vampires. Without using our compulsion charm, we scare them, right up until we drink their blood."

"And then?" In spite of myself, I'm curious. How do I not already know more about my best friend?

Probably because supernaturals aren't encouraged to mingle. There's a reason we learn almost nothing about the other life forms the akero brought. The wizards and witches were placed at the top of the hierarchy—children of the mighty akero—and the rest of us are meant to stay in our lanes.

"When a vampire drinks a human's blood, it makes him or her stronger. You know that, surely."

I nod.

"Drinking a human's blood doesn't need to be a big deal. If a vampire wants, he or she can even erase the experience from the donor's mind. But."

"But what?" I'm not sure if the alcohol is already leaving my system, or if I'm just interested enough that I'm able to focus.

"If it's a human the vampire has had sex with—or even more so, if the blood is consumed during sex—the human will sort of. . .imprint. The vampire will become irresistible to the human."

"That's why you refuse to ever date anyone you've drunk blood from."

"Other way around," he says. "It's why I won't drink blood from anyone I've been with." His cocky smile is always so self-assured. "But yes. That's right."

"But it sounds great. Why not pick someone you really like and—"

"This is the important part." Izaak peers at my face. "I want to make sure you're sober enough to understand it."

"I'm listening," I say.

"Since we met, all you've wanted was to fix your parents' mistake. You want to be part of a pack. You want a position so that you have their support, so that you can have a place to belong, and most importantly, so that one day, instead of meaningless one night stands, you can find a real mate."

I don't even bother agreeing. He knows all that. I've never hidden what I wanted.

"My dad loves my mom. My mom loves my dad." Izaak's eyes are sad. Why are they sad?

"Okay."

"But how would either of them know whether it's *real?*"

"Huh?"

"My dad had no choice. From the moment my mom drank his blood and then talked him into bed, he was hers. He didn't get to pick her. He didn't slowly fall in love. He's as good as a blood slave."

Izaak wouldn't use that word casually. "But you said they're in love."

"That's like saying a dog that's in heat is in love. It didn't choose to be in heat. It just *is* in heat. But we aren't animals." Izaak looks down at his hands, his face cast in shadows from the harsh light of the streetlight over our heads. "You don't want that. I've seen what it has done to my mother."

"I can't have it," I say. "I'm a werewolf."

"You don't want to find a pack the wrong way," Izaak clarifies. "If you do, it'll always feel *wrong*. You can't start your happily ever after by ending someone else's, especially someone you know and care about."

Roxana. That's what he's talking about.

"I don't know her that well," I say again. The alcohol's definitely leaving my system, because that doesn't sound nearly as convincing as it did the last time I thought it.

Izaak shakes his head. "Fine, let's say that's true. But you know your pack, and if you're brought in because you complied with some rule to rat out someone else? That's not the way to join a family. They'll never really welcome you. It'll be a new pack in name only."

I've been so caught up obsessing over the fact that I could earn myself an invite that I didn't think about what the invite would mean. The pack alpha hates me. Lo Ren'll honor his word. He'll let me in, but what would really change when he does? I'll still be the shredder no one wants. I'll still be the member that wasn't born in and didn't even marry into the pack. I'll be a part of it, but not really.

I can't solve my problem this way.

I may never be able to solve my problem at all. My dad saw to that with his epically stupid behavior. And now the stupid sympathy that usually rears its ugly head shows up again.

My dad didn't have any options once she got pregnant.

My mother wasn't really his mate. She was hurting as badly as he was.

None of that changes how their behavior ruined my life, though.

"What do you suggest?" I ask. "Should I just go back home and keep spending every day alone?"

Izaak slings an arm around my shoulder. "Not alone, idiot. With your mates."

"None of you are even wolves. You can't possibly be my mate."

"Mates means friends, too, dummy."

I'd never thought about it that way before, but he's right. Mates also means friends, and I may not have the pack that most wolves need, or the pack I actually want, but I do have a group of friends whom I can rely upon to help me.

And if that pack has grown by one, even if she's a little whiny and a huge liability, I should be happy about that. I shouldn't be contemplating ways to turn her over to her enemies so that I can eliminate my own problems.

"I'm a bad person," I say.

"Good thing you're not a person," Izaak says. "You're a werewolf, and you're pretty decent at it."

I don't even need Izaak's help to walk back to our apartment, so I must have already burned through my pathetic attempt at an excuse for betraying Roxana. I'm headed into the main door of our building when Izaak stops me. "Let's take the stairs."

"Why?" I worry a screw has been knocked loose in his brain.

"You're almost sober," he says. "But a little physical activity will burn off the rest."

"Why were you drinking?" Bevin asks from behind us. She's just locking up her shop. "That's not normal for you—you've got to drink so much, it almost never helps."

"Oh," I say. "Hey Bevin." I kick Izaak. He's got a big mouth.

"You know the pack has offered to let him join—if he surrenders Roxana."

"Where are you going?" I ask. "Don't you live over your shop?"

"I got a call from Minerva," Bevin says. "She's got her mother coming and—"

"She needs backup," I guess.

Bevin nods. "But I can't believe you're thinking of selling Roxana out. Again." She glares.

One flight of stairs into the climb, and I'm already tired. "Why are we taking the stairs again?" I groan.

"It's good for you." But she's huffing, too.

"I guess it keeps my buns tight," Izaak says. "But even so, I should've taken the elevator. I get no complaints."

"Oh," Bevin says at the top of the second flight, finally understanding. "You were going to turn Roxana in while you were drunk."

"Right," Izaak says. "As if that would give him an out."

"That's kind of pathetic," Bevin says.

I jog ahead of them, but they don't let it go.

"But you're not going to do it, right?" Bevin asks. "Because I've got a *tail* thanks to Roxana, and still, I would never hand her in."

"That's my point," I say. "It's almost like I'd be doing the rest of you a favor. I mean, I won't, okay? But she's my ticket to a pack, finally, and it's not like I'm sentencing her to death by handing her in. I'd be calling her *family* and telling them where she is! Imagine how worried they must be."

"The family that wanted to marry her off to that ogre, without her consent." Bevin stops at the top of the third flight of stairs, wheezing. "Wow, we are all in really bad shape."

"Speak for yourselves," Izaak says, but he's breathing heavily, too.

"Just one more flight to go," I say. "At least I don't feel even a tiny bit drunk anymore."

"Which is good," Izaak says. "Minerva's mom hates you enough when you're sober."

"Are you kidding?" I ask. "Mrs. Lucent loves me." We all start up the stairs, slowly but steadily.

"And not a word to her about Roxana," Bevin says. "With Clark's spell from this morning, she won't recognize her, and that's for the best."

"Is it?" Roxana's standing at the top of the stairs, and her mouth is turned down. Her hands are trembling at her sides.

How much did she hear?

"Oh, hey, Roxana," Bevin says.

"I'm sorry you descended for a lie about me." A tear rolls down her cheek. "I'm sorry your pack is in trouble because of me." Her eyes drop to her feet. "I'm sorry that I'm ruining everyone else's lives because I'm a selfish coward."

"No," Bevin says. "That's not—"

"It's alright," Roxana says. "I'd rather know the truth." She points. "I'm going to go in there right now, and stand beside Minerva. Her mom's here, and she's stressed out. But in the morning, Xander, you can turn me in. That should make it better, right?"

"That's not what we want," Izaak says.

"It's what they want," Roxana says.

"It's not," Bevin says.

"No," I say. "Not for me, either."

"I've never had much say in my life," Roxana says. "But the last thing I ever want to do is make the lives of my friends worse. You're right. It's my family, and it's my mess, and none of you should suffer for it."

Before we can argue any more, she spins around and races down the hall. She's small, but she's fast. By the time we reach the top of the stairs, she's already ducking inside Minerva's apartment door.

"Well, that went well," Bevin says. "Who had the stupid idea to take the stairs?"

I point at Izaak.

She kicks him.

And then she kicks me, too.

"What was that for?"

"You're the moron who got drunk and made that idiot push us toward the stairs."

I can't argue with her logic.

"Now, let's try and salvage this night if at all possible." She marches toward Minerva's apartment, her shoulders square and her head held high.

Izaak and I slink in behind her. I can't speak for my vampire bestie, but I'm just hoping not to screw up anything else. If I could manage that, it would be a small miracle.

20

MINERVA

Nothing with my mother is ever easy.

"Aren't we talking right now?"

"Yes, Mom, we are, but what I mean is—"

"I heard from your brother that you applied to be a guardian. Again."

I suppress my groan.

"And that you still weren't chosen. *Again*."

"The reason—"

"Just because your father did something doesn't mean that it's the right thing for you to do. You have to be realistic about your expectations or you'll live your life in a state of constant disappointment, dear."

Mom's always been a firm believer that adding the word 'dear' to something makes everything you say constructive.

You are an utter failure at baking, dear.

Your hands are far too manly to be able to wear a ring that dainty, dear.

Oh dear, some people can get away with short haircuts. You just aren't one of them.

"If you never try anything, you never succeed," I say. "I'm going to keep applying until they pick me."

"Even if that happens by process of elimination." Her bemused voice has always irritated me a particular amount.

"Dad always said—"

"Your father's platitudes are the one thing I don't miss about him. Have I mentioned that?"

I almost hang up.

But I need answers, and since Dad's gone, she's my only hope. "Mom, can you come over for dinner tonight?"

"You know I play bridge every Thursday."

I most certainly did not know that. "What about tomorrow, then?"

"Fridays are—"

"It's important, Mom."

She sighs. "Alright, fine, I'll skip bridge, but make sure Clark's there too. I never see him, and I miss him terribly."

She has a regular lunch the first Tuesday of every month with Clark—a lunch I've never been invited to by her and only know about thanks to my brother asking me to come. I imagine the more likely truth is that she can't bear the thought of wasting an entire night with just me. "I'm sure that Clark will come tonight." He's here most nights, but I don't mention that. I can't deal with her being jealous that I see him often.

"There's no chance you'll be introducing me to a nice young wizard this evening, is there?"

"Uh-oh," I say. "There's a big work problem. I better go. See you soon." I hang up. If she knew I worked nights, that might seem suspicious. But since she has no clue that my partner's a vampire or what my schedule is, I can get away with this kind of thing.

I immediately start planning out a menu. The only thing Mom likes to criticize more than my love life is my clearly deficient—in her estimation—cooking skills.

It's not that I'm bad. I can make most anything that comes prepped in some way. Rice-a-roni. Spaghetti with store-bought sauce. Tacos with the crunchy shells and the taco seasoning packets. Ravioli, if I buy the pre-made kind that you just boil. Anything they have in the frozen section at the store. I even know how to make a few things from a list of ingredients. Most people rave about the pasta salad I make, with olives and fresh tomatoes. At every holiday party, my boss tells me that my asparagus dip is the best he's ever had.

But Mom's a chef.

As in, she's a professional chef who quit working to marry my dad. Actually, saying that she quit working is a stretch. She stopped working in a commercial kitchen and began creating works of art in our home.

I was actually pretty chubby in grade school, because Mom made lavish dinners almost every night. My parents always joked that's why Dad fell in love with her and why he'd never leave her. But it makes her impossible to please when she comes over to eat a meal made by someone else.

She almost never goes out to eat, certainly not in the city. Maybe I could pass off take-out as my own food. It bears thought.

Roxana's on her way out the door as I get home. She waves. "I'm late. Gotta run."

"One second," I say.

She pauses. "Yeah?"

"Please, please, *please* don't ever let Giggles out of her cage. I promise she's not in danger in there."

"But she's a wild pigeon, right?" She frowns. "Why does she need to be in a cage?" She glances at Giggles where she's perched on my shoulder and drops her voice to a whisper, as if the bird can actually understand us.

"You still want her to D-I-E, right?"

I cast my eyes heavenward. "I mean, yes, that would be great for me, and surely pigeons can't live *that* long, but I can't be culpable in any way."

"Yeah, I remembered that," she says.

"But she doesn't die when you let her out," I say. "She just follows me to work and embarrasses me horribly."

Roxana blinks, her enormous, cartoon-character eyes practically shining. "Wait, do you think that I let her out last night?" She looks pointedly at where Giggles is sitting on my shoulder.

"I'm not suggesting it," I say. "I'm asking that you never do it again."

Even when she frowns, she's stunningly beautiful. "I haven't ever let her out of her cage. Not one single time."

"I can't imagine anyone else would have done it," I say. "And someone definitely let her out last night."

"Look, I'm not trying to pick a fight. I've done a lot of things wrong," she says. "But I haven't ever opened her cage, I swear."

She must be lying. There's no way Clark would have freed Giggles—he knows I've been trying to keep her existence a secret at work. Xander gets it on a molecular level —he's not exactly welcomed at his job either. Izaak's afraid of all birds, so...Bevin?

I'll have to talk to her later.

"Alright, well, thanks for agreeing never to do it." It's hard, but I don't say 'again.'

She shrugs. "Of course. Alright, gotta run."

After she's gone, I realize I never told her about the dinner with my mom. I'll have to call her later and make sure she's there. With my mom, the key's having a lot of other warm bodies to distract her from fixating on me.

Plus, my mom lies to me all the time, but when other people are there, people like Xander and Clark especially, who listen and pounce on every wrong word, she can't do it as easily.

And I need her to tell the truth. I have to know.

I bake a frozen lasagna, but it looks too dry. I can hear

what she'll say about that already. I throw it away. I make a pan of enchiladas, but I'm not sure why I even bother. They're total mush. I think about stir-fried rice, but I can hear her already. *Fried rice? That's. . .simple.* I set the pan of enchiladas on the patio and let Giggles eat her fill. As if she has some kind of pigeon broadcasting system, minutes later there are a dozen pigeons out there, helping her clean it all up.

Of course, then I'm stuck cleaning their poop off the patio.

"Giggles! Stop inviting all your friends. You poop enough as it is."

She just coos at me.

I should give up and order pizza, but I've never been good at admitting defeat. That's my dad in me—he never could do it either.

Mario Leehack.

I hate that name—it feels like an unwelcome intrusion in my life. He's not my father. It's a name I've never heard before. What kind of a last name is *Leehack*, anyway? A quick web search turns up NO ONE named Leehack. So, maybe it's a transcription error or something. Or a joke? I mean, my mom and I may not always have gotten along perfectly, but Dad was like my twin. He laughed the same way I did. He talked like I did. He wanted the same things I wanted, and he fought against the demon-spawn who tried to destroy the safety of our world.

Just like I've always wanted to do.

My dad was always my hero, so how could he not be my real dad?

I've never questioned whether my parents were my biological parents. After all, what kind of mother would be so critical and picky and irritating to an *adoptive* child? Plus, I look just like my dad. Everyone always said so.

But the name Mario Leehack is right there on my file,

listed right after the word, Father. That nonsensical, not-even-a-bit-familiar, weird name is printed in the place that should say Holden Lucent.

I want my mom to tell me it's a mistake. I want her to look me in the eye and laugh her rude, high-pitched laugh and tell me that there's been an error at the department and that *of course* my father is my father. Holden Lucent, former Chief of the Paranormal Affairs Department, former guardian extraordinaire, decorated veteran of the Werewolf-Vampire wars, is one hundred percent my biological dad.

Once the patio's clean, I admit defeat. Even though today's my day off, even though Mom won't be here for hours yet, it's clear I'm not going to make something that would have any chance of impressing her.

It's time to come up with a plan B. Chinese food is out. She'd never believe I could make it. She made pastries and specialized in French food, so I'll avoid all of that. American basics were Dad's favorite, so Mom learned them well enough that those are out as well.

But Mexican food?

That she might buy. I can certainly slice and dice tomatoes and cilantro and onions. I mean, I won't, but I *could*. I call in a take-out order and as a finishing touch, I slice the end of my finger and cover it with a Band-Aid. A less insane person might just put a Band-Aid on her finger, but clearly they don't know my mom.

Or my luck.

I'm sure to get it wet, and my mom would notice if I happened to have a Band-Aid on for no reason.

And now I think about what I've just done.

I sliced my finger open to perpetuate a lie I'm planning on telling my mother. How do I really expect to get the truth from her about my file? Clearly our relationship doesn't exist on anything close to the truth.

None of that stops me from picking up the Mexican food and then disposing of the takeout boxes before Mom arrives. I fluff the pillows. I sweep the floor. I wipe all the counters down. Luckily, thanks to all my failed attempts at cooking earlier, my dishwasher's believably full of dirty dishes. I'm as ready as I'll ever be.

Giggles is cooing on my shoulder, and I'm frantically calling everyone to tell them to come over ASAP when there's a knock at the door.

How can Mom be the first one here?

I'm almost to the door when I realize I haven't locked Giggles in her cage. I swear under my breath and spin on the ball of my foot.

"I can hear you," Mom says.

"One second," I say. "I forgot, erm, to put on my shirt."

"You walk around your apartment naked? What on earth—" She's opening the door.

I fling my hand at it and shout, "*Claudere.*" The door slams, alright. Mom's going to be ticked, but I'd rather make her mad than let her know I've bonded a pigeon. With a flick of my wrist, I flip the deadbolt. "I'll be back in one minute."

Giggles glares at me when I lock her up, but I don't even have time to feel guilty. This matters too much.

"You'll just have to try and understand," I mutter. "My mom's the devil, and if I let her meet you, well. Let's just say she won't see the cute things about you. You'll be another failure in a long line of them."

As if she understands me, Giggles fluffs up and then settles down on one of the rods in her cage. She's burbling when I walk back out.

My mom is much more upset than my familiar about being locked away. Her entire face is red, and she's fuming. "You slammed the door in my face, and then you locked me out." She stares pointedly at my chest. "Are you operating under the mistaken delusion that I've never seen what you have under there? Because I have. And the next time you insist on frolicking naked in your apartment, you can answer the door and then pull a shirt on instead of leaving me out here like a door-to-door saleswoman." She's tapping her foot, her nostrils flared.

"I'm sorry, Mom," I say. "I'll be sure to remember that for next time."

She sniffs the air. "Is that. . .Mexican food that I smell?"

I nod.

"I hope they didn't use too much cilantro. I hate when they chop up too much."

"They?"

She blinks. "I'm assuming you got take-out." She breezes into the kitchen and spins in a circle, looking at the pans of enchiladas, the bowls with queso and guacamole, and the pile of slow-cooked pork carnitas. Then she turns to face me. "You weren't really going to try and pass this off as though you made it, right?" Her eyes are sparkling. Her hand drops to her hip. "I've seen you try and make Mexican. You remember that, right?"

And now I look even more ridiculous than if I'd just left the food in the take-out boxes. "No, Mom, I wasn't trying to pretend I made it. I just thought it would look nicer if I put it into bowls and dishes of my own."

"So if I open your trash can, I'll find the to-go packaging?" She walks toward the trash can. She's incapable of letting anything go, ever. "You wouldn't have rushed out to stuff the evidence down the garbage chute since you weren't trying to fool me, right?"

Seconds before she would have opened the trash can, the door pops open. "Minerva," Roxana says. "I am *starving*. Please tell me I'm not too late for your famous—" She sniffs the air. "Enchiladas?"

"She knows I ordered take-out." My voice is even flatter

than I feel right now—squashed about as small as I can go. I should have suspected I was adopted all along. Could it possibly be any more obvious that Mom doesn't even like me?

"The others are right behind me," Roxana says.

"And who's this absolutely breathtaking creature?" Mom asks.

"This is my new roommate." I can't introduce her as Roxana, because Mom will immediately recognize who she is and knowing my mother, probably turn her in.

"I'm Roxana Goldenscales," my friend says. "Your kind, brave, caring daughter has been helping hide me from an overbearing father and an unbearable fiancé." Roxana leans against the counter. "She may try to pass off take-out as her own cooking so that her mother's proud of her, but she's also brave and self-sacrificing."

Mom's eyes widen and her mouth dangles open satisfyingly. I wish I had the guts to snap a photo.

"I'm sure that's no surprise to you," Roxana says. "Seeing as she's a police officer in this dangerous city."

"A paranormal affairs officer." Mom's categorically incapable of letting anything slip past.

"I'm not sure whether you know this, but we were good friends in school, and even though we went our separate ways, I always admired Minerva for being such a trailblazer, and for always doing her own thing. So of course, after I decided not to get married, I thought of her right away."

"She knew I was in New York," I say. "And I wasn't invited to the wedding, so I was likely to be at home."

"I'm not sure what to say," my mom says.

That's a first.

"How about hello?" I suggest.

"Well, of course. Hello."

"You raised an amazing child," Roxana says.

The door opens and the rest of my magical misfit

friends stumble through. "Hey, Mrs. Lucent," Xander says. "Always a pleasure."

"Enchiladas?" Izaak's grinning broadly, and I'm suddenly worried I didn't order enough.

"Did you get any without meat?" Bevin asks. I still can't believe she's vegetarian—always has been. She's always thought that killing animals in order to consume them might put her on the naughty list.

"I did order one pan of cheese." I point.

"Great." She's the first to grab a plate, but the boys aren't far behind her.

"Where's Clark?" Mom asks.

She's always looking for her golden boy. "He's coming," I say. "But he may be late. He had an interview on campus."

"I can hardly believe that he's going to be a professor at the New York Institute of Magic." Mom's voice is soft and wistful.

"Yes, he's as wonderful as ever," I say.

"He's been casting a spell on me every morning," Roxana says.

"Oh?" Mom's eyes widen. "So are the two of you dating?"

Roxana blinks. "What?"

"You're under his spell?" Mom's smiling now.

Roxana coughs. "Uh, no. I meant that he's been casting an actual spell, so that no one will know who I am."

"Which won't really work, dear, if you go around blurting out your identity to everyone." Mom always recovers quickly.

Roxana does, too. "You're not just anyone, Mrs. Lucent. You're my dear friend Minerva's mother. Of course I can't keep you in the dark."

Izaak and Xander are pulling out chairs.

"It's such a beautiful day," Mom says. "Why don't we eat outside?"

I can't even argue with her. The sun's shining, and the weather's relatively warm for a New York Fall. "Sure." I toss my head at the chairs. "Can you guys carry a few out so we have enough?"

We've barely been outside for two minutes when a pigeon lands on the railing and coos.

My heart stops in my chest for a moment, until I realize it's not Giggles. Thank Gabriel for that. I toss it a piece of a tortilla chip.

"What a cute little guy." Izaak chucks a hunk of enchilada to it.

"Ew, gross," Xander says.

"What?" Izaak straightens his shoulders. "I love pigeons. I don't care what you say about them. They're cute, and they're soft, and they're smarter than people give them credit for."

"Easy, Erin Brockovich," Xander says. "I was saying you shouldn't toss it *chicken*. Isn't that a little like feeding someone their cousin?"

But it's too late. The big piece of chicken enchilada's already gone.

We all stare at the pigeon for a moment to see if he reacts, but he simply tilts his head.

"You really shouldn't let them come on your patio," Mom says. "Feeding them's a bad idea."

"I know," I say.

"They're dirty creatures," she continues. "They're the flying rats of New York. I read an article that said that pigeons can carry fungal *and* bacterial diseases."

"Yes, thank you for the warning." I will not shout at her. "We'll do our best to keep the terrible threat of pigeons away from our very important and otherwise quite secure back patio."

"You may joke around," she says. "But wait until you catch botulism from one of them."

"Botulism?" Xander asks.

"It's rare," Mom says, "but potentially fatal."

"You don't say, honey," Xander says. "Or do you prefer canned goods?"

"What's he saying?" Mom stands up and begins to shoo the pigeon away.

As if that stupid pigeon is also bonded to someone, it flies away, only to circle back around. Because pigeons are almost as dedicated to anywhere they can find food as my familiar is to me.

That's a depressing thought.

"Coo." Another pigeon coos from behind me. Only, this one actually *is* Giggles. She flies over in an attempt to land on my shoulder and I wave her off, much as my mom just shooed the other one.

I glare at Roxana.

She shakes her head.

But when I think about it, I realize that it couldn't have been her. I watched her walk inside—and Bevin too. No one left and went to my room. None of them *could* have let her out.

How in the world is she escaping?

Clark pushes through the back porch door, and I have my answer. Though why he'd go into my room to release her is beyond me. Is he trying to make this day harder?

"Clark!" Mom crosses the patio to pull him into a huge hug. "I'm just so delighted about your new job."

"Actually—"

"I've told my friends, and they all agree. We'll have to celebrate. Would you prefer a small, intimate party or a large dinner?"

"Mom," he says.

"I'm thinking a dinner. I haven't cooked in a really long time, and I just perfected the most amazing puttanesca—"

"I didn't get the job, Mom."

She freezes. "You didn't. . .what did you say?"

"When I saw the time commitment, I realized that it's not going to work. I can't work the hours they want without risking my current job, and it's only an adjunct position for the time being."

"I could give you money, if it came to that," Mom says. "I'm happy to give you money now. With your scholarship, it's not like your college cost us a dime. It would only be fair for us to help out. Tell me, how much do you need?"

Clark shakes his head. "It just wasn't good timing. There will be other positions," he says. "Trust me."

"Did you get something to eat?" I ask. "There's plenty of food left in the kitchen."

Clark's just ducking back inside when a feeling of complete and utter joy suffuses me. The sun is shining. The sky is blue. Nothing in my life could possibly be better.

"Why are you smiling like an idiot?" Mom asks.

I don't even care if she's mean. I don't care about anything at all. I'm just. . .happy.

"What's going on over there?" Roxana's staring at the edge of the patio.

Where Giggles and the other pigeon are circling one another. . .and biting each other's beaks. And then, oh no. Giggles is huddling down. And the other pigeon!

I race toward them, realizing that the feelings of joy aren't mine. *They're my familiar's. And she's about to. . .I can't even think the words.*

I shoo them both away, but Giggles launches into the air and lands on my shoulder.

"See? What did I tell you?" Mom asks. "They're disgusting creatures, and now that one's sitting on you."

Like the feelings are an explosion in my brain, I just can't take any more. I'm done hiding who I am to try and make her happy, because even with an airbrushed version of me, it's still not good enough. "She's my familiar, Mom," I say. "And her boyfriend, apparently." Which is pretty gross, but also kind of cute.

"It's your. . .it's your *what?*"

"This is Giggles, my familiar."

"You couldn't bond a familiar," Mom says. "You tried and tried."

"Well, apparently I can."

"But why did you bond such a terrible one?" Mom's face couldn't look more horrified if I told her I was going to stop shaving my legs and join a boy band. "No familiar at all is better than that—at least people can think that you just didn't want one."

"I kind of like her," Izaak says. "She's got swag, and she's friendly, and her coo soothes me."

Mom rolls her eyes. "What do you know, *vampire?*"

Giggles fluffs up and warbles at her. She's staring directly at Mom, and she's making the most noise I've ever heard, for all the world like she's telling her off.

My familiar, my disease-carrying rat of the sky, is braver than I am.

I'd better do what I asked her to come for right now, or I might chicken out. "I asked you over here for a reason." I gulp.

Clark's just stepping back out onto the patio. That's good. I want him to hear this, too. I want to see both their faces when I ask the question.

"Was I adopted?"

Mom's mouth dangles open.

Clark drops his plate.

Giggles and her boy toy lose no time at all fluttering down to clean up the mess.

"Was I?" I ask.

"Why would you think you're adopted?" Clark asks. "That's crazy."

"I pulled my own file at work," I say. "And the first

funny thing I noticed is that almost all of it's been redacted. Like, ninety percent of the words in my file are black blocks."

I watch her eyes, but they don't look shocked. They look...guilty.

Which is my cue to plow ahead. "Except for the words that list my father's name. That isn't blocked out, and the name that's listed isn't Holden Lucent."

"What?" Clark shakes his head, and his hands are trembling. He looks like I felt when I read that file. "You must've been looking in the wrong folder, and how would you know, if everything is blacked out?"

"Who's Mario Leehack, Mom?" I'm not even sure whether I said his name right. Or whether he even exists.

Her sigh's long and beleaguered. "Your father was an activist. Did he ever tell you that?"

"Huh?" I glance at Clark, but he looks confused, too.

Mom collapses into a chair and presses her hand to her forehead. "He went to rallies and meetings and all sorts of things. In fact, I met him right after one of those rallies."

"An activist for what?" Clark pulls up a chair next to her, like he's comforting *her*.

"Years later, when I couldn't have a second child, your dad thought it was a sign. He thought that it must be the will of God or something."

"What?" I ask.

"He wanted a daughter, you know, and he thought you would be good for Clark. I wasn't so sure. I thought the whole thing was misguided, but he was so positive."

Misguided? Is my mom saying she didn't want me? "So Mario Leehack really is my father?"

She finally turns and looks at me. "You're asking the wrong question. His name is irrelevant."

And finally, all the pieces click into place. The reason Mom never liked me, but Dad did. The reason she always,

always, always favored Clark—her real child. "You didn't want to adopt, and he did."

Mom's lips compress tightly. "You're *my* daughter. Don't think for a second that you aren't. We made the decision together."

I swallow but the lump in my throat won't go down. "So I am adopted?"

"We adopted you, knowing it would be a hard road for you. For us, really."

What's she not telling me? "Why is my entire file redacted?"

"That's still not the right question," Mom says.

My brain's full of so many questions that I don't know where to start.

"You'd think it would have occurred to you by now. You've essentially been asking the same question your whole life," Mom says. "The answer's finally staring you in the face, and you still don't see it."

What question have I been asking my whole. . .then it hits me.

Like a dump truck in an alley.

Like a zombie, high on the blood of someone on speed.

Like a werewolf running at a dead sprint, the truth lays me out cold.

Why am I such a terrible witch? Why do all my spells misfire? Why is it so hard for me to follow in Dad's shoes?

My voice is wobbly when I ask, "Not who, but what. That's where I went wrong, isn't it?"

Mom actually looks sad—terribly, terribly sad. "Your father was so positive that it was the right thing to do. He felt that we handled half-humans all wrong, and he was determined to prove it."

Is she saying I'm a social experiment? Is she saying my dad adopted me so that he could prove something? "What was my biological father?" I need her to say it.

"He was a human, of course." The words I've dreaded, deep down, for my entire life. "That's why you're terrible at everything you try to do. That's why your spells constantly misfire. That's why you can't bond anything better than a rat-bird." She sighs. "You really should be grateful you can work any magic at all, dear."

And that's what the Chief meant, too.

I'll never be a guardian. I'm probably only a paranormal affairs officer *at all* thanks to Dad's legacy. Now it's time for me to accept what everyone else already knew.

I'm a magical misfit, and I'll never improve because it's not what I'm doing that's the problem.

It's who I am.

And even with hard work, or a fancy familiar, or remedial spell classes, or private tutoring, that's not something I can ever fix.

21

IZAAK

I'm not an idiot.

It's just that my friends are all really smart, and that's never been my thing. Even so, sometimes I notice things that they don't. Being book smart isn't always the thing a situation needs most.

"So, your mom finally left," I say.

Minerva shrugs. "I guess."

"And you're okay, right?" I ask.

She flops back against the cushions of the sofa. "Define 'okay.'"

"Well, you're half human, but so is Bevin, and you don't hear her complaining."

Bevin looks pensive. "Actually."

"What?" Minerva asks.

"I'm half-human. Xander's half-human. And so is Izaak, if we're being technical."

"It doesn't really work like that with vampires," I say. "If one parent's a vampire, then the kids are all born with—"

Bevin waves her hand through the air. "All I'm saying is that you're just like all of us, and we're all doing fine."

"So I shouldn't be upset?"

"You have every right to be upset." Roxana perches on the edge of the sofa and drops a hand on Minerva's knee. "Your parents have been lying to you, and your mom didn't handle that well."

"Mom never handles things well," Clark says.

"That's an understatement," Minerva says. "When I started my period, she laughed and asked me if I was ready to die."

"She didn't," Bevin says.

"I had to tell her that every girl goes through it," Roxana says. "And dragona don't. So the fact that I was explaining it was pretty strange."

"She thought it was funny," Minerva says.

"Maybe it's good you're not related to her," Xander says. "I'm kind of surprised Clark's alive. She seems like she'd eat her young."

"Hey now," Clark says. "It was probably a hard conversation on Mom, too."

"How do you deal with it?" Minerva asks. "They make a big deal out of it with packs, right?" So she's clearly asking Xander.

"It's the reason I'm an outcast," Xander says. "It's the defining part of who I am every day of my life." He doesn't often look serious, but he does right now. "As hard as it's been to find out this way, maybe you should be grateful they kept it a secret."

"I'm lucky to have the job I have," Minerva says. "If people knew, I'd be, what? A glorified bouncer?"

Xander flinches.

"I'm sorry." Minerva straightens. "I didn't mean it like that."

He shrugs. "It's the truth. I'll probably never be welcomed into a pack, because I'm defective."

"You're not, though." Roxana's eyes flash. "I know that I'm pure bred dragona and all that snot, but I can't shift. Every single male that hatches can, but I can't. I understand feeling defective—I've felt inferior my entire life. But now that I'm watching it from the outside, I realize it's not true." She stands up and stares straight at Minerva. "You're brave. You're bold. You're strong. You're smart. And even when you don't get what you want right away, you just keep going. There's a word for that too, hanging on for dear life and trying harder than anyone else, even when something's hard."

"Tenacious," Xander says.

"That." Roxana points at him. "You're tinay—say it again."

"Tenacious," Xander says loudly. "You're tenacious! And beautiful. And you're resilient. And you're not alone."

"No, you're not," Bevin says. "You have all of us."

"I may be one hundred percent pure vampire," I say, "but I haven't ever killed anyone, and I'm my mother's greatest disappointment."

"I married a human, who subsequently left me, and I just turned down that university job," Clark says. "Looks like we're a whole cadre of magical misfits." He pats Minerva's head from behind the sofa. "But I love you just the same as I always have."

"I may never find a pack, or a mate of my own," Xander says, "but you guys are the best mates a guy could ever have, and I don't think we'd all be here without you, Minerva."

"Um, I feel bad that you don't have a girlfriend," I say, "but—"

"He means friends," Clark says. "In England, people use the word 'mates' to mean friends."

"Oh, then, yeah, totally," I say.

"We all love you, Minerva." Roxana perches by her again and holds out her arms.

It takes Minerva a moment, but eventually she leans in, and they hug. Bevin hops up from the chair and drops onto the sofa next to them, joining the hug. And then Clark wraps them around from behind, and Xander and I rush to join, too.

"I'm sorry you had to find out this way." Roxana's voice is muffled, but still confident. "But I'm more proud of you now."

"What?" Minerva's voice sounds strange.

I poke Xander's side until he squirms, and I can shift enough to see her face.

She's crying.

"I'm more proud," I say. "If I get—no, *when* I finally get a role that's not a villain, it'll mean more, because it's hard for a vampire to do it."

Minerva's quiet tears shift into shaking sobs. "You guys."

"And gals," Bevin says.

"I love you." Minerva looks like she might be slacking off, but Giggles chooses that moment to circle above us and dive until she's resting on Xander's head, which puts her close to Minerva's face. She rubs her face against Minerva's and coos.

"Thanks," Minerva says, "you flying rat."

"You look like you're doing better," Clark says.

"A little," Minerva says.

"Then I'm going to just—" Xander eases away, pulling his arm out from under mine. He brushes Giggles off, too. "It's not as bad as pigeon poop on my head, which I was also worried about, but one of you is not *Sure*."

"Sure? About what?" Roxana asks.

I take a good sniff and realize he's right. I swear under my breath. "That's not cool."

"It's a deodorant reference," Minerva says.

Clark drops his arms, too. "I noticed that, but I didn't want to be rude."

"It's me, alright?" Bevin asks. "But it's not a problem. It's a good thing."

Minerva slowly pries Bevin's arms away. "How is smelling like BO a good thing?"

"It's full of parabens and glycol and aluminum," Bevin says. "All of you are going to get cancer or not be able to have kids. Mark my words."

"You won't be having any kids either, if you keep smelling like that," Xander says.

"I doubt the IVF doctors will rule me out based on my smell." Bevin smirks.

"Fine. Let me amend my joke for the record to, 'You won't ever find a wife to raise your kids with if you keep smelling like that,'" Xander says.

"It loses a little bit of the zing when you have to change it," I say.

"You think?" Xander rolls his eyes. "But for real—life's all about risks. Smell better."

Bevin folds her arms and glares. "I think we have bigger things to be worried about today."

"I'm alright," Minerva says.

"Are you really?" Roxana asks.

Minerva's smile is forced, but at least she's smiling. "I always knew I had great friends, but I didn't realize how great." She sighs. "It's probably best that the world doesn't know the truth, but I think it's better that I do."

"Really?" Bevin asks. "Will you keep applying to be a guardian?"

Minerva's shoulders slump a bit, and then they straighten again. "I will."

"Are you sure? Clark says it's really dangerous," Roxana says. "He said a lot of them get hurt in the line of duty."

"Did I ever tell you why I want to be a guardian?" Minerva looks around.

Even Clark shrugs. "Because Dad was one?"

"He was also the Chief, and I don't want to do that." She sighs. "There are a lot of guardians who don't treat the demon-spawn like people. They act like they're all criminals."

"Some of them are," Bevin says.

"But you know better than anyone that many of them aren't," Minerva says. "I think the team needs someone to help the demon-spawn who are scared and confused."

Bevin takes her hand and squeezes. "Some of them are really dangerous."

"My dad never told me that I'm half-human. Why do you think that is?"

Bevin shrugs. Actually, no one seems to have any ideas.

"Mom said he was an activist, and maybe that's part of it, but Mom always treated me like there was something wrong with me. She always acted like I was doomed to disappoint her, and I get why now." She sighs. "I was."

What's she saying?

"Dad never acted like that. He always treated me like I could do anything I set my mind to, like my possibilities were limitless. I plan to carry on as he taught me to live."

We limit ourselves sometimes. That's what she's saying. Her dad gave her a gift, of not defining her by what she's not.

"That's really brave," I say.

"Thanks," Minerva says.

"I'm proud of you," Clark says. "Maybe even more proud now than I was before I knew."

"If we're all feeling better," I ask, "is there any chance we might eat some dessert?"

Minerva actually laughs, but then she stands up and brushes off her pants. "Sure. Why not?"

I only take one brownie, to be polite, but once the others have all had one, I finish off the pan.

"By Gabe," Xander says. "How do you stay fit, eating all that?"

I pat my belly. "Vampire."

"I'm a wolf, but every time I try to lose some weight, it just finds me again."

"We need some kind of restraining order," Clark says. "On days your jokes are bad like that, you have to go sit outside."

"Not every joke is going to be funny," Xander says. "I have to try them all and see what sticks."

"Try harder," I say. "We're supposed to be cheering her up, not bumming her out."

"I'm honestly fine," Minerva says. "Or you know, I will be. I'm mostly surprised that you're still paying attention."

"Hey, what does that mean?" I ask. "I'm a considerate guy."

"Just not an observant one," Clark says.

"You didn't even notice when I cut my hair a few months ago," Minerva says.

"A few months ago?" It didn't seem that long ago. "It wasn't that big a difference."

"I cut twenty-one inches off it." Minerva sits up straight and glares at me. "I decided to see how long it would take for you to notice. I gave up at three weeks and told you."

"Yeah, you're not usually the one checking in on people," Bevin says. "I'm kind of proud of you."

"Well, then you'll be really impressed when I tell you what else I just noticed," I say.

"What?" Clark asks.

"Now that I'm pretty sure Minerva's doing alright, I thought you might like to know that Roxana's gone."

"She probably went to take a nap." Clark looks totally calm.

But Bevin and Xander leap to their feet.

"She could be going to the bathroom or maybe showering," Minerva says, "But thanks for being obsessed with where she's located, Mr. Perv."

"Hey," I say. "That one time was an accident. The water sounded like a white noise machine."

"The door was locked," Minerva says.

"Vampires are stupidly strong," I say. "Sometimes I don't notice things like doorknob locks, especially when I've had bean and cheese burritos."

"I was shouting for you not to come in," she says.

"I really needed to go," I say. "And it's not like I looked." Or at least, not much, anyway. It *was* a hot girl in the shower.

Bevin grabs her purse off the counter. "Xander and I can go look for her."

I stand up. "I'll come too."

"Why would anyone go to look for her?" Clark frowns. "Her spell should be fine until morning. Maybe she went to get a present to cheer up Minerva."

"She probably did. You two stay here." Bevin mutters under her breath. "And hopefully we'll catch up to her quickly."

"What's going on?" Minerva asks.

Xander shakes his head at Bevin.

"Those two were talking about how much they wish she never came here," I say. "And Roxana overheard."

Clark and Minerva may not biologically be brother and sister, but their faces look *identical* in that moment: their mouths and eyes are round, and their eyebrows are slanted. It's pretty scary, and not much scares me. I'm a black vampire whose mom's an assassin.

"Now that we all know what's going on, anyone have ideas about where she might have gone?" Xander asks.

"I'm sure she went back home," Clark says, "to turn herself in."

"What?" Xander dashes for the door. "She can't do that. If she wants to go home, she should let me take her."

"This guy is unbelievable," Clark says. "Are you really upset because you can't turn her over for the bounty?"

"It is a lot of money," I say. "I mean, I wouldn't sell her out, but if she wants to go. . ."

"Not the bounty, idiots," Bevin says. "Xander wants the spot in the pack."

"Right," I say. "I keep forgetting about that."

"We need to stop her," Minerva says, "not convince her to let us get some prize." She throws her jacket on and heads for the door, whipping her phone out as she moves.

"Of course we do," Xander says. "That's what I meant too. Obviously."

Clark shoves past him and manages to be the first one out.

"Did she answer?" I ask.

"Yes." Minerva waves her phone at me. "She answered, said she's taking a shower, and she wants you to join her."

"Wait, really?" Because that's a huge relief.

Xander whaps me on the head, which I think is pretty rude. She *could* have answered. It would have been really nice.

Bevin's the one who grabs us a cab. Maybe that's why she climbs in the front, next to the ruddy-faced driver. He frowns when we all pile in. His lip curls at me when I squeeze in next to Clark and the cigarette dangling from his mouth nearly falls. "My cab seats five. One of you gots to get out."

"Right," Minerva says. "There's five of us."

"With me, there's six," he says while exhaling a cloud of smoke.

"Please, sir, this is important," Bevin says. She doesn't

even lecture him on the evils of smoking, so clearly she's worried.

He grumbles, but he puts the car into gear. "Where to?"

Why does that always work for her? If I asked, he'd probably put his cigarette out on my knee.

"Where exactly are we going?" I ask. "I mean, she could be anywhere."

"She went back," Minerva insists again. "We head for Dagobar Plaza."

The cabbie's eyes widen and he drops his cigarette in the ash tray. "Back?"

Minerva shakes her head. "I know what you're thinking. We're not after Roxana Goldenscales." She laughs. "I wish, am I right?"

The cabbie frowns.

"Wait," I say. "Why—?"

Minerva kicks me. "I mean, if we knew where she was, wow, would that be worth a lot of money." Her laugh is forced.

That's when it hits me. If we tell the cabbie what we're doing, even if we talk her out of turning herself over, the cabbie could follow us and hand her in. So clearly we need another reason why we're headed that direction. We can't be chasing our friend Roxana there.

"I could really use some cash, too," I say. "But sadly, we're going there because one of our friends is getting back together with the footman."

"The footman?" The cabbie blinks.

Xander sounds pained. "Yes, a *footman*. Just like in Cinderella." He groans. "I know how stupid it sounds, but we didn't make this up."

"Is there a pumpkin there, too?" the cabbie asks. "Does it turn into a carriage?"

"Just drive," Clark says. "Please."

And finally, we're on our way. I wonder what Roxana's

thinking right now. She didn't talk to anyone. She didn't even let us know she was leaving. We can't even talk about a plan on the way over, not without the cabbie listening in.

"You can stop here," Minerva says.

We're two blocks away, but she's probably thinking what I am—we need to come up with some kind of idea for what to do when we arrive.

Clark throws money at the cab driver before anyone else can, which is good, because I don't actually have any money to throw. "Why are we standing around?"

"We need a plan," I say. "Right? I mean, are we just going to walk up there and say, 'Roxana's coming, and you can't let her in'?"

"Of course not," Minerva says. "If you were her, how would you approach your old family?"

"She's someone who puts things off," Bevin says. "She doesn't deal with stuff until she absolutely has to, right?"

"Why do you say that?" I ask.

"She knew she caused me to get a tail," Bevin says. "She knew there was a bounty, and that Xander wanted to join a pack, but she didn't actually take action until she heard us talking about her."

"I still can't believe you three," Clark says. "The nicest girl ever, and her family is horrible, and she runs away, and you three are arguing over how she's ruined your lives."

"Leave me out of this," I say. "I was trying to keep Xander from doing something stupid."

"And I was telling him that I understood how he felt, but that it would be a mistake," Bevin says.

"Yeah, yeah, we all know I'm the only bad guy. Horrible, greedy, selfish Xander ruined everything again."

"No one said that," Minerva says.

"We were just thinking it," Clark mutters.

"Look, this isn't helping," I say. "Can we please just think of a plan?"

"Like I was saying," Bevin says. "She puts things off. She'll walk all the way here—"

"It's thirty-five blocks," Clark says.

"Or she'll take the subway," Minerva says. "But when she gets here, she'll approach from the back."

"I bet she sneaks back in through the fire escape," I say.

Clark sighs. "You can't do that, Izaak. They suck up when they're not in use. See?" He points at a building behind us. "You can go down, but then they pop back up. Otherwise, burglars would just crawl up the fire escape every time."

"Oh." Sometimes I hate being the normal one in the bunch, the one who doesn't already know all the answers to everything.

"Alright, so we should circle around the back and wait?" Xander asks. "I know you're all mad at me, but I will fix this, I swear."

No one has any better ideas, so we set off. We walk as quickly as we reasonably can, without drawing attention to ourselves, and we're nearly to the building, making good time, when there's a commotion.

Shouting. Sirens. People shrieking.

We rush toward the entrance. Minerva and Clark whip out their wands, the tops of Xander's hands grow bushy, and Bevin's tail whips back and forth wildly, but we're too late.

The cause of the commotion is pretty clear. Roxana Goldenscales did not walk around the back of the building. She didn't sneak in or take the slow route. She drove up to the front doors in a cab and climbed out. Then she marched right up to the guards posted by the door.

She may try to avoid things in general, and she may have done it her entire life. But when her friends are miserable, when she's causing them suffering, apparently she does not pass go, and she does not collect two hundred dollars.

"Were you kidnapped?" A reporter shouts.

Another reporter waves. "Who took you?"

"Are you injured?"

"Why are you back now?"

"Is the wedding still on?"

Roxana's calm, collected, and almost serene. She turns to face the reporters, and probably unbeknownst to her, the five of us as well, and she says, "The wedding's not going to happen. I wasn't kidnapped. I ran away."

"You what?" To say her father's face looks thunderous from where he's standing in the double doorway of the Dagobar Building, backlit by bright yellow light, would be an understatement. He clenches his fists, and scales ripple down his face. Horns sprout on his forehead. "You *ran away?*"

"Hi, Daddy," Roxana says.

"Now that my daughter has returned, the wedding will take place tomorrow." He crosses his arms over his chest. "A formal apology will be issued to her fiancé, Ragar the Ruthless, and she will immediately travel from New York City to Moscow."

Clark's nostrils flare. His fingers tighten so much on his wand that his knuckles turn white. He rushes toward the cab Roxana's standing in front of, clearly meaning to protect her. I had no idea he liked her quite that much. I just noticed his crush, and now I'm wondering if it's more than a crush.

But before he can say a word, before Roxana even knows he's there, a tall man in a long, tailored black coat steps into the space at her side. "I'm afraid that the mage's council can't condone Roxana's apology for her departure." The man turns toward Roxana, and I can only make out his profile, but it's one I'd know anywhere. It's one that everyone knows. "You see, the reason your daughter ran away is that we fell in love, so she most certainly can't say she's sorry and marry Ragar."

Clark drops his wand.

Every one of the reporters goes absolutely insane.

Minerva looks just as shocked as everyone else. "Wait, Roxana's in love with Lionel Sol?" If she sounds a little breathy when she says his name, well, I don't blame her. He's the son of the Grand Chancellor of the Illuminae, the most powerful mage organization in this part of the world.

"How does she even know him?" Bevin asks. "She never once said his name."

Roxana's dad is spluttering. His face is red. And wings are rippling out behind him. I'm going to go ahead and guess that he's not pleased. His bellow nearly knocks me backward with its intensity. "Is any part of this true, Roxie?"

I wish I were standing closer. Roxana's saying something to Lionel. He's saying something back. And then, in front of all these people, in front of the gathered crowd, Lionel kisses her.

It does not look fake.

They *look* like they're in love.

If it was anyone else, it would mean war, but I'm not sure that even Ragar the Ruthless can face off against Orion Sol. Not to mention, as the leader of all the mages, he's one of the few humans in contact with the akero. As the leader of the Illuminae, he meets with them once a year. The dragona are powerful, but even they don't dare challenge the akero.

"What's going on?" Minerva asks. "Does anyone know?"

I shrug.

"No idea, but it kind of looks like she doesn't need our help," Bevin says.

But when an enormous blood-red dragon shoots across

the sky, shrieking at the gathered crowd, I'm not at all sure that's true.

Ragar's back, and no matter how beautiful I think Roxana is, there's not a force on Earth that would convince me to trade places with Lionel Sol right now.

I'm pretty sure he's about to be turned into a sooty little pile of ash.

22

ROXANA

One of my earliest memories is of my dad shifting into his dragon form and my mother climbing up onto his back. When my father launched from the top of the Dagobar Tower, Mom clung to his tallest back ridge. Her smile was broad, her hair whipping around her face.

I felt *lucky* to be dragona. I couldn't wait for the day when my husband would launch into the sky with me on his back.

It never occurred to me then how monumentally unfair it was. I'm not some normie who just happened to meet a dragon lord. I'm dragona myself—only, I can't shift. I'm stuck hopping rides and popping out eggs.

And to make matters worse, no one ever pointed out this terrible injustice. They all taught me that I was blessed and that my role was noble. I had the *honor* of creating the next generation of dragona. Without me, our species could cease to exist. I would be cherished and honored. All the dragona from my mother's line—from my line—were the most powerful. The most fierce. The most gifted.

What a load of crap.

But it's not fair for my generous newfound friends to suffer for that lie, either. They didn't create my misogynist world or its rules. It's not their fault that I drew the genetic short straw. They didn't cause me to be one of the only people on Earth who can create new baby dragons, and it's not their fault that I can't take a dragon form myself.

But they're suffering because of me.

As I watch Minerva, navigating the lies that formed her entire life, to find the truth she may have already known, it gives me confidence. If Minerva, half-human Minerva, can face off against her mom, if she can accept who and what she is, if she can dig and dig and dig until she uncovers her limitations and then she can accept them, then why can't I do the same?

It's time for me to stop huddling and hiding and running. It's time for me to march right up to my family and do what they never taught me to do.

Stand on my own.

Refuse the proposal that was never made.

Take control of my own life firmly and boldly.

With my new friends all talking, buoying Minerva up, it's easy to sneak back onto the patio. Giggles coos at me, and tilts her head, like she knows exactly what I'm planning, and she's unimpressed.

"What do you know? You're a pigeon, and even you can fly."

Before I can second guess myself, I swing my legs down over the fire escape and leave the same way I did the first time I ran away. I try not to think about the irony that my plan to face up to my fears is beginning in the same way as the last time I cowarded out.

Unfortunately, the further I move away from my friends, the lower my confidence ebbs. I'm debating between walking the entire way—to clear my head, but also because I ate not one, but two pretzels from a vendor on the way home today before eating an enchilada—and taking the subway when a cab stops right next to me. "Need a ride?"

It's almost impossible to get a cab most of the time, but now they're flagging me down? Is it a sign? "Okay." I open the door and climb in. Before I even have time to think about them, the words just spring out. "Dagobar Plaza."

Luckily, the woman with the big straw hat who magically appeared in her cab has almost nothing to say to me. I spend the ride there going over and over my plan in my head. I'll try and find my mother first. Surely she'll be sympathetic. Surely she will understand how I've felt. Even if she loves her life, even though she loves my dad and my brothers, she must have felt a little trapped. Right?

When I find her, I'll explain how I felt, and then how scared I was when Ragar just ran all over me. She'll get it. She has to get it. Then she can help me explain to my dad, and surely he'll be able to smooth things over with Ragar and his even more horrible father.

I'll be sure to credit Xander with convincing me to return so that his pack isn't upset with him.

And poor Bevin won't need to lie for me ever again.

Maybe once things settle down, I can find a job on my own and get an apartment. Hopefully it'll be close to Minerva. Before I've had time to review much else, I'm suddenly there. Dagobar Tower looks even higher from the very bottom than it does from the top. I can't believe I really climbed that many flights down.

I start walking toward the front of the building, prepared to look for any guards I might know. They won't recognize me right away, obviously, thanks to Clark's careful disguise. But if I can get a message through to my mom. . .

Only there are loads of people on the ground floor for some reason.

"Thank you for meeting with us," Dad says.

Dad's down here? Why? My heart rate feels practically thready. My hands go clammy. I bite my lip.

And then a familiar voice answers Dad. "It was my pleasure. My dad's had me doing so many things for so long—he's always insisted fluency in six languages is a bare minimum, for instance." It's Clark's friend, Lionel Sol.

"Your father sets high standards for a reason," Dad says. "If you don't ask a lot, you don't get a lot."

"So true," Lionel says. "But I shouldn't have put him off as long as I did. I'm delighted to be the new liaison between the Illuminae and the dragona."

Dad shakes his hand briskly. "We hope it never comes to that scenario we discussed, but just in case."

"Of course." Lionel half bows, and then pivots on his heel. . .and nearly marches right into me.

"Roxana." His voice emerges in a whoosh, like a gust of uncontrollable wind.

Why? Why did he have to use my name?

I'm probably the last person he expected to see here.

Like a school of sharks when a bucket of chum has been upended next to them, the reporters milling around swim toward me frantically.

"Did he say Roxana?"

"Is that her?" A woman asks. "Roxana Goldenscales?"

"Were you kidnapped?" A grey-haired reporter shouts.

A terribly short reporter waves. "Who took you?"

"Are you injured?"

"Why are you back now?"

"Is the wedding still on?"

So much for pulling Mom aside and enlisting her help. So much for slowly convincing them, one by one. Well, the best defense is a good offense. That's Dad's favorite play. Hopefully he'll appreciate it in his daughter. "The wedding is not going to happen. I wasn't kidnapped. I ran away." Let them choke on that news.

Only, it's not the reporters who have the most trouble with it. "You what?" Dad's nostrils flare, tiny tendrils of smoke wafting away from them. Golden scales pop out along his neck and jawline. Bright golden horns, the first real sign of his upcoming shift, sprout from his forehead. "You *ran away?*"

"Hi, Daddy." I hate baby talk, but when your dad could literally roast you and eat you for dinner, it has its place. I open my mouth to explain, but he's not in a listening mood.

"Now that my daughter has returned, the wedding will take place tomorrow." He huffs. "A formal apology will be issued to her fiancé, Ragar the Ruthless, and she will immediately travel from New York City to Moscow."

Oh! Has he already gone back to Russia? That's the best news I've heard.

"Go upstairs, right now, and prepare your apology."

If he really thinks I'm going to apologize, he's going to be sorely disappointed. Perhaps he'll know how I felt when I realized he'd pledged me to marry the Vin Diesel of the dragona world.

Mom tosses her head upward, toward the skies.

I follow her glance and notice a dragon hurtling toward us. It's not a normal dragon. It's a bright red one, enormous, at least double the size of the usual dragon around here. My chauvinistic Prince Repulsive, decidedly not in Moscow.

What am I supposed to do now? I may not be scared of Dad, but Ragar's another story. He's unpredictable, selfish, and savage. He really might toss me over his shoulder and fly away with no regard for any objection I make.

The last time I saw Lionel, he looked nothing like he does on television. His hair was unkempt. His clothing was casual—unimpressive, even. But today, he's wearing a beautiful black suit, covered with an even darker black trench coat.

The one thing that looks the same is his indolent stare. His swagger. That's unchanged. Even when he steps toward me and says, "I'm afraid that the mage's council can't condone Roxana's apology for her departure." Lionel pauses, and when his eyes meet mine, there's a surprising amount of sincerity in them. "You see, the reason your daughter ran away is that we fell in love, so she most certainly can't say she's sorry and marry Ragar."

The reporters lose their minds.

Dad looks like he might explode. Golden wings ripple to life behind him. "Is any part of this true, Roxie?"

"I know you don't love me," Lionel whispers into my ear. "I know you barely know me. But trust me when I say, this is your best play right now unless you were looking forward to marrying Lenny up there."

"Lenny?"

"Not a Steinbeck fan?" He sighs. "Guess not, or that joke would have killed."

"My fiancé may do all the killing you'd ever want to see," I say. "What in the world do you think you're doing?"

He shifts a little closer—close enough that I'm uncomfortable about it. But it's not like I can afford to shove any knights in shining armor away at this moment.

"You need help," he says simply, "and I'd be lying if I didn't admit I was interested in you from the start. The idea of a little fake dating doesn't alarm me."

"We're not even remotely compatible," I say. "I'm only valuable for my ability to lay eggs, in case you hadn't heard."

"Oh, I think you have a little more value than that."

It's a little depressing that the first time I hear that, it's from a mage who's hitting on me. Right before we're about to become char. "You're willing to risk war for it?"

"Actually." His voice is husky and low. "Let's just say that my dad and I have issues with Ragar and his father that aren't new. Hardly surprising, given that your fiancé is a real thug. Since curbing his power and keeping you safe are goals that align, this is the best thing for me *and* you right now. A naughty dragon and a beastly one with the same stone, as it were."

"You're not worried that Ragar might gut you?" My eyes shift, drawing his attention to the dragon rocketing toward us. "He's coming in hot, and he looks ticked."

"Time for a big performance, then," Lionel says. "You ready?"

He gives me no time to respond. His mouth simply closes over mine, hot, hard, and demanding. My hand clenches into a fist, ready to punch him, but before I can, he releases me.

"That was really stupid," I whisper, the second he releases me.

And then, there's no more time to talk, because Ragar lands next to us, his fiery breath puffing over us, his talons digging furrows into the previously smooth concrete.

If I'm not mistaken, brave, big-talking Lionel is about to dearly regret his hasty proclamation. Ragar's not called ruthless for no reason, and he looks seriously pissed.

※

I hope you enjoyed My Pigeon Familiar, where Minerva's the focal character. There's plenty more to come, and each of the magical misfits will get a book where their story is the most prominent. Of course the others will show up in each book, but that title character will have a *little* more page time.

Up next? My Mongrel Pack (Xander's story!) You can grab it now!

Looking for another book to check out? You might like my HORSE shifter book series, starting with My Queendom for a Horse if you haven't tried that yet.

ACKNOWLEDGMENTS

OH MY WORD, this is going to be long. I had the idea for this book almost a full year ago. For me, that's a long time between idea and execution. (Although, I do have some babies who have been fully written and still sat on the shelf for years. Sorry, books.)

But this story would not be out today if it weren't for Demetrius Rouse. He was EPIC. And supportive. And he gave so freely of his time. Friends like him are not common. THANK YOU. (And to his lovely wife Stephanie, whom I adore, for sharing his time with me.)

Thanks to Aurea Jenson and to Milaine Fernando Espino. I love you both for your support and your time and your willingness to help me make this book as "right" as I can. <3

Thanks to Tamie Dearen for an early read and insight. I love you, lady!

Thanks to my kids for their support and their cheering.

Thanks to Elana Johnson for holding my hand. Sorry I was so whiny.

Thanks to my narrators, and a special thank you to Jennifer Jill Araya for lining up the circus that the audiobook for this has been. SORRY for writing so many POV characters.

A huge thanks to my husband, because he puts up with me and he cheers me endlessly. And in this case, he also poured over an early draft and helped me brainstorm jokes. <3

And last but never least, thank you to my readers and fans. Without you, I never would have even endeavored to write this book. I love you all more than you know.

ABOUT THE AUTHOR

Bridget's a lawyer, but does as little legal work as possible. She has five kids and soooo many animals that she loses count.

Horses, dogs, cats, rabbits, and so many chickens. Animals are her great love, after the hubby, the kids, and the books.

She makes cookies waaaaay too often and believes they should be their own food group. In a (possibly misguided) attempt at balancing the scales, she kickboxes daily. So if you don't like her books, maybe don't tell her in person.

Bridget is active on social media, and has a facebook group she comments in often. (Her husband even gets on there sometimes.) Please feel free to join her there: https://www.facebook.com/groups/750807222376182

ALSO BY BRIDGET E. BAKER

The Dragon Captured Series: (dragon shifter romance!)

Ensnared

Entwined

Embroiled

Embattled

The Russian Witch's Curse: (horse shifter romance!)

My Queendom for a Horse

My Dark Horse Prince

My High Horse Czar

My Wild Horse King

My Trojan Horse Majesty

The Magical Misfits Series: (paranormal humor!)

My Pigeon Familiar

My Mongrel Pack

The Birthright Series:

Displaced (1)

unForgiven (2)

Disillusioned (3)

misUnderstood (4)

Disavowed (5)

unRepentant (6)

Destroyed (7)

The Birthright Series Collection, Books 1-3

The Anchored Series:

Anchored (1)

Adrift (2)

Awoken (3)

Capsized (4)

The Sins of Our Ancestors Series:

Marked (1)

Suppressed (2)

Redeemed (3)

Renounced (4)

Reclaimed (5) a novella!

A stand alone YA romantic suspense:

Already Gone

I also write women's fiction and contemporary romance under B. E. Baker.

The Scarsdale Fosters Series:

Seed Money

Nouveau Riche (2)

Minted (3)

Loaded (4)

The Finding Home Series:

Finding Grace (1)

Finding Faith (2)

Finding Cupid (3)

Finding Spring (4)

Finding Liberty (5)

Finding Holly (6)

Finding Home (7)

Finding Balance (8)

Finding Peace (9)

The Finding Home Series Boxset Books 1-3

The Finding Home Series Boxset Books 4-6

The Birch Creek Ranch Series:

The Bequest

The Vow

The Ranch

The Retreat

The Reboot

The Surprise

The Setback

The Lookback

Children's Picture Book

Yuck! What's for Dinner?

Printed in Great Britain
by Amazon